HENDRIXSON'S HANDS DROPPED TO HIS SIDES, INCHES AWAY FROM HIS .45s.

"You pull either of them Colts, boy," McLeary said in a voice cold as mountain ice, "and I'll splatter your insides all over this saloon before you clear leather. I hate to disappoint you, but I aim to stick around this town for a spell."

"That creates a problem," Hendrixson said slowly.

"For you, maybe. Not for me."

"I'd purely hate to throw down against you, Mister McLeary," Hendrixson said. "But if my boss says somethin' . . ." He shrugged as if to say he would have no other choice.

McLeary dropped his right hand so that it rested on the ivory grip of his Smith and Wesson.

"Best think about it before you try it, boy," he said with no hint of mercy in his voice . . .

SADDLE UP FOR ADVENTURE WITH G. CLIFTON WISLER'S TEXAS BRAZOS!

A SAGA AS BIG AND BOLD AS TEXAS ITSELF, FROM THE NUMBER-ONE PUBLISHER OF WESTERN EXCITEMENT

#1: TEXAS BRAZOS (1969, $3.95)

In the Spring of 1870, Charlie Justiss and his family follow their dreams into an untamed and glorious new land – battling the worst of man and nature to forge the raw beginnings of what is destined to become the largest cattle operation in West Texas.

#2: FORTUNE BEND (2069, $3.95)

The epic adventure continues! Progress comes to the raw West Texas outpost of Palo Pinto, threatening the Justiss family's blossoming cattle empire. But Charlie Justiss is willing to fight to the death to defend his dreams in the wide open terrain of America's frontier!

#3: PALO PINTO (2164, $3.95)

The small Texas town of Palo Pinto has grown by leaps and bounds since the Justiss family first settled there a decade earlier. For beautiful women like Emiline Justiss, the advent of civilization promises fancy new houses and proper courting. But for strong men like Bret Pruett, it means new laws to be upheld – with a shotgun if necessary!

#4: CADDO CREEK (2257, $3.95)

During the worst drought in memory, a bitter range war erupts between the farmers and cattlemen of Palo Pinto for the Brazos River's dwindling water supply. Peace must come again to the territory, or everything the settlers had fought and died for would be lost forever!

Available wherever paperbacks are sold, or order direct from the Publisher. Send cover price plus 50¢ per copy for mailing and handling to Zebra Books, Dept. 2660, 475 Park Avenue South, New York, N.Y. 10016. Residents of New York, New Jersey and Pennsylvania must include sales tax. DO NOT SEND CASH.

SHOWDOWN AT SIX-GUN MINE

John Legg

ZEBRA BOOKS
KENSINGTON PUBLISHING CORP.

ZEBRA BOOKS

are published by

Kensington Publishing Corp.
475 Park Avenue South
New York, NY 10016

First printing: May, 1989

Printed in the United States of America

For Mary Maw Hires:
Since words are inadequate
Simply:
Thank you, with love

Chapter 1

Charlie McLeary sat with his back against a boulder, listening to the bullets whining off the jumbled mass of rocks protecting him. Damn if this didn't beat all, he thought—a week on the run with the Otero County Cattle Association "detectives" hot on his trail.

In his mind, he could hear his father's cackling voice saying, "This here's damp powder, boy, and no use sayin' elsewise to it."

McLeary grinned, but there was little humor in it at the moment. Things, indeed, were looking bad. But there was some mirth—at least in the remembrance. His father, a tough man who had been a mountain man for a dozen years long before fathering McLeary, would not have stopped there. No, McLeary thought, he could hear the old, gray-haired, strong-till-the-end father adding, "How'd ye ever get caught up in such foolishment anyway. Goddamn, boy." And his father would have launched into some long-winded tale of how he had done this or that wondrous deed.

Trouble was, McLeary found out when talking to some of the old men who would know for sure, after he had grown and was back from the Civil War, many of the tales his father had told were true.

The grin widened. He *had* been a damned fool, he knew full well now, to have hired on to protect a group of cash-poor sodbusters on the Colorado prairies, trying to buck the hired gunmen that the powerful cattlemen's association called range detectives. Well, he vowed, as he whirled and fired half a dozen quick shots from his well-worn, well-used Henry .44/40 rifle, he would not be so foolish again. That was damn sure.

McLeary scrunched down behind the rock again as another volley was flung at him from the unseen men below. He pulled off the plain, gray, stained Stetson and mopped his head and brow with a large red bandanna. It was hot, and would only get hotter.

McLeary stuffed the bandanna back into the right rear pocket of his Levi's and settled the hat back on his head. He looked around, eyes searching for a way out. He knew that he could not hold out here much longer.

There was another lull in the gunfire, and McLeary spun again and snapped off several more rounds, lest the men below think he was sleeping. Once again with his back to the protective boulder, he searched for an escape. He had seen two of the dozen gunmen below moving up the rocky hillside and knew he had little time.

McLeary spotted a crack in the rocks above. It looked like there might even be a trail that way, but he could not be sure from here. It was mostly hidden by brush and a shrub of some kind growing sideways out of the whitish rock on the right side. He waited a few more minutes, waving at the gnats and mosquitoes, looking. But there was no other likely possibility. McLeary whirled, fired off several shots, then whirled back. Jerking to his full six-foot height, he ran for his horse, which was tied behind some other rocks, out of danger.

Grabbing the cinnamon gelding's reins, McLeary tugged. "Come on, boy," he said, heading for the rock cleft, hoping it was wide enough for the horse, hoping it would lead to safety.

The cinnamon balked a little as the foliage caught at its legs and sides. McLeary yanked, urging the horse forward. The saddle scraped on rock, and for a moment McLeary thought the horse was going to get stuck. But the animal managed, with much snorting and whinnying, to work its way through.

McLeary wiped the sweat from his head and face again, looking up the trail, for that's what it was. Only an animal path perhaps, but it was usable enough for him, considering the alternative. From where McLeary stood, the rock-strewn path wound between boulders and giant chunks of granite in the mountain, curling around out of sight.

McLeary reloaded his Henry rifle. His long, thin fingers worked rapidly but calmly as his eyes scanned the land around him.

McLeary was tall, and lean, with an angular face, full lips and thin, pointed nose. His eyes were a faded blue, under sandy eyebrows and a matching patch of hair that curled slightly at the longish ends. His cheekbones were prominent, and his cheeks and jaw were coated with more than a week's worth of short, sandy beard. A mustache curled around his upper lip, running down the sides, and dangled off his jaw. In addition to the Levi's and Stetson, he wore a scruffed pair of black, pointed-toe boots, and a shirt of white calico with a floral pattern in green woven through it. The shirt was buttoned up to the neck.

He finished reloading the Henry and stuffed it into the saddle scabbard, butt facing upward at the front. Then he moved off on foot, tugging the cinnamon gelding behind him. For two hours McLeary hiked up the scarred face of the mountain, stumbling over broken slabs and chunks of granite. Once he had to clamber over a rockslide that had blocked the narrow trail cut between the mountainous cliffs. He made it all right, but the horse, nickering nervously, had a tough time before it, too, was safely on the other side. And they pushed on.

McLeary was drenched in sweat, his shirt soaked through, when he rounded the back side of the mountain near its stubby peak. The trail leading down into a rocky, barren canyon a mile or so away was not wider than the one he was on, but it was far less constricted—and it sloped gently downhill. McLeary breathed a little easier since the trail looked a bit better and he had heard no sounds of pursuit all the while he had been walking this trail.

He walked on, pulling the horse. There was still not enough room for comfortable riding. In another hour, he reached a point where the ground leveled as it opened into the narrow canyon. Soon after, McLeary found a spring among the rocks, with two stunted, wind-twisted cottonwoods standing sentinel over it. He welcomed the relief of the meager shade. He opened his shirt and tossed his hat on the ground while the cinnamon drank from the muddy water where the spring dripped off a rock and pooled at its base.

When the horse was done, McLeary drank his fill before splashing some of the cool water on his face and head. Then he filled his canteen. There were still no signs of pursuit, but McLeary knew better than to stay here too long. After all, it wouldn't take those gunmen long to find the way he had come.

He let the horse drink a little more, all the while wishing he had not been in so much of a hurry to leave Otero County that he had done so without food, other than the little jerky he almost always kept in his saddlebags. That had run out two days ago, and he had had nothing more than berries and such ever since. He grimaced as his stomach emitted a resounding rumble. "Come on, horse," he growled as he pulled himself into the saddle, "time we were movin' on."

With a last glance behind him up the mountain—and seeing no one; nothing but a swooping hawk high above—he touched his heels to the cinnamon's flanks and rode off.

By the next afternoon, McLeary had entered a high mountain meadow, with numerous aspens, cottonwoods and willows; chokecherry, blueberry and blackberry bushes; oaks and pines. There was plenty of water and abundant game: elk, mule deer, rabbit, beaver, antelope, hawks, grouse, quail, raccoon and more. Having still seen no signs of pursuit, he figured he was safe enough by now, so he dropped a deer with a well-placed shot from the Henry.

That night, for the first time in more than a week, he had a fire and a full belly. He had even found a half-pint bottle of whiskey wrapped in his other shirt in one of his saddlebags. He polished that off with his supper. It was, he decided, almost pleasant, and his humor returned. He pulled the deer carcass high up into a tree with a rope to keep it away from marauding bears and other scavengers, and then fell asleep to a chorus of coyotes, owls, crickets and cicadas.

The next morning, he ate hearty again, though by now he wished he had had some coffee stashed away. Then he cleaned his weapons. They were his life, and he took exceptional care of them. First he cleaned and oiled the Henry. In the ten years he had had it, the rifle had never failed him. While it was the same caliber as the newer Winchesters, he found the Henry's heaviness an asset.

Then he worked on the Smith and Wesson American—also .44 caliber, meaning he could use the same cartridges for both his pistol and the rifle. Finally he took care of the .38 caliber Colt Lightning that he carried in a shoulder holster underneath his shirt in case of emergency. The small, powerful Colt with the three-and-a-half-inch barrel had saved his life on more than one occasion.

McLeary took the time after that, and during the next day, to let himself recover from the ordeal, and to think over the folly of his last job. He shook his head when he thought about how he had let himself be swayed by the fervor—and the hopelessness he had sensed—of the farmers trying to eke out an existence on the Colorado plains. There was never enough water for them, and they lived lives of squalor, huddled in soddies while trying to raise a brood of kids—and enough crops to improve their lots in life.

How they had gotten his name, he never knew, since they never told him. All they had said was that they had managed to scrape up a hundred dollars for him, if he would chase way the two—for that's all there were at the time—"range detectives" hired by the cattlemen's association to intimidate the would-be farmers and drive them out.

Against his better judgment, he had agreed to do so, and soon after rode off toward Timpas, the nearest—well, only—town in the vicinity. He spoke to the two gunmen, neither of whom he knew—though they knew of him by reputation. But they had not listened to his advice to head out. Instead, they went to their bosses and told the cattlemen that the farmers were hiring gunmen.

Within days, another dozen men hired by the association were in town. The first two called McLeary out while they were all drinking in a saloon late one afternoon. McLeary gunned both down.

But the sheriff, whose salary came in large part from the association, told him he was under arrest. McLeary, knowing his time in the area was up, clobbered the sheriff on the side of the head, and then rode hell for leather out of town. He had no particular direction in mind when he left, but quickly decided that California might be a nice place to visit.

So here he sat, on his second full day in the pleasant mountain meadow in the San Juan Mountains—if he was not mistaken—sharpening his horn-hilted Bowie knife. It had been his father's knife, back in the waning days of the fur trade, and old man Rob McLeary had passed it on to his son.

McLeary scratched at his face and the new beard. He had decided it was time to hack it off, and so had started honing the blade. He whistled an old tune—*When Johnny Comes Marching Home Again*—as he worked.

Suddenly he was aware of a bullet striking his saddle right next to him, but not sure how he knew. He moved almost instinctively. Two seconds later, when he heard the crack of the rifle, he was behind a cottonwood, pale blue eyes searching frantically for the source of the shot.

He lay sweating, wishing he had the Henry. The gunman had to be up in the rocks off a quarter of a mile or so—much too far for a shot with the Smith and Wesson. It would be a long shot even for the rifle; with a pistol it would be impossible. Besides, the Henry was in the scabbard attached to the saddle some feet off to his left.

McLeary waited, more than a little worried, watching. The

nervousness began to wear off as he realized it would be difficult for anyone to get him across the meadow leading to the copse of trees. However, if there were still a dozen of them—for he figured it to still be the association's gunmen—all they had to do was charge. He could never get them all—unless he had the fifteen-shot Henry.

Or they could wait till nightfall, and then sneak up on him. He shook his head. The horse was back in the trees, cropping grass, safe. All McLeary had to do was grab the saddle, mount the horse and ride out.

"No," he snapped quietly. He was tired of running, and he would do no more of it. He waited, watching intently, and was finally rewarded when he saw a brown hat move behind a rock, ever so slightly.

Suddenly he rolled over and over, finally stopping behind the saddle. Bullets kicked up dirt to his left, then right; another thudded into the thick leather of his saddle. It was eerie laying there, seeing the bullets hit, but not hearing the sound till several heartbeats afterward.

McLeary yanked the Henry from the scabbard, and rolled again. Figuring the unseen gunman was waiting for him to dash back to his tree, McLeary rolled the other way, toward another cottonwood.

Several shots hit the tree, and he grinned in tense satisfaction. He had made it safely by the time the gunman had realized his intention and was able to swing around and fire.

McLeary slowly stood and edged the Henry out around the tree. Then he waited. It seemed an eternity, but finally he spotted the gunman's hat creeping around a rock. McLeary's lip twitched in anticipation as he levered a round into the chamber, cocking the rifle at the same time.

Again he waited. Suddenly, he saw a face, dim and unrecognizable at this distance. He squeezed off a shot, and the face disappeared. McLeary looked up at the blue sky beyond the high ceiling of cottonwood leaves. It was well past noon, and it would be some hours before it got dark. So he waited.

An hour later, vultures began circling over the rocks where he had last seen the gunman. He smiled. But he was not stupid enough to venture out. The gunman might have friends waiting.

At last dusk painted the meadow purple, and McLeary stepped from behind the tree. He built up the fire and hung a haunch of deer meat over it to cook, then sat back in the gathering shadows. He ate the meat with gusto, and then washed it down with water from the brook behind him.

It was dark now, and the sounds of the night were comforting. But McLeary would not relax his vigil. He moved back into the trees and sat with his back braced on a tall, thin aspen.

Before dawn had pushed its pink nose over the ridge where the gunman had been, McLeary was moving. He saddled the horse and ate again. Then he moved to the brook where he drank before plunging his head into the cool water. Wiping his face off, he stood next to the horse. There was enough light to see, so he mounted up. With the Henry in hand, he rode south through the trees and brush for a mile, before swinging out onto the grassland and moving east toward the rocky ridge.

Cautiously he worked his way up into the rocks. But he had worried needlessly. There was only the one man, and McLeary's shot had been deadly. The coyotes, buzzards and other scavengers had been busy during the night, and there was little left of the gunman but his weapons, bones and shreds of clothing.

"Damn fool," McLeary muttered, almost in sympathy. He found the man's horse and the tracks the man had made coming in. There were no other tracks, as far as McLeary could see, and he figured the other hired guns had turned back, not thinking it worthwhile to pursue McLeary any longer—as long as he was far gone from Otero County. McLeary reckoned this man was the exception and had for some reason determined to find and kill McLeary.

McLeary breathed a sigh. He did not think there would be any more pursuit, but he did not want to stay here much longer, either. He took the dead man's Colt and stuffed it in the back of his own gunbelt, and then took what .44 caliber cartridges the man had. He searched through the man's saddlebags and found nothing of interest—or value—except some more shells, which he took. Then he pulled the saddle off the animal and sent the horse racing away with a hard slap on the rump.

McLeary did not feel the man who tried to kill him deserved a burial, especially since there was little enough of him left to bury, so with a shrug, he mounted his cinnamon horse and rode back to his camp. He stuffed the dead man's Colt and ammunition in his saddlebags, cleaned his rifle again, and then ate once more.

Done, he kicked dirt over the fire, made sure his canteen was filled, and then rode out without so much as a glance over his shoulder. Maybe, he thought as he made his way westward, life wasn't so bad after all. At least if he could refrain from any more damnfool crusades. However, that, he reasoned ruefully, was going to be difficult, knowing as he did how he was.

Chapter 2

Charlie McLeary reined in the cinnamon gelding in front of the Pick and Shovel Saloon. Gaps could be seen between the logs of the building, as well as in the false wood front. There were no windows, and the place looked decrepit. He glanced across the street at the Silver Nugget. It was rather fancy, and looked quite inviting. But such places usually meant trouble for him, and he did not need any more of that for a long spell. So he stepped down off his horse where he was.

Eight days had passed since he had killed the gunman in the rocks off the meadow. He had kept a close eye on his back trail as he rode for the first several days, before he relaxed and took a couple of days to rest up in a well-watered glade. Though most people did not know it—and couldn't see it in him even if they did—he was a superstitious man, and overly cautious. But it was his way, and he could do nothing to change it now.

The small, hand-painted sign he had seen when he rode into the town had announced that this was Silver Canyon, Colorado. It was a good-size place, though that didn't surprise him. It often happened that way in mining towns. Someone would make a strike, and within months there would be a few thousand people living there.

There weren't that many in Silver Canyon, McLeary figured, but he estimated there were close to that number. He saw at least two dozen saloons, but only the one fancy one. The Pick and Shovel, in front of which he was standing, looked the least foul of the poorer establishments.

There were two general stores, a milliner's a photographer's shop, barber shop-doctor's-dentist's office, a carpenter's, two blacksmiths, a livery, tinsmith, wheelwright, three hotels that he could see, a school, and even a church.

There were at least four streets paralleling Silver Street—the main street of the town—and perhaps twelve cross streets, plus a number of alleys. There were plenty of houses, almost all of them shabby, hastily thrown together affairs made of wood hauled in from the tree-covered mountainsides all around town.

There were, however, four truly fancy houses: one in the center of town, the other three near the far—north—end of Silver Street. In the windows of the one in the center of town, McLeary could plainly see a number of women, most wearing little or no clothing. The other three ornate houses apparently were regular homes. McLeary guessed those houses belonged to the mine owners—or at least the managers, if the owners were absentee types, which was common enough.

Each of the three houses was Victorian in size, shape and ornamentation. And all three were of red brick, with carved wood trim. There was real glass in the many windows. Even at this distance, McLeary could tell they were populated by people of wealth.

There were several other nice houses that he had seen while riding in, most off on the side streets. Those, he figured, would belong to store owners, bankers, and other fairly well-to-do businessmen in town.

The town sat in a canyon, with the walls rising steeply to the east past a glade and to the west on the other side of the river. Animas Creek ran coldly, just beyond the last north-south street of Silver Canyon.

At the north end of town, beyond the three opulent houses, McLeary could just barely see the mine. It seemed to be off just a bit to the east, down in a gulch. Outside it sat the smelter, belching smoke. And edging into the gulch, McLeary found out later, were the homes of the miners, delapidated shacks, mostly, a living testament to the vast disparity in income between the miners and the men who owned the mines.

McLeary looped the reins over the cross pole of the hitching post. With what would seem to others to be a casual glance, he carefully scrutinized the area around him. All seemed peaceful.

Satisfied, he peeled off the long, tan duster and flapped it hard, sending up a cloud of dust. He tucked it into the rawhide thongs holding the bedroll behind his plain saddle. It had been hot on the trail, even this high up, since summer was almost here. And wearing the duster had only made it worse. But a storm yesterday had been a drenching one, and he was happy to have had the garment. He had left it on this morning when he rode out of his small, lonely camp because the sky then had still been thick with bunched, black clouds.

With another brief look around, he stepped onto the wooden sidewalk and pushed through the saloon's creaking wood half-doors.

McLeary paused just inside. He slipped to his left, making the move look natural, so he would not be framed in the doorway. Within a few moments, his eyes adjusted to the dim light of the lantern-illuminated interior, and he moved slowly toward the plank bar on his right. As he did, his eyes carefully swept the room, alert. There was no danger, he decided, since few people were inside. Three men sat at a table toward the back, playing poker being dealt by a hefty, scantily clad woman who wore an abundance of face paint. Two men stood—widely separated—at the bar.

With his left hand, McLeary pulled off his wide-brimmed gray hat and slapped it on his knee to get rid of the trail dust.

The bartender shuffled over and asked nervously, "What'll it be, mister?"

McLeary dropped his hat on the bar and said, "Shot of redeye. And a beer."

The bartender brought over a brimming mug of cold beer and a shot glass. He placed them in front of McLeary and reached under the bar. McLeary stiffened a moment, but the bartender only brought forth a bottle of whiskey. He uncorked it and filled the shot glass.

As he picked up the coins McLeary had tossed on the bar, he cleared his throat nervously and said, "I'm surprised you're here, mister. All your friends are probably over to the Silver Nugget."

"I don't know anybody here."

"You ain't with the others?" the barkeeper asked, looking anxiously around.

"Others who?"

"You know." The bartender looked pointedly at the ivory butt of the Smith and Wesson American at McLeary's right hip.

"I have no idea what you're talkin' about, mister," McLeary said in some annoyance. He was hot and tired and wanted nothing more than to have a cold beer in peace—for now.

"Ain't you one of the boys the company hired?"

"What company?" He jolted down the shot and smacked his lips.

"Consolidated Silver and Mining."

"Never heard of it." McLeary took a deep, satisfying swig of beer.

The bartender looked at him suspiciously, gaining a little courage. But he was still doubtful. "You sure?" he asked.

"Just said so, didn't I."

The bartender poured McLeary another shot. "It's on me," he said.

"Thanks, mister . . . ?"

"Just call me Lem."

"Thanks, Lem. Mind tellin' me what in hell you've been talkin' about?"

Lem Wilson drifted off to fill the glasses of the two other men at the bar, chatting briefly with them as he did. Then he wandered back to McLeary and filled the shot glass and empty mug.

"Well, it's like this . . ." he started, then paused. "By the way, what's your name, mister?"

"Charlie McLeary." It was said flatly.

Wilson's eyes widened, and fear flickered across his face. McLeary's lips flinched into an almost smile. He was used to it by now. It was the same everywhere.

"I better not say no more," Wilson mumbled, turning away.

McLeary sipped his beer, knowing Lem could not ignore him forever. It took some time, but Wilson finally drifted back and asked tightly, "Want anything else?"

"Yep. Information," McLeary said quietly. "You got nothin' to fear from me, Lem."

Wilson finally found his voice. "I ain't sayin' nothin', mister. No sirree."

"Why not?"

"If you're one of the company's men, you know. . . ."

"I ain't."

"And if you ain't one of 'em, it's none of your affair." He turned away.

McLeary's left hand snaked out and caught Wilson's shirt. Roughly he yanked the bartender around to face him. "Tell me," he ordered, his voice filled with menace.

Wilson swallowed hard and started to speak several times before the words actually came. "The mines here in Silver Canyon been open nearly four years now. Silver was found back in '73, maybe '74, by some old coot named Tyler. The Stoughton brothers—

Tom, Alva and George—came in about a year later."

He paused. He was still suspicious of this gunman, and he could be in deep trouble. But he pushed on, figuring he had no choice. "They bought the mine from Tyler pretty cheap. Some say they got it while Tyler was drunk and they was all gamblin'."

He felt a little more assured when this produced little reaction from McLeary. "Anyway, around the same time they bought Tyler's claims, they bought up several others. In fact, a few people had claims in Squaw Gulch were never seen again. Then the Stoughtons come in here in a big way, bringing in a lot of men to work the place, putting in the smelter, a couple donkey engines, ore carts and such. They been pullin' ore out of them mines by the trainload, it seems, ever since. But the miners ain't makin' no more money now than they was when they was first hired by the Stoughtons."

"How much they pulled out of the mine?"

"Mines. There's three of 'em workin' over in the gulch. Six-Gun Mine's the biggest, and the main one. Last I heard, the Stoughtons had pulled about four million out of the three mines."

McLeary's eyes widened. "That's mighty damned good."

"Right." Wilson grew more self-assured. "They got plenty of cash, the Stoughton brothers do. But they ain't givin' any to the poor bastards workin' down in the holes. So the miners have been threatening to strike—close the mines until they get better pay. Soon's the brother's heard that talk, they started bringing in gunmen"—again the worried glance at McLeary's deadly-looking pistol—"to scare the miners." Wilson held his breath, afraid again.

"And you thought I was another one?" McLeary asked in some amusement.

"Yep." Wilson laughed nervously. "I mean, you are a . . . a . . ."

"Yeah, I am, Lem. But I ain't been hired by the Stoughton brothers. Never heard of 'em till now. I'm just driftin' through. Decided to stop by for a drink, a meal—" he paused a moment—"and maybe a woman."

Wilson sighed with relief. He considered himself a good judge of people, and he thought he could trust this tall, thin, hard-eyed stranger.

"Well," Lem said with a small smile, "you've had the drink. If you want food, there's Lankshire's down the street. Nobody knows for sure if the Stoughtons own it or not. Don't matter much, though. It's the only decent place to eat in town—except for the Silver Nugget. Rest of the restaurants"—he snorted—"are rat holes. Not for the likes of decent people."

Wilson paused. Then: "We got some women in cribs out back. Unless," he added, his voice trembling some, "you go to the Silver Nugget, where you can get all three—and better quality, too—all at once."

"That the Stoughton place?"

"Yep. They own a considerable piece of Silver Canyon—includin' the Silver Nugget and Lucy's place." He pointed to where McLeary had seen the brothel.

"I kinda like it here."

Wilson beamed. "Let me get you another beer, Mister McLeary."

"No thanks, Lem," McLeary said, setting his hat on. "You know where I could get a shave and maybe a bath?"

"Parker's." He said it with distaste. When McLeary gave him a questioning look, he explained, "That belongs to the brothers."

"Anyplace else?"

"Old woman named May Vanderloon lives next to Lankshire's Restaurant. She's got a tub in back, and she gives a pretty fair shave if you don't mind a few nicks in your chin." He grinned.

"I've had worse. Thanks, Lem."

"Be seein' you again, Mister McLeary?" Wilson asked, with a combination of fear and hope. "Maybe for a woman, eh?" He winked lecherously.

"Never can tell, Lem." McLeary grinned. "Thanks for your hospitality." He turned and headed for the door, spurs clanking rhythmically.

Chapter 3

McLeary was playing poker at the Pick and Shovel Saloon, watching his small stash of money dwindle, when two men approached and stood over him. After they observed him for two hands, with McLeary ignoring them, the younger of the two men coughed almost discreetly.

McLeary tossed down the cards for another lousy hand, aware of the thick silence that had started slowly when the two well-dressed men had entered the saloon and built as they waited. Finally that silence was complete.

Pushing his Stetson back on his head, McLeary tilted his chair until it teetered on its two back legs and rested against the log wall of the saloon. "You boys want in the game?" he asked politely, eyes looking over them.

The older of the two was perhaps forty. He had a well-fed look about him, like he had adjusted well to a life of ease, comfort and wealth. He wore a dark wool suit, with a starched white shirt, black string tie, and a vest that matched the suit. A tall, silk top hat was perched on his oiled black hair, and a silver watch fob dangled from the watch pocket of his vest, visible where the suit jacket was open over the substantial middle. His jowly face was clean-shaven, and his hands were soft, as if they had never done a hard day's work.

The other was close to McLeary's age—maybe thirty-two. He had a perpetual sneer on his bowed lips, and a challenging look in his eyes, as if trying to project a sense of hardness. He looked to be strong, but McLeary doubted the man was anywhere near as tough as he attempted to appear. He wore a brown derby on his slick, longish black hair. He, too, wore a dark wool suit over a starched stiff white shirt, and the inevitable silver watch fob curved across his slim midsection. Under the man's suit jacket, McLeary could see the pearl handle of a Colt, probably a .32 or .36 caliber,

McLeary figured.

"We'd like a word with you, mister," the younger one said. "We've been waiting some time now, too."

"I've been busy," McLeary said cooly, casting calm eyes over them.

"Why you . . ." the younger man started, until the older brother touched his arm and said quietly, "Easy, George." Then he looked at McLeary and said, "My name is Alva Stoughton. This is my brother George."

"So?" McLeary asked. The cards were being dealt again, and he turned his attention back to the game, leaning the chair forward so it was sitting flat again. He gathered up his pasteboards and cupped them closely in a large hand.

"We have a proposition for you, Mister McLeary."

"Ain't interested." McLeary laid down his cards, backs up, and tossed a paper bill into the pot. He pulled a cheroot from his shirt pocket, bit off the tip, and lit the small cigar.

"I think" Alva said calmly, while George seethed quietly, "that it would be worth your while to listen to what we have to say, Mister McLeary."

McLeary took three cards and looked at them carefully again. A pair of sixes, a three, a king and a nine. Another terrible hand. The betting came around to him again, and he tossed in the cards. "I'm out," he muttered, annoyed. He shrugged. He knew damn well what the Stoughtons wanted, but his luck with the cards tonight was lousy. He might as well listen to the two brothers. Maybe he could get a free drink or two out of it. He stood, shoving the chair back with his legs as he did. "All right," he said. "Let's go talk."

He shoved past the brothers and walked to an empty table. He sat and waited patiently for the other two men to catch up. When they had sat, McLeary looked at them calmly. His eyes widened when George said abruptly, "We want to hire you, Mister McLeary."

Alva caught the raised eyebrows and grinned. He seemed a pleasant enough man, McLeary thought, but he was still cautious. "Please excuse my brother, Mister McLeary," Alva said. "He is yet young, and does not know the finer points of life. George, order a bottle."

"But—"

"You can't expect us to do business when our 'guest' has a dry mouth, George."

"But he's just a goddamn gunfi—"

"Another thing you'd best learn, boy," McLeary growled, voice hard as flint, "is manners. You may have money, boy, but that don't impress everybody you meet." He stamped the cheroot out on the table with angry stabs, aware that everyone in the saloon was gathering around, watching them.

George sputtered, and then started to say something, but Alva snapped, "Enough, George. Get us a bottle." He looked toward McLeary and said, "Unless you'd rather have a beer?"

"I would."

"Fetch it, George."

Then Lem Wilson loomed up at the side of the table. "What'll it be, gents?" he asked nervously. This was the first time any of the Stoughtons had been in his saloon, and he did not like it.

They ordered, and sat waiting until the barkeep returned with a foaming mug of beer for McLeary and one for George. Alva uncorked the bottle the bar owner had brought, and poured a shot. He raised the short, stubby glass in a sort of salute before downing the shot in one gulp.

McLeary nodded curtly and poured some beer down his throat. He placed the heavy mug on the table and then swiped at the foam residue on his mouth with the back of a hand. "Well?" he questioned.

Alva threw back another shot before saying, "As you know, Mister McLeary, we are owners—with our older brother Tom—of Consolidated Silver and Mining."

McLeary nodded and sipped at his beer.

"We have, in the almost four years we have owned the Squaw Gulch mines, tried to treat our workers with respect and dignity. They are well paid, well cared for. Their safety is paramount."

"That ain't what I heard," McLeary said easily, almost grinning as fire leaped into George's eyes.

"Undoubtedly," Alva muttered. He sighed as the weight of business problems settled heavily on his shoulders. "As you might figure, there are some . . . agitators, shall we say . . . who are trying to stir the miners up. They talk of higher salaries, shorter work days, other things. . . ." He waved a hand in the air, as if dismissing the miners' concerns as not important enough for him to even mention, let alone consider.

"So?" McLeary reached into his shirt pocket for another cheroot.

"Wait," Alva said with a smile. From an inner pocket of his suit jacket, he produced a silver case. He opened it to reveal half a dozen fat, expensive cigars. He took out one and handed it to McLeary, who nodded his thanks. Then he pulled one for himself.

McLeary scraped a match on the table and held it out so Alva could light his cigar after biting off the end. Then McLeary lit his own. Both men leaned back in their chairs, puffing quietly, enjoying the fine tobacco.

"Good cigar," McLeary said. It was true, too. A man like him didn't often have such amenities.

Alva nodded and said, "To get back to the subject at hand . . ."

"About time," George muttered, barely audibly.

". . . we need regulators to keep the peace at the mines. Men such as yourself."

"You mean you need gunfighters to intimidate the miners, don't you?" McLeary said amiably.

There was a shuffling and low rumble from the men who had gathered in a half circle behind the Stoughton brothers, facing McLeary.

"Heavens no," Alva said with a fine display of horror passing across his face. "No, no, no. Our regulators are duly hired company employees, drawing their salaries along with all others on the company payroll. Let's just say they are kind of like having our own Pinkerton men. They keep agitators from stirring up too much trouble, guard our silver shipments, and keep watch over the working men, so that none start pocketing a nugget here and there. No working man is beyond that, as you might well imagine. The temptation of so much silver laying around is, well . . ."

"Mister Stoughton, you are full of shit, pure and simple," McLeary said. He was smiling. He liked Alva Stoughton, but that did not mean he had to side with him.

George's face clouded over with anger, but Alva grinned back at McLeary. "You are a direct man, Mister McLeary," he said through the cloud of cigar smoke. He downed another shot.

As he did, George jumped in, saying angrily, "Why you broken down excuse for a gunman. Christ, you can't even do the jobs you're hired on for. We heard what happened over in Otero County." He grinned maliciously when he saw McLeary's eyes darken with anger for the first time. "Oh, yeah, we heard all about how—"

"Stop!" Alva ordered sharply, and George snapped his lips shut. He fumed silently. "You must learn to control these outbursts, George," Alva said quietly. Turning his fleshy face back toward McLeary he said. "I may be full of shit, Mister McLeary, but we still need men of your talents. George was right—we did check on you. You have a considerable reputation, you know, despite what happened in Otero County. You would be a benefit to us, and the Consolidated Silver and Mining Company, if you were to join us."

"No thanks, Mister Stoughton. I ain't lookin' for a job just now. Didn't even know what was goin' on here till I rode in yesterday. All I plan to do is stay a day or two, fill up on some good grub, entertain myself a little"—he winked man-to-man at Alva, who nodded and smiled—"and then ride on out."

"Have you another job somewhere, then?"

"No, Mister Stoughton. But I have no plans to stay here either. I'm on my way to California."

"Call me Alva. May I call you Charlie?" When McLeary nodded twice, Alva continued: "California's a long way off. And it can offer you nothing we can't offer you here. We have fine food, a plush bordello, one of the best saloons in the state in the Silver Nugget."

"You make it sound tempting, Mister . . . Alva. You purely do."

The crowd groaned.

"But I still reckon not."

The crowd seemed relieved.

"What can I do to change your mind?" Alva asked, ignoring the crowd that moved in closer behind him. "We pay well. You can have an open account at the Silver Nugget, as well as at Lucy's. Taylor's Mercantile will be open to you."

"I said no, and I meant it. You have enough guns, I reckon."

"You yellow-backed, chicken son of a bitch," George sputtered. "Got no—"

McLeary turned hard, glittering eyes on the young mine owner. "You continue on with that sentence, boy," he snarled, "and you'll be dead before you finish it."

George was florid with rage, but he retained enough sense to keep his mouth shut.

"I think our business is done, eh, Alva?" McLeary asked, looking at the older brother.

Stoughton looked at the hard edge to McLeary's jaw, and he nodded. "I would say. However, should you change your mind, please look me up. I'm usually to be found at the Silver Nugget." He held out his hand, and McLeary shook it. "Good day to you, sir," the older Stoughton said as he stood and swept up his hat. He turned and, with a furious sibling in tow, pushed through the crowd, which responded with rude cheers and catcalls.

The saloon gradually fell back to normal as McLeary finished his beer and the cigar. He thought to get back into the poker game, but then decided against it. Instead, he went to Lankshire's to eat. Afterward, he wandered to Markham's General Store. Since Alva Stoughton had mentioned Taylor's, McLeary figured the brothers owned it. So he chose the other.

He bought a shirt, and some cheroots. As he turned after paying, he almost ran over an attractive, well-dressed young woman. "Sorry, ma'am," he said, tipping his hat to her.

"My fault entirely," she said softly, batting long eyelashes over doe-brown eyes at him.

"If you say, ma'am. If you'll excuse me." He stepped around her and headed for the door.

"You could buy a girl dinner," he heard the woman say, and he turned back toward her.

"Ma'am?" he asked, a little stupified.

She closed the gap between them and looked up at him. "I said," she repeated, "that you could buy a girl dinner. As a sort of apology."

He seemed unsure, so she added, "I could make it worth your while." Desire smoldered in her deep eyes.

He grinned. "I reckon I could do that," he said. He stared at her beautiful face, wondering. Either she was from Lucy's, where the women would be fancy, and not as obvious as those who plied their trade at the Pick and Shovel; or she was a strange woman, to offer herself so freely like this. Good women simply did not do such things. Well, he decided, he would find out. If she was one of Lucy's girls, he would get away cheap with a dinner. If she was not, well . . .

Chapter 4

Janie May Dillon looked stunning sitting across the table from Charlie McLeary at Lankshire's Restaurant. She wore a high-necked dress of dark green satin, with a lighter green collar, hem and wrists. Matching buttons ran the length from neck to cinched waist, and the bodice was ornamented with white lace. Her hair hung in dark ringlets down to her shoulders.

She smiled at McLeary, showing small, white teeth. Her smile was a bit crooked, with one side of her trim upper lip lifting fractionally higher than the other. Her lower lip was full and pouty. Her cheekbones were regally high, and her forehead wide over thick eyebrows. Her bosom rose out above her tiny waist dramatically.

Dillon was, McLeary thought, startlingly beautiful. He smiled back at her, thoughts of what the night might bring careening through his mind. And he did not just think they were idle thoughts. After he had almost run into the delectable Miss Dillon, he had done some discrete checking.

Dillon, he found out, was a recent addition to the parlors and comfortable bedrooms of Miss Lucy's pleasure palace. He had also learned that she did not usually dress so formally, even while "in town." Therefore, he deduced, she had been sent after him. And it could only have been done by the Stoughtons.

And, while assumptions were sometimes dangerous, he felt safe this time in assuming that the brothers were still trying to bring him into the fold. With that in mind, he had decided in the afternoon that he would enjoy the plush body of Miss Janie May Dillon, availing himself of her services as frequently as he could—at least until she found out he knew she was a plant from the Stoughtons.

They had made small talk on the short walk to the restaurant and then while waiting for their food to be delivered. Both were relieved when the meal came, since making small talk was difficult under the circumstances.

Besides that, McLeary was hungry, and it was with gusto that he tore into the ham steak, peas, boiled potatoes and biscuits. Dillon ate her baked chicken, carrots, yams and biscuits with more restraint.

Afterward there was coffee, and cherry cobbler. Finished, McLeary leaned back, stuffed, and lit a cheroot.

Dillon looked at him and said, "Aplology accepted."

He nodded, smiling. "I can but try, ma'am."

"You try quite well, Mister McLeary." She hesitated demurely a moment before saying, "If only there was some way I could show my appreciation . . ."

"I'm sure we could think of something."

"Whatever do you mean, sir?"

She was a good actress, McLeary thought. "Well . . ." was all he said, drawing the single word out.

She tried to show horror, but failed. "Well, I never . . ." she started, faltering.

"Maybe you should," he said easily, with a roguish grin.

"You don't think I do this kind of thing as a matter of course, do you?" She sounded concerned.

"Certainly not," he replied hastily, assuringly.

"Well . . ." Now it was she who drew that single word out. She cast her eyes down briefly, before looking up at him again. There was an impish smile on her lips. "I guess that would be all right," she said conspiratorially. "But where? . . . How? . . . I don't know much about these things, you know."

"It'll all work out, don't you worry," he said soothingly, playing the game.

"Now?" she asked, almost gulping in her mock fright.

"Might as well." He stood and settled his J.B. on his head. He held out a hand for her. She took it and squeezed lightly as she rose from the chair. Arm in arm they strolled back to the Casa de Plata Hotel. It, too, was owned by the Stoughton brothers, but so were the other two hotels; and McLeary had no choice but to stay in one of them, since all the boardinghouses were full.

No one seemed to pay them any mind as they strolled through the soft mid-June night in the San Juan Mountains. McLeary enjoyed the coolness and the scent of wild flowers. And no one paid them heed as they entered the elegant hotel and walked up the carpeted, curving staircase to his room.

Inside, McLeary tossed his hat on the table. As he turned to face Dillon, she said, "Well, what now?"

"Don't make this any harder than you have to," McLeary said stiffly.

Real surprise leaped into her eyes, but she quickly quelled it and continued with her charade. She smiled. "Well, I must admit, I was married once. I'm widowed."

"Then you ought to know what to do."

"I reckon, but it's different like this, somehow."

"You still know how to kiss a man, don't you?"

Her smile spread, and it was a wonderful thing to see. "Reckon I do." She slid up to him and wrapped her arms around his slim, hard middle. Tilting her head up, she said, "Well?"

He bent and kissed her hard. She responded in kind—her tongue toying with his; her lips moving—forgetting for the moment the part she was supposed to be playing.

Finally she pulled her lips away. "That was something," she said breathlessly.

He grinned and peeled her arms from around his waist. She looked a little frightened. McLeary began undoing the buttons on the front of her dress, and she looked more scared. She's a fine actress, McLeary thought. Almost worthy enough for the stage in someplace like Denver or San Francisco.

With her bodice loose, McLeary peeled the top of her dress off her pale, white shoulders. It fell to her waist, showing the new corset. Even McLeary could tell the corset had never been used before. He worked at it steadfastly, until finally he peeled the stiff garment away, exposing Dillon's large, firm breasts.

He smiled as her eyes closed and she leaned back, providing him better access. His head dipped and his lips brushed hers before moving southward across her chin. He kissed the hollow of her neck and then slid his tongue in a trail through the valley of her bosom.

She moaned, and McLeary figured she was not acting; but considering her profession, he couldn't be sure. Her eyes were closed, and her breathing erratic.

He straightened and quickly stripped off his shirt and shoulder holster, not really wanting her to see it. A secret weapon would do no good once it was not a secret any longer. He tossed them aside, and Janie partially opened her eyes as he removed the rest of her clothing. "Hurry," she muttered, forgetting her role again. McLeary nodded and shucked his boots, and pants.

Soon after, when they were trying to catch their breath, McLeary was sure Dillon had not been faking. Her skin was blotchy, as it would get only after. . . . He grinned to himself, and nuzzled her neck.

Eventually he sat up, then stood and picked up his shirt. Pulling out a cheroot, he lit it and sat on the side of the bed. Janie dreamily ran her hand up and down his back.

"That was fun," she said softly.

"I'm glad." For some reason, he was rather annoyed now, and wanted little to do with her.

"It wasn't like that with my husband," she said. "Never."

He clamped his lips shut over the retort that threatened to spill out. He had been about to tell her he knew who—and what—she was. But he decided to wait and see if it would lead anywhere. So he said nothing.

After McLeary stubbed out the cheroot, Dillon asked, "Could we . . . again? . . . You wouldn't think I was a . . . was . . ."

"No, I wouldn't," he answered. Just as suddenly as he had decided he wanted nothing more to do with her, he reversed course and desired her badly again.

In the morning, Dillon rose first. "I have to get home," she said, picking up her stockings and putting them on, oblivious to McLeary's ogling. Dawn's pink glow was edging past the sides of the curtains. She picked up a petticoat and pulled the garment on.

McLeary didn't much care, but he thought he should be polite. "Want me to walk you home?" he asked.

"No, that ain't necessary." She had on the last of her petticoats and was struggling to get her dress on. "People might talk." She sounded worried, though she certainly didn't look that way.

"All right." She was beautiful, and a delight in bed. But he grew tired of playing the game, of hiding what he knew about her; of having her also playing the game, trying to convince him she was just some poor, lonely widow.

"Will I see you again?" she asked.

"If you like."

"I would," she said enthusiastically, and McLeary wondered for a moment if perhaps she had stopped playing the game there for a moment.

"Fine. Tonight?"

"Yes," she answered somewhat breathlessly.

"Eight o'clock?" he asked. She nodded. Stifling a grin, he asked, "Where do I pick you up?"

Real fright blinked onto her face, and she hesitated in buttoning up the dress. It passed in a moment, and she said, trying to sound modest, "I'll come here."

"Sure." He did grin then, but he turned his face toward the window so Janie May Dillon could not see it.

She came up to him and kissed him lightly on the lips. Then she was gone, closing the door softly behind her. McLeary rose and watched out the window, barely parting the curtain. He saw Dillon walk out of the hotel. Halfway across the street she stopped and looked back up at his room. He grinned, knowing she could not see him. She turned and hurried the short distance to Miss Lucy's and went inside.

McLeary stretched. He padded naked across the room and picked up his clothes; then he dressed and went to the Pick and Shovel. The bar was full of miners this time, and was noisy.

"Give me a beer, Lem," McLeary said after elbowing his way through to the plank bar.

"Sure thing, Charlie." Lem Wilson hurried off and was back quickly with a mug of frosty beer. "Nice'n cold, just like you want it," he said proudly.

"Thanks."

Wilson rushed off, adroitly dodging the two bartenders he had on duty to handle the crowd. McLeary smiled and sipped at the beer. It tasted good, especially in the hot, malodorous saloon. He looked around the room—at the unbroken line of dirty men standing at the bar; at the tables of disheveled miners playing cards and drinking; at the groups of men sitting, talking, arguing and laughing.

He noticed that several men kept glancing his way. It did not unnerve him, since he was rather used to it. But he kept his guard up.

As he was starting on his second beer, he saw two of the men who had been watching him start marching in his direction. He placed the beer down and surreptitiously dropped his arm to unhook the small loop over the hammer of his Smith and Wesson American.

Lem was nearby, pouring a shot of whiskey for someone. "Hey, Lem," McLeary called quietly. When the barman looked up, he said, "Who're the two boys headin' my way?"

Wilson looked. "The tall one's Pete Bowers; the other's Duncan McGregor. Both are kind of leaders of the miners."

McLeary nodded. The two men stopped in front of him. Both wore stained wool shirts and blue duck pants, plain, heavy brogans covered with clay, and tattered felt hats that were covered with dirt and candle drippings. McGregor was barely five and a half feet tall, if that; Bowers, maybe an inch shorter than McLeary's six-foot-one. Both looked strong, and their eyes—McGregor's dark blue; Bowers' brown—were determined.

"A word with you, if you'd please, Mister McLeary," Bowers said. There was authority in his voice, and McLeary could understand why men would follow him.

"Ask away, boys."

"Shall we take a table?"

McLeary shrugged and followed Bowers and McGregor.

Chapter 5

"My name's Pete Bowers," Bowers said as he sat. He pointed to his companion. "This here's Duncan McGregor."

McLeary nodded at each.

"We represent the miners."

"What do you mean 'represent'?" McLeary asked harshly. He could see what was coming already, and was in no mood for it.

"We talk for them," Bowers said, a little taken aback. He had thought this was going to be easy. Now he was not so sure. "We have gone to the owners and talked with them about the men's concerns. We advise the workers in areas of mine safety, pay, other working conditions."

"You ain't doin' such a good job of it, are you?" McLeary said in some annoyance. "You boys ain't had a pay raise in, what, three years? Longer? That's what I heard."

Bowers growled, and McGregor looked down, ashamed. "We been tryin', but the Stoughtons"—he just about spit out the name—"won't give an inch."

"Then go on strike," McLeary said without mercy. "All you boys walk out, the Stoughtons won't have nobody left to work the mines. They'll come around to your way of thinkin'."

"They'd just hire more from up in Denver, or any of the other minin' camps around here even," Bowers said angrily.

"Besides," McGregor snapped, showing no trace of Scottish burr in his speech, "they got the guns—and the men that know how to use 'em." He was angry, and it showed in the eyes peering out from the dirty face.

"Face 'em down."

"With what?" Bowers demanded. "We got nothin' but picks and shovels and axes. What're we supposed to do, throw rocks at mounted gunslingers?"

"Get some guns. You boys could afford to buy a pistol each—if you wanted to enough."

"Stores around here won't sell 'em to us. The Stoughtons own Taylor's. The owner of Markham's is afraid of the Stoughtons, and won't sell us any."

"Order 'em by mail, if you have to. Or, hell, scrape up some money, pick one of your men—one you trust—give him the cash, and send him off to Ouray or Silverton and buy some there. I don't reckon the Stoughtons hold much power there."

"What're we gonna do with guns, even if we get 'em?" McGregor asked, more calmly. "We are facing hardened gunmen. Killers each and all. We are but miners, Mister McLeary. We cannot face down those men."

"How many of them are there?"

"Two dozen, or thereabouts," McGregor answered.

"And how many of you miners?"

"Seventy-five, maybe eighty," Bowers answered.

"Seems," McLeary said as he drained the last of the beer, "that the odds are in your favor, Mister Bowers."

Bowers waved toward the bar, and soon another mug of beer appeared in front of McLeary. The gunman lifted it and sort of saluted both miners before taking a sip.

"We are not fools, Mister McLeary," McGregor finally said. "Of course the numbers are in our favor. But, just as obviously, we know that half our men would get killed if we were to go against the Stoughton brothers' 'regulators.' We are, after all, miners, not killers."

There were a number of arguments McLeary could make, things like figuring that probably a substantial number of the miners had fought in the Civil War and would be unafraid of bloodshed; that a good many of the miners had crossed the Plains, facing death every day from hostile Indians, wild animals, raging rivers and more; that they could ambush the gunmen, thereby negating the hired gunmen's talents and advantages.

However, he knew equally well that neither of these two men would listen to such arguments. They—and most likely the rest of the miners—had their minds made up, and there was nothing he could say to change them.

"And just what do you want of me?" McLeary asked, knowing, but still wanting them to voice it.

"We want you to join our cause, Mister McLeary," McGregor said with dignity and conviction.

"No." McLeary liked the short, powerfully built Duncan McGregor, but he would not let himself be sucked into this foolishness—especially since the miners seemed to want him to do everything for them. No, it was too reminiscent of his fiasco with the sodbusters in Otero County. He would not be drawn into another such idiocy so soon after it.

Indeed, he could hear his old dad's cackling high voice saying, "If you don't want to git yer ass et up, boy, ye don't go bitin' a griz on the nose."

"But why?" McGregor blurted out.

" 'Cause it's a damnfool idea, is why," McLeary said, growing angry. How dare these men question his motives and decisions. "I may not be the smartest man God ever put here, but I ain't the dumbest neither."

"But we'd pay you," Bowers started.

"I know that. But . . ." He paused to collect his thoughts, and to sip some more beer. "I ain't but one man, boys," he finally said. "I can't do nothin' against all them gunmen, especially if there's any good ones in the bunch. I didn't come here to get involved in all this. I just rode in 'cause it was the first likely place I saw—"

"While you were runnin'?" Bowers sneered.

McLeary's eyebrows raised. "Yep, while I was runnin'. Seems like I got my ass in a situation very much like this one back in Otero County. Wound up facing down more than a dozen hired guns. If you boys think I'm a coward for not standin' up under them kind of odds, that's your business."

Bowers looked like that's exactly what he thought, and McLeary said mercilessly, "Of course, it ain't quite the same as not facin' down some gunmen when the numbers are four or five to one in your favor."

He leaned back and sipped beer, while Bowers fumed and McGregor sat looking thoughtful.

"Like I said, boys," McLeary said after a short spell, "I was just ridin' through. I had aimed to leave tomorrow, but—" he chuckled—"you see, I met this here woman and—"

"That trollop Janie May?" Bowers sneered.

"That's the one."

"She's a strumpet over at Lucy's, you know," Bowers said, using the words as if they were daggers.

"I know."

"She's workin' for the Stoughtons."

"I know that, too."

"They probably set her onto you to get you to join their side—become another one of the goddamn 'regulators.' "

"I reckon so."

"You know all this," Bowers asked, almost incredulously, "and yet you're still gonna go on seein' her?"

"Reckon so. She's the finest piece of woman flesh this old boy's had in a long, long spell. I ain't gonna pass it up just 'cause she works over in a joy house. Hell, I kinda like the idea of havin' me a high-class whore all to myself, even if for a little while, when somebody else is payin' the freight."

"Why you goddamn—"

"Shut up, Pete," McGregor snapped. "We had hoped you might want to join us, Mister McLeary. But we cannot force you to do so. However, if I may ask, are you plannin' on joinin' the Stoughtons?"

"No more than I am you. I ain't no more in favor of runnin' roughshod over a bunch of workin' folks than I am in facin' down an army. My old pap had a sayin' about such things. He used to say, 'Whether the wind's a blowin' east or west, hard or soft, you don't piss into it.' "

McLeary stood and said, " 'Night, gentlemen." He wandered back to his hotel room.

He took his leisure the rest of the day, waiting with a combination of excitement, interest and curiosity for the arrival of Janie May Dillon. There was no denying that her body was one of the finest he had ever seen, and she knew well how to use it, even when she was holding back in her roll of innocent widow.

He ate a substantial dinner and bought a bottle of whiskey to have in the room. Then he dressed in the best clothes he had—which, he must admit, were not all that good. However, he thought with a grin, he probably wouldn't be wearing them long anyway. And he made sure the shoulder holster was out of sight.

He sat in one of the plush chairs at the table, reading one of the town's two newspapers. The one he was reading, the Silver Canyon *Telegraph,* obviously was owned, or at least controlled, by the Stoughtons. It was far larger than the *Bulletin-Times,* it had much more advertising, and was quite slanted in favorable coverage of the Stoughton brothers and the Consolidated Silver and Mining Company.

There was a light tap on the door. McLeary dropped the papers and stood. He took the three quick steps to the bed and pulled the Smith and Wesson from the holster hanging there. Thumbing back the hammer, he went to the door. Standing slightly to the side, he pulled it open quickly.

Janie May Dillon gasped in surprise.

"Come on in," he said cheerily as he eased the hammer of the pistol down. He slid the revolver back into the holster. When he turned back to face Dillon, she was naked. She had worn nothing but a long, brown dress and soft, felt slippers. Both were lying on the floor at her feet.

She stood coyly, seeming ever so tiny without the high heels on. McLeary felt a warm tingling in his groin. He didn't care who Dillion worked for; she was too ripe a woman to ignore. Slowly he began to unbutton his shirt.

McLeary was loathe to leave Silver Canyon. He had come to like Janie May Dillon, and enjoyed their interludes. He had planned to tell her soon off that he knew what she was up to, but he could not bring himself to do so. He knew that as she learned that, she would be gone, taking the pleasures of her body away forever.

So he kept silent, continuing the deceit, even after she began to hint in the two days after their second night together that perhaps he would be wise to hire on as a regulator for Consolidated Silver and Mining.

"Why?" he had asked innocently.

"Well," she had said slowly, as if this was of great importance to her, "you've got little money, or so you've told me. It'd give you a regular job—with regular pay."

"You got a point there, Janie," he said, pretending to think it over. "But I reckon not."

"Why?" she asked, face falling. She thought she had him there for a few minutes.

"Just not to my likin' is all."

"What do you mean, 'not to my likin'?" she exploded.

He almost grinned. He figured she stood to gain a substantial bonus for this job, and would not get it unless she brought him into the fold. "I don't hold with intimidatin' plain folks," he said, meaning it.

"That's not what you'd have to do," she said, almost pleading. "You'd—" She clamped her mouth shut.

"What do you know about it?" he asked her sternly.

"Nothin'," Dillon mumbled, embarrassed. She had almost given it all away. "Just what I hear around town."

A few minutes later she had left, angry, and a little worried. But she was back that night, and the next, willing and eager. The night after that, though, she stormed into his room when he opened the door. There was fire in her eyes, and he knew the game was up.

"You bastard!" she screamed at him, trying to kick him. "Rotten, filthy, lyin', evil, two-tongued son of a bitch."

"Somethin' wrong?" he asked, grinning, and adroitly avoiding her small fists and occasional kick.

"Wrong? *Wrong?*" She was screeching now. "You know. When did you learn? How? Why'd you? . . ."

She could go on no more, but still she tried to reach him with fist and foot. He continued to dance out of the way, before he finally grabbed her in a bear hug. She fought for a while, but her strength ran out fast; and she stood, shaking in his tight embrace.

He let her go, and she sank onto the bed, sitting and crying.

"Don't you go pullin' that nonsense with me, Janie May—if that's really your name. The game's over. You needn't continue it."

The tears stopped, and she looked up at him. She grinned. "Had to give it a last try."

He nodded.

"How'd you find out?" she asked.

"First day I met you, I thought it was a little odd. Did some checkin' about town and found out you worked at Lucy's. I didn't know at the time you were sent to try to get me to become a regulator, but I figured it."

"You knew from the beginning and strung me along?" She wasn't sure whether to be angry or to laugh.

He shrugged, nodding. "You ain't the only one can play act."

"And so get yourself a woman like me for nothin', eh?"

"Yep. But I reckon you got your money for the time you've been spendin' with me."

"Sure did. But you cost me a hundred dollar bonus."

"Sorry."

"Don't be." She stood and shucked her dress and shoes. Standing there nude, she said, "I ain't. I could've used the hundred dollars, but, damn, we had us a fine time, didn't we?"

"Yep." He grinned.

"Well come on and take me, big boy, one last time. Next time, you'll have to fork over the cash, and let me tell you, sweetheart, I'm the most expensive girl at Lucy's."

"I believe it," McLeary said, smiling. "And because of that, I doubt I'll ever get over there. I'll be leavin' town soon anyway."

Sadness tinged Dillon's face as she nodded her acceptance. Then her face brightened. "Well, hell, cowboy, we still got this night. Come on over here and do me proud."

McLeary moved to her and took her in his arms. "Yes, ma'am," he muttered.

Chapter 6

McLeary tensed when the three men entered the Pick and Shovel. He quietly set down the shot glass he had just emptied—the redeye still trailing warm down into his insides—and unhooked the loop over the hammer of the Smith and Wesson.

There was no question the three men were guns hired by the Stoughtons, and McLeary could only assume they were looking for trouble—or him, which amounted to the same thing.

All three stopped just inside the swinging doors, eyes searching the interior. They seemed almost to be preening, letting and sundry bask in their importance. It was, McLeary thought, ridiculous, since he was one of only four customers in the place.

The three gunslingers spotted McLeary. One took up a position next to the doors, while the other two headed for McLeary's table. Charlie looked them over with seeming indifference.

All three were young, lean and hard. The first was of medium height, and wore Mexican-style striped pants of heavy wool, with a crisp white shirt and black vest. The shirt was buttoned up to the neck, and he had on a string tie. A sombrero shaded his boyish eyes. Two Colts rode his hips, butts facing forward, and he wore Spanish spurs with gigantic rowels that rang with each step.

The one walking with him was an inch or so shorter. He looked down on his luck, with a pair of well-worn brown denim pants and no shirt other than the top of his once white long johns. His hat was felt and once might have been a derby or short-brimmed Stetson, but you couldn't tell now, so battered and moth-eaten was it. But the polished butt of the heavy-duty .44 caliber Remington showed care.

McLeary had a less-clear picture of the one by the door, but he was tall, thin and had a decidedly deadly air about him. His eyes were shaded by a Boss-style Stetson hat, and he wore two fancy Colts—one on his left hip, the other in a shoulder rig on the right side of his chest.

McLeary waited, alert. He had eaten breakfast a short while ago over at Lankshire's—after one final session with the delectable Miss Janie May Dillon. He had figured on leaving town right after breakfast, but on the short walk back toward the hotel, he had decided to stop at the Pick and Shovel, have a few snorts of redeye, maybe say his farewells to Lem Wilson, and then leave. He had just downed his second shot and was trying to decide whether to refill his glass one last time when the three gunmen had entered.

The two were at the table now. "You McLeary?" one asked. He seemed nervous, but the coating of sweat on his face could have been from the oppressive heat.

McLeary fought back the grin. This arrogant young punk knew of his reputation and was afraid, though he was trying manfully not to let it show. Charlie stared at the young man with flat eyes. His left forearm was on the table, crosswise to his body. His right elbow was cupped in that hand, and his right hand slowly stroked the long, dangling mustache. He said nothing.

"I ast you was you McLeary," the young man demanded again.

"And if I am?" McLeary finally said.

"I got a message for you."

"From who?" McLeary never took his eyes off the young man. He had exceptional peripheral vision, and used it to keep an eye on the other.

"Mister Stoughton."

"Which one?"

"It don't matter. One's the same as the other."

"They talk and you jump, eh, boy?" McLeary said with a sneer.

The young man started, anger flushing his face. With his lack of intelligence, he was stuck without something to say. His hand twitched uncomfortably close to the Colt's pearl grip.

"What's your name, boy?" McLeary asked in a hard voice.

"Cale Oakes." He seemed a little befuddled.

"Well, Cale," McLeary said, dropping the hand from his mustache so it was resting on the table, "speak your piece, and then get your ass out of my sight before they haul it away in a pine box."

Again the flush of anger splattered over Oakes' bitter face.

"Can we sit?" the other asked in a stutter.

McLeary turned his eyes on this one. He would bear watching, McLeary thought. Despite the stutter, the ratty clothes and general air of disreputableness, he had a look of competence in his greenish eyes. He must lull a lot of people into a sense of security, McLeary thought, with the outward appearance. It would give him an edge against many people. But McLeary would not be taken in by it.

"Name's Karl Hendrixson," the young man stuttered.

McLeary nodded and waved a hand at the chair across from him.

Hendrixson and Oakes sat, the former's face open and almost friendly; the other's still contorted with anger and an inability to voice the thoughts that slammed around inside his jumbled brain.

The bartender—one of Lem Wilson's helpers, since Lem was not in yet—brought two shot glasses, set them on the table and then scurried back behind the bar. He was pale with fright.

The other three customers also were scared, but would not chance trying to walk out past the lanky gunman leaning nonchalantly against the wall next to the door.

McLeary poured out three shots, and all the men were silent as they chugged the drinks back. Done, McLeary said, "Now, like I said before, speak your piece and then leave me be."

"Well, Mister Stoughton wanted us to bring you a message," Hendrixson said, fighting to form the words around the stuttering.

"I'll tell it," Oakes snarled. "Goddamn flabber-mouth fool."

McLeary watched silently. It was obvious that Hendrixson was far more intelligent and had more book learning than Oakes, but because of his stutter, he was afraid to speak. It was obvious, too, that he did not like having his handicap pointed out to him.

"Mister Stoughton said to tell you that you got a choice." Oakes paused in self-importance, watching McLeary's face, and it worried him. He decided to hurry on. "He says he wants you to throw in with us—or leave town."

"That your message?"

"Most of it," Oakes said haltingly.

"You got more to say, spill it. I got more important things to do than sit here jawin' with the likes of you."

Oakes' face twitched, and his breathing rasped in and out.

McLeary's mustache quivered as he battled down a grin. He quietly dipped into his shirt pocket and pulled out a cheroot and a match. He lit the small cigar and blew smoke across the table. "If you're through makin' faces at me, boy, finish up what you got to say," he snarled.

Oakes shoved his chair back, the legs of it scraping on the dirt floor. His hands dropped to his sides, halting inches away from the Colts. His ruddy, moronic face twitched and jerked as anger coursed through him.

"You pull either of them Colts, boy," McLeary said in a voice cold as mountain ice, "and I'll splatter your insides all over this saloon before you clear leather."

Hendrixson held out his hand toward Oakes. "Don't," he said softly, stuttering the simple word into half a dozen syllables before it was fully out. Then he turned to McLeary. With a great effort, he formed his words carefully, "Mister Stoughton says he wants you to join the regulators. He's treated you well, what with a good room over at the Casa de Plata and"—he even managed a lecherous grin that was not too offensive—"the services of Janie May. But you got a choice: Join us, or get out of town."

He shrugged at the hard look that snapped into McLeary's eyes. "Those're Mister Stoughton's words, not mine." He paused, then added, "Mister Stoughton told us to tell you, though, that he'd much rather you joined the regulators than leave town. He"—Hendrixson grimaced as if about to say something intensely distasteful to him—"values your services, and thinks highly of your reputation."

"Too much," Oakes mumbled.

McLeary was angry now. He did not take well to being issued ultimatums. He immediately put aside his plans to leave this morning. He would be perverse and hang around a while, if for no other reason than to antagonize the Stoughtons.

"You tell George Stoughton"—and he knew from the looks in the eyes of the other two men that he had scored right in his choice of Stoughton brothers—"that I'll leave town when I'm damned good and ready. Which might be today, and just as easy might be next month."

Oakes choked on his rage, but Hendrixson remained calm, though his eyes and voice took on a new hard cast. "I'd advise you to heed Mister Stoughton's words."

"Or?"

Hendrixson stared flatly at him. There was no need for words.

McLeary was quiet, staring at the two men. Oakes had calmed some, now that the possibility of gunplay was there. It was about the only thing the young man understood. Time dragged on. Sweat tricked down McLeary's back, and along his ribs.

Finally he smiled slightly. "Well, boys, I hate to disappoint you—or your boss man—but I aim to stick around a spell. On my own hook."

"That ain't good," Hendrixson said slowly, the stutter less evident. "That creates a problem."

"For you boys, maybe. Not for me."

"I'm gonna kill—"

"Shut up, Cale," Hendrixson snapped with no sign of a stutter. Authority—and the expectation of action—seemed to do something for him. To McLeary he said, "I'd purely hate to throw down against you, Mister McLeary, but if Mister Stoughton says somethin' . . ." He shrugged and raised his hands as if to say he would have no other choice.

"Best think about it before you try it, boy," McLeary said with no hint of fear—or mercy—in his voice.

Hendrixson bobbed his head once, and then stood. "Come on, Cale," he said.

Oakes rose and cast a hate-filled look at McLeary before spinning and clanking across the saloon at Hendrixson's side.

McLeary dropped his right hand so that it rested on the ivory grip of his Smith and Wesson. His left hand grasped the edge of the table tightly. And he waited.

Oakes and Hendrixson were halfway across the saloon when they stopped and spun. But McLeary was ready. As soon as the two gunmen began to turn, reaching for their pistols, McLeary moved. With his left hand, he shoved the table up and over. The three shot glasses and the bottle went flying, clattering onto the dirt floor, unbroken.

At the same time, McLeary fell to the side off of the chair to his left—toward the bar—while yanking out the Smith and Wesson. He rolled several times before surging up to a stand, revolver out, cocked, held at arm's length, and braced by both hands.

In that fraction of a second of movement, Oakes and Hendrixson had drawn their pistols and fired twice each before they had completed their spin. All four shots thunked holes into the overturned table where but a moment before McLeary had been sitting.

McLeary fired all five shells he kept in the Smith and Wesson. Two smashed into Hendrixson's lungs, sending up an explosion of blood. The gunman was spun by the impact and fell half-sideways, gasping his life out on the dirt floor of the saloon.

The second two punched holes in Oakes, one in the belly, the second up in the shoulder as Oakes fell backward, as if yanked by an invisible rope, missing the heart. He curled into a ball on the floor, moaning as the agony pierced him.

McLeary tried following the falling man with the fifth shot, but he was wide with that one.

Smith and Wesson empty, McLeary leaped behind the cover of the bar where he slid the Smith and Wesson away. Yanking open his shirt—tearing off two buttons in the process—he pulled out the smaller .38-caliber Colt Lightning. He slipped down the bar about halfway, then popped up, Colt cocked and ready.

But the third gunman was gone, leaving only two lazily swinging doors in his wake. McLeary looked around carefully, making sure no one else was going to make a play against him. The other patrons were behind tables, scared, and a frightened bartender scrunched in the corner behind the bar, watching McLeary with wide eyes.

McLeary uncocked the Colt and shoved it back into the shoulder holster. He emptied the spent shells from the Smith and Wesson and reloaded it. With the weapon in hand, he went to check on the two gunmen.

Hendrixson was dead in a puddle of his own blood. Oakes lingered on, but his eyes were glazed over in pain. McLeary kicked Oakes' Colt out of the way before dropping the Smith and Wesson back into his holster and hooking the loop over the hammer.

"Give me a hand here," McLeary ordered the three customers, who had finally risen. They still looked rather frightened, but they had seen death—violent death—before.

"What do you want us to do?" one asked, approaching. He was scared, but at the same time pleased to see that two of the gunmen who had been taking over the town with the Stoughtons' consent had been taken down.

"Help me drag this garbage out into the street." He grabbed one of Oakes' legs, while the man who had spoken grabbed the other. The two other men each took one of Hendrixson's legs. Together they dragged the bodies—one still gasping in the throes of impending death—out into the street and dropped them there.

"Thanks, boys," McLeary said as he re-entered the saloon. He set his table back upright, and briefly inspected the bullet holes in it. With a small smile, he set his chair back up and then sat. "Bartender," he said jovially, "I do believe such excitement calls for a cold beer. And set up my helpers there, too."

He figured he would have more visitors soon, and he probably should ride out of town now, like he had planned to. But, hell, he decided, he had been doing too much running lately. He would do no more.

He could hear his father's high whining voice saying, "Don't nary run when trouble's afoot, boy. Ye do that, and ye'll not see it when it comes on ye and bites yer ass."

McLeary smiled and relaxed.

Chapter 7

McLeary didn't have to wait long. There had been some commotion outside, and under the half-doors McLeary could see several men finally cart away the two bodies.

Then the swinging doors burst open, and three men entered the saloon. One was the young gunman who had stood guard over the door earlier. Another was also fairly young. He was of medium height, and rather pudgy, with a sun-darkened face. He wore black Levi's and a sky-blue, bib-front shirt with a black string tie. A derby was perched on his head, and a gunbelt with two ivory-handled Colts girded his waist.

The third man, who led the way, was the one who made an impression. He was a big man, six-feet-four and weighing two hundred and thirty pounds. There was a thatch of wild straw hair that would stick out in all directions when he took off his Boss-style black Stetson with the rattlesnake-skin band.

He wore brown chino-cloth pants that bagged a little at crotch and knee, above which was a black and red checked flannel shirt that strained to cover the girth of the man's broad midsection and wide, powerful chest. The sleeves of the shirt were rolled up to his forearms, exposing the dirty ends of faded red longhandles.

The man carried a Colt Walker that he had convinced some gunsmith to convert from percussion to cartridge a few years ago. It was an odd weapon, but the almost five pounds of pistol fit nicely into the man's beefy hand. There was a .38-caliber pocket Colt in one of his copious pockets, and several other weapons were secreted about his person.

He thumped up to McLeary's table, spurs ringing, and sat across from McLeary. The two younger men flanked him, standing one to each side and a few steps back.

"Hello, Bodie," McLeary said with a grin.

"Charlie," Bodie Wheeler said, smiling. "Long time no see, eh."

"Been a time. How you been?" He stuck out his right hand.

Bodie shook McLeary's hand, saying. "That it has. I'm doing well. You look fit and sassy."

"Same's ever. I didn't know you was runnin' with this bunch."

Wheeler tossed his hat on the table and ran a thick hand through the mass of hair. Wheeler was one of those men who, no matter what he wore or how neat he tried to be, would always be disheveled looking. He had long ago decided to give up the effort at trying to look sharp.

"I'm ramroddin' 'em. I kept myself out of it for a while, once I knew you was in town. When you rode in, I was off up north with some of the other boys ridin' herd over a shipment of the Stoughtons' silver. When I got back, I heard you was here. I also heard you didn't want no part of joining our little group." He shrugged. "I told the Stoughtons I knew you, and might be able to change your mind, but they said they'd as soon try some other things first."

"Like Janie May?" McLeary asked with a huge smile of pleasure and remembering.

"How was she?" Wheeler asked joyfully.

"You remember that gal took us on together up in Cheyenne that time a few years back?" When Wheeler nodded, licking his lips at the thought, McLeary said, "Janie May's better'n she *ever* was."

"Gawd-damn," Wheeler breathed, smiling hugely, showing the gap where he had lost two teeth.

McLeary remembered when his friend had lost the teeth. They had finished up a job over in Texas, and were heading to Denver. They had stopped in Santa Fe to resupply and then rode out. A week later, high in the mountains, they were struggling through wind and snow in a swirling spring blizzard. Their mule, carrying their supplies, was getting more cantankerous by the minute, and finally got bogged down in a snowdrift. Bodie, big as he was, got behind the mule to help the animal out. He succeeded, but after the mule was free, it thanked its benefactor with a kick in the jaw.

McLeary had tied the horses and the mule off, and then made a camp. He had been worried about his friend, who was unconscious for an hour or so. Then Wheeler awoke and shook his head to clear out the cobwebs. He reached inside his mouth and with his fingers yanked out two teeth loosened by the mule's kick.

"Goddamn," he muttered. He stood, a little woozy still. After a cup of hot coffee, he seemed more like his old self. He found a stout log—one weighing about forty pounds—and went to discuss his differences with the mule.

McLeary and Wheeler ate well over the next several days, feasting on mule stew and mule soup and mule steaks and mule chops.

McLeary grinned, thinking back on it, as Wheeler said again, "She was that good, eh?"

"Yep."

"Damn, it's been a time since I had me a woman like that."

"Me, too."

Wheeler ran a hand through his hair again as the bartender put a beer and a shot glass in front of him, and a bottle of whiskey in the middle of the table. Wheeler and McLeary drank a bit, unhurried.

Then Wheeler asked, "How's the old man?"

"Died just last year," McLeary said sadly.

"Shit," Wheeler mumbled. He was touched. He had liked McLeary's crusty old father. He raised his beer mug in a small salute. When McLeary returned it, Bodie drank, then said, "He was the best sort, Charlie, and lived a full good life."

"That he did." Suddenly the sadness lifted. "Hell, what're we sittin' here so gloomy for? He was near seventy. Outlived most all his old friends—Bridger, Carson, all of 'em. Hell, I can just hear him sayin', 'Ye boys ain't lived yet till ye've gone under once or twice.' "

He had done a creditable job at imitating his father's voice and manner, and he and Wheeler sat laughing loudly at that—and at the statement, which old Rob McLeary had actually said once.

The laughter finally dribbled away as the two men worked at their drinks slowly, remembering with fondness the hardened old trapper who had spawned Charlie at a late age.

The two young gunmen stood quietly, but impatiently. They were too full of self-importance to take well to being ignored so.

Finally Wheeler asked, "Well, Charlie, what're we gonna do?"

"About what?"

"You know damn well about what. I can't have you runnin' around town, maybe sidin' with the miners."

"I got no intention of doin' such. I tole that to them two idiots you sent over here before."

Wheeler grimaced. "I didn't send 'em. That was George's idea."

"I figured."

"I told him it was a stupid idea. That if he was gonna send somebody, he should send me. First off, I'm the only one of the regulators who could take you." He winked. "And besides, I know you. But he didn't trust me 'cause we're old pardners. So I told him that if he wasn't gonna send me, he ought not send Oakes and Hendrixson. Told him he was sendin' them to their deaths. Ass wouldn't believe me."

"What in hell are you doin' workin' for such a damn fool for anyway?" He stroked his mustache.

Wheeler belched proudly, then said, "Man's got to do what's necessary. The Stoughtons offered a job and good pay." He shrugged. "There's times . . ." He trailed off. Then he grinned. "I hear you didn't do so well on your last job, either," he said with a chuckle.

McLeary got angry, and it took some seconds before he calmed himself. Then he saw Wheeler's gap-toothed grin, and he broke into a smile. "Hell, let's just say I took the path of less valor and more smarts."

Again they fell silent, drinking, listening to the sounds of the busy town outside, of the impatient click of spurs as the two young gunmen shifted positions occasionally.

"We still got us a problem, Charlie," Wheeler said quietly.

"Ain't no problems, Bodie, 'less you make some."

"You gonna join the regulators?"

"Nope."

"Then we got a problem." He paused. " 'Less you're plannin' on ridin' out of town."

"When I feel the urge," McLeary said slowly. "I had felt the urge already, but things seem to be gettin' interestin' around here of late. I just might stick around some—see what happens."

"Like I said, Charlie, then we got a problem."

"And like I said, Bodie, we got no problem unless you—or one of your boys—want to force a play."

"I'd hate to have to go against you, Charlie." He shrugged the great humped shoulders.

"I could think of better things myself," McLeary said easily. "But it doesn't need to come to that, Bodie. If it comes down to where the Stoughtons are tryin' to force us against each other, I'll ride on out. Unless," he added pointedly, "you—or they—try humiliatin' me in the doin'."

"They try that, and I'll ride on out of town with you—after I shoot each and every goddamn one of 'em." He drained his mug of beer and tossed back another shot. Smacking his lips, he said, "You ain't plannin' to side with them damnfool miners, are you, Charlie?" There was almost a pleading in his eyes.

"Nope. Told you that before. Just like I told it to those pistol-totin' peckerwoods the Stoughtons sent over here this mornin'."

He was aware of the anger budding inside the young gunman who had been the third of the three who had approached him earlier. The man wanted nothing more than to gun McLeary down where he sat. McLeary stared up at him.

Smiling, Wheeler watched McLeary's face. He almost wished the young pistoleer would make a play against his friend. It would be one less punk he'd have to worry about.

But the gunman, sweating, saw death in McLeary's eyes. His own death. And he held himself in check.

McLeary finally broke off his gaze. "And I'll tell you, Bodie, I ain't plannin' on sidin' with the miners. I got no place in particular to be—or go—and stickin' around here a spell to see what happens is as good a thing to do as any."

"Then join us," Wheeler said, leaning forward onto the table to emphasize his words. "Get paid for hangin' around doin' nothin'."

"Can't do that, Bodie. I couldn't work for someone like George Stoughton."

"Hell, he's the baby of the family. Alva runs the business and all. The oldest, Tom, don't have much to do with the business, other than countin' his money. George would like to take over, but he's afraid of Alva."

McLeary leaned back. "That might all be true, Bodie. But he's still a Stoughton, and so he could give you—and me, if I was to join you—orders. That don't set well with me. Especially seein's how the miners got some real complaints, from what I hear."

"You don't know it all," Wheeler growled. He knew McLeary was right; but he had hired on, and there he would stay.

McLeary shrugged. Wheeler sat angry for a few moments, before he relaxed. No use getting angry with his old friend over nothing, he figured. Of course, though, he could have a little fun. "Why'd you kill them two boys before?" he asked with a grin and a wink.

McLeary picked it up, knowing Wheeler wanted him to goad the two young gunmen into a fight to test their mettle—or scare the hell out of them.

"Couple reasons," McLeary said, affecting a drawl. "For one, they called me out. There was nothin' I could do. Can't let a challenge pass."

"That wouldn't do at all. Nope."

"Other reason was that they was bein' pests, pure and simple. Damn fools got to annoyin' the hell out of me. And you know how I hate to be bothered mornin's."

"That I do." He laughed, aware that behind him two young men were itching to go for their pistols but were too frightened—especially the one who had seen less than an hour ago just what Charlie McLeary could do with that ivory-handled Smith and Wesson American he carried at his hip.

Finally Bodie stood. "Well, reckon that's where it all lies."

"Yep."

"Just don't go and change your mind and side with those goddamn miners," he cautioned again, but it was a friendly warning.

"I won't."

"Good. Why don't you stop over to the Silver Nugget of an evenin'. I'll stand you to a beer and a few swallows of redeye. We'll show some of these punks just how a couple of real old boys drink."

"I'll do that," McLeary said with a grin.

As Wheeler turned, the gunman who had been there earlier said, face contorted with anger, "Ain't you gonna do somethin', Bodie?"

"Like what?" Wheeler asked, face and voice stony.

"Shoot him down or somethin'."

"For what?"

"For gunnin' down Cale and Karl."

"Why?"

"But . . . I told you how he shot 'em down in cold blood."

"You, boy," Bodie said slowly, each word sharp and distinct, "are full of cattle shit. Charlie McLeary ain't ever killed a man in cold blood. *Ever.* You keep that in mind, boy." He waited.

"You afraid of him? That it?" the young man asked, finding some small reservoir of bravery. "Just 'cause he's your friend?"

Wheeler swung one meaty hand, catching the younger man backhanded on the side of the jaw. The gunman went flying, skidding along the dirt floor. When he stopped, he lay, his head ringing, bells and lights going off inside his skull.

"You got anything else to say, Creed?" he asked harshly.

"No," Creed mumbled, getting shakily to his feet.

"Didn't think so." Wheeler turned back to face McLeary. He winked and grinned. "See you around, Charlie." Then he thumped out, two young, nervous gunmen trailing in his wake.

Chapter 8

Charlie McLeary stepped out of the Pick and Shovel Saloon. It had been sunny early in the morning, but now dark, bloated clouds blackened the sky. He headed up the street, toward one of the many Chinese laundry places that dotted the streets. He had brought in his only other shirt the day before, and figured he would pick it up now. It would save him buying another one to replace the one he wore—ripped when he dug for his emergency pistol in the shoulder holster.

He started to enter and almost ran full into an attractive young woman, who was accompanied by an older, more matronly woman.

"Excuse me, ma'am," he said quietly, touching the brim of his hat. He stepped back outside, holding the door for the two. The woman filed out, the first—the more attractive, and younger—woman looked at him briefly, somewhat as if he were a bug.

He almost smiled as he watched her for a moment as she sashayed up the street, her shiny brown dress swaying. In the darkness of the store, he had not seen much of her, but when he had moved back and she had stepped into the light, he was struck by her beauty. But he could tell from the quality of her clothes, by her patrician bearing, by her hauty demeanor, that she was not the type for him.

McLeary grinned and got his shirt from the laundry and went back to his hotel, where he changed. It had been interesting, he thought, seeing his old friend Bodie Wheeler. But it was disturbing to find Wheeler working for Consolidated Silver and Mining—and the Stoughtons. It was not like Wheeler to side with the monied interests against a group of hard-working—if poor—men.

Well, there would be time later to find out how Wheeler got himself into this. It was raining now, and hard, so he sat in the chair by the window overlooking the street, reading the newspaper.

After an hour or so, the rain eased, thought it did not stop, and McLeary realized he was hungry. He set out for Lankshire's. He still did not know whether that restaurant was owned—or managed—by the Stoughtons; but he didn't care, and it was the only decent place in town.

He stepped inside, dripping, and peeled off the long, sopping duster. Then he saw that the place was full. "Damnit all," he muttered to himself. He saw only one empty seat—across the table from the attractive young woman he had almost run into that morning.

With a shrug, he weaved through the crowded restaurant to the back—and the empty chair. He loomed over the woman, and asked, "Might I join you, ma'am?"

She looked at him, repelled. "I should say not," she said firmly in a voice like fresh honey.

"It's the only seat left, ma'am."

She looked around, as if seeing the crowded restaurant for the first time. "I suppose it is," she muttered, unhappy. She gazed up at him. "Are you one of those regulators for the mine?" she asked in some annoyance.

"No, ma'am."

Oh," she said sarcastically, "just a drifting saddle bum, eh?"

McLeary's eyes flashed anger, but he stayed outwardly calm. He stroked his mustache with his left hand. Then, in a soft voice, he said, "It's a good thing, I reckon, that at least one of us has got some manners. If I didn't, I'd knock you off that chair."

He had to admit some pleasure at the look of shock that dusted her pretty, high-cheekboned face. "I suppose I deserved that," she said coldly. "Well, then," she continued gruffly after a short pause, "sit, if you must."

"Thank you, ma'am." He sat, taking off his hat as he did so. He hung the duster on the back of the chair and tossed the Stetson on the table out of the way. Then he looked the woman over. She was twenty-five or twenty-six, he thought, with wide, clear eyes of hazel. The silk dress she wore complemented those eyes. Her hair was honey blond, laying in long, tubed curls down the side of her pale face and onto her shoulders in the back. She was not nearly as well-padded as Janie May Dillon was, but her figure was still quite plush. Full lips covered perfect, small white teeth, beneath a tiny, pert nose.

A harried waiter hustled up and slapped some plates in front of the woman, who nodded her thanks. The waiter did not notice, and that annoyed the woman even further. The waiter had already turned to McLeary and asked, in surly tones, "What do you want?"

McLeary placed his order slowly, making the waiter fume, and when McLeary turned his eyes back to the woman, she was smiling at him, "Very good," she said.

"What?" he asked innocently.

She only smiled, wishing she had been able to anger the waiter so easily. She picked up her knife and fork, and started eating, her long slim fingers handling the cutlery with flair. She felt slightly uncomfortable knowing McLeary was staring at her.

Staring at her was easy to do, he realized. He could not quite fathom it. She was not the best looking woman he had ever seen, though she certainly was very high on the list. But there was something about her that caught him up.

"If you are not a regulator, then what are you doing in town, Mister? . . ."

"McLeary. But you can call me Charlie." He paused and looked around the room. The crowd had not diminished any. "I was just passin' through," he said finally. "Thought I'd stick around a few days."

"So you're the famous—or perhaps I should say infamous—Charlie McLeary, eh?" she said with another smile, dazzling him.

He lifted his shoulders in self-deprecation. "At your service, ma'am. But I reckon you have me at a disadvantage." When she looked blankly at him, he said, "Your name?"

"Ah." She gazed at his handsome face for a few moments. She was becoming intrigued by this tall, lanky, hard-edged stranger. He was quite unlike any other man she had met before, and he interested her. "Molly," she said finally. She started to give a second name, but clamped her lips shut before even the first syllable was out. She did not know why she had done it; only that she was interested in this man, and letting him know too much about her already might not be good.

"No last name?" he asked, not certain whether to be angry or amused.

"No," she said, smiling to ease the awkardness of it. "Molly's good enough for now."

"All right, Miss Molly." He sat forward, resting one forearm on the table. The other hand stroked the mustache. "And what of you?" he asked.

"What about me?" she countered around a mouthful of peas.

"You know all about me. Seems like everybody in the town knows all about me. But I know nothin' of you."

Molly shrugged and took a bite of baked chicken. "A woman must retain a certain aura of mystery, don't you think, Mister McLeary?"

"I reckon. But such things can be taken too far." He smiled, to let her know it should not be taken badly. But he was annoyed just a little. He figured she just thought she was too much a lady for the likes of him. She had the aura of mystery, he realized, but she also carried an aura of money and respectability, class and breeding.

"Tell me about yourself, Mister McLeary," she said quietly, indicating she was at least a little bit interested in him. However, she knew, it would not do well to have him thinking she was *too* interested.

"There ain't a hell of a lot to tell, Miss Molly. Like you figured, I'm a saddle bum. I go where my horse takes me. I—"

The waiter's arrival interrupted him. The server slammed down a plate with a giant beefsteak filling it to hanging over the sides, a bowl of hot yams, and a small bowl of carrots. As the waiter turned to leave, McLeary said, "You forgot my coffee."

The man spun, a snarl on his face. He started to say something, but McLeary cut him off: "Unless you're fixin' to compliment me on my clean shirt," he said quietly but with unmistakable menace, "I'd suggest you not say anything at all."

The waiter fumed, face coloring over with anger.

"Now, in your profession," McLeary continued, "I would think that some manners and a friendly face would take you far. You got to figure, boy, that bein' in such poor humor all the time is gonna get your ass in a heap of trouble one day." He paused, then said, "Today just could be that day, if you catch my meanin'."

The waiter stomped angrily away, but when he returned a few minutes later, he was more calm; and he quietly placed a coffeepot and two cups on the table, along with a small pitcher of milk and a bowl of sugar.

"Thank you," McLeary said cheerily.

"You're welcome," the waiter said, surprising both McLeary and Molly, though the woman was the more startled of the two.

"How'd you do that?" Molly asked as the waiter left.

"Do what?" McLeary asked, digging into his food.

"Get him to change like that."

"It's my cheerful nature, my handsome, boyish smile, and clean livin'," McLeary said with a grin.

Molly giggled, the first real sign that she was human, McLeary thought. It was a nice sound, soft, and warming.

"You sure it's not 'cause you're wearing that big gun?" she asked.

Had someone else said the same, McLeary might have been angry, but her tone—and open, smiling face—let him know that she was not criticizing.

"Could have somethin' to do with it," he said agreeably, forking a piece of meat into his mouth. He turned serious. "I try to be nice to folks, given a chance. I don't hold with bein' mean, 'less it's necessary. But bein' nice don't get you much in life sometimes. My bein' nice to that waiter wouldn't have made a damn bit of difference to him without him knowin' I could get mean if he didn't improve his humor some. The words and way they're said sometimes don't mean much—it's what's under the words that counts."

Molly shuddered. "You mean you would have shot him had he still been so nasty when he returned?" she asked in some horror.

McLeary grinned. "I ain't so bad as all that. I've never shot a man for somethin' so unimportant. Have thought on it several times, though," he added with a chuckle.

Molly relaxed a little, as McLeary continued: "But he didn't know that. Sometimes havin' a reputation can be a good thing. Mostly, it's a pain in the ass. Oops, pardon me, ma'am."

"It's all right." She ate a bit, then asked, "So it was your reputation that changed his attitude?"

"More or less. All he knows is that I'm some big-name gunfighter. Didn't matter what I said to him; I just give him a tough look, and he figured I'd shoot him down should he continue his rude ways with me. Don't matter that I wouldn't really do that—though I might have knocked him flat on his ass for it. It just matters that he *thinks* I'd do that."

"Must be nice to be able to do that," Molly said almost wistfully.

McLeary shrugged. "Like I said, havin' a reputation sometimes helps. But most times, it only leads to trouble. Everywhere you go, people've heard your name—and high-falutin' stories about you, most of 'em untrue. There's always some pissant pistol punk aimin' to take you down a peg, tryin' to make his own name." He grimaced and ate.

"Why don't you stop doing it, then?"

"Can't now. Far too late. My pap had a sayin': 'If ye be aimin' to git a good night's shut-eye, boy, don't go layin' yer sleepin' robe in a pile of buffler shit.' "

Molly sat stunned for just a moment, then broke into laughter. McLeary joined her in it.

"Well," McLeary said, still chuckling, "I already put my sleepin' robes in the buffalo shit, and its too late to pick 'em up and move 'em now. Even if I did move 'em, the stink'd be on 'em for all time."

She still giggled. "You are an interesting man, Mister McLeary," she said, meaning it. Then: "But you have heard of laundry, haven't you?"

"What?"

"Laundry. You could take your sleeping robes, as you say, and get them laundered. Once you did that, no more buffalo—" she looked around, as if thinking someone might hear her—"shit." She giggled, then got serious again. "Meaning, of course, that you *could* give up the ways of the gun if you really were of a mind to."

"It might be nice to think so," he said solemnly. "But there are other things involved. For one, other people might not make it easy."

"You don't look like the type to let other people dictate your actions, Mister McLeary."

He smiled wanly. "Sometimes you get forced. . . ." He paused, then said, "Besides, I don't know of anything else to do. It's been my life so long now. . . ."

"You could be a farmer, or a miner, or a rancher or—"

"I don't know shit from beans about any of those things," he said, a little more harshly than he had planned. "Sorry, Miss Molly," he mumbled. "But I don't know anything about those things. And I can't see me workin' in some store. Good God, that'd be the end of me for sure."

He was surprised at the gravity with which she looked at him. She seemed close to tears. "I understand, Mister McLeary," she said softly. "Sometimes people are trapped in lives from which there can be—or at least seems to be—no escape. It is not easy."

"I reckon not," he mumbled, suddenly unsure of himself.

Then she brightened. "Then, again, most good people—strong people—make the best out of the cards life deals them, isn't that right?"

"Yes, ma'am," he said with a smile. "And it helps sometimes when you get a chance to draw more cards. Once in a while the draw goes your way. If not, well, there's always another hand to be dealt."

Chapter 9

McLeary held open the door for Molly, who stepped out. It had stopped raining, but the street was a morass of mud and the sky black. Thunder growled, ricocheting off the still snow-covered peaks around town.

McLeary and Molly had spent another hour or so in the restaurant chatting, with Charlie regaling the woman with tales—both his own and those remembered from his father. But outside, she looked a little nervous, casting anxious glances up and down the street, as if she feared being seen.

"Well," she said, knowing she should get away, "it was pleasant talking with you, Mister McLeary. But I must go."

He nodded, saddened by the news, even though he knew it had to be. "Will I see you again, Miss Molly?" he asked.

Molly stared up at him, and for the first time he realized just how small she was. She searched his face solemnly, and then said in a somber tone, "I think so, Mister McLeary. Yes . . . I certainly do think so."

She turned and strolled away, back straight, parasol in hand. Her hat, a flowery thing that matched her dress, bobbed with the rhythm of the large bustle on her dress.

McLeary walked the other way, toward his hotel. He got about half a dozen steps when he stopped and turned. Silently he watched Molly grow smaller as she sauntered along her way.

McLeary was rather stunned by his attraction to this woman. She had an almost mystical pull on him. "Well, I'll be damned," he breathed as he turned. She had disappeared into the crowd now, and he started walking. But he knew now he had a reason—a real reason—to stay around Silver Canyon awhile. It made him happy, but at the same time, it annoyed him. He had never felt this way before, and he was not sure it was a comfortable feeling.

It was with some distraction that he walked down the street, puzzling over his feelings—and he was not even sure yet what they were—for this woman. He knew that she was wealthy, and that she must be married; that she probably would want to have nothing to do with him, other than an enjoyable afternoon of sitting to lunch. He grinned. He would have to see to it that if she really did feel that way, she changed her mind.

McLeary crossed the street, dodging the horses, carriages and wagons, and noisy, running children. He thought he would check on his horse, something he hadn't done in several days. Mud slopped over his boots as he walked through the brown lake.

When he reached the other side, Duncan McGregor was standing on the sidewalk, watching him, apparently waiting for him. "Mister McGregor," McLeary said, touching the brim of his hat politely.

"A few words with you, if I may, Mister McLeary," McGregor said with little preliminary—and apparently with a great deal of reluctance.

McLeary shrugged. "Speak your mind," he said warily, and with little friendliness.

"Not here," McGregor said, looking from side to side. "Too many people about," he whispered conspiratorially.

"Anything you have to say to me ought to be said out in the open, Mister McGregor," McLeary said testily. He wanted no part of the fight between the miners and the Stoughtons, and he was getting angry with being tugged at by each side. He had better things to do with his time—like trying to get close to the beautiful Miss Molly Whatever Her Last Name Was.

"I think you might want to hear this," McGregor said stiffly. "And I'm not going to discuss it out in the street." McGregor was not anxious to do what he had been asked by the miners to do, and McLeary was not making it any easier. It troubled him, and he was not one to be troubled easily.

"Then good day to you, Mister McGregor," McLeary said sharply. He stepped around the short, muscular miner.

"Wait," McGregor said, almost pleading. He grabbed McLeary's sleeve lightly.

McLeary stopped and turned back.

"Please, Mister McLeary," McGregor said. He had been assigned to do this by men who trusted him and relied on him.

He had to do it, even if it meant subjugating his own feelings. He paused. "Please. Let's go to the Pick and Shovel. I'll buy you some redeye. We can talk privately there, in peace, as men should."

McLeary looked down, thoughts of Molly lingering in his brain, the scent of her perfume loitering in his nostrils. He shook those feelings off. The miner was a good man, he decided, and probably should be listened to, even though McLeary thought he knew what McGregor was going to say.

"All right, Mister McGregor," he said calmly. "But," he added, somewhat harshly, "I wouldn't go gettin' my expectations up was I in your boots."

McGregor looked rather crestfallen; but he had a job to do, and he meant to see it through. He nodded. "I understand. But you'll give me a fair hearing, won't you?"

"Yep."

They walked down the street, the tall, lanky gunfighter slowing his steps to match those of the short, powerful miner. It had started to rain again, souring McLeary's disposition a little. Thunder still rolled off the mountains, booming and ringing around the town. Occasional flashes of lightning sizzled and sparkled. The sidewalks were almost deserted as most people stayed indoors, though traffic on the street was still fairly heavy.

McLeary and McGregor entered the Pick and Shovel. "Bring a bottle, would ya, Lem," McGregor shouted over the crack of a particularly loud thunderclap. He and McLeary headed for a table near the back. McLeary draped the duster over the back of his chair. Almost as soon as they sat, Lem Wilson brought over a bottle and two small glasses.

"Thanks," McGregor said. McLeary said nothing, only nodded at the bar owner.

McGregor pulled the cork on the tall, green bottle and poured whiskey into the two glasses. Setting the bottle down, he lifted his glass in a salute toward McLeary. The gunfighter did not respond. McGregor shrugged, face darkening momentarily with anger, and he tossed back the shot. He poured another right away.

"Well, Mister McGregor, you have something to say, say it." He had not touched his glass.

"You're rather unmannerly, Mister McLeary," the miner said.

"If I was really unmannerly, I would've never come in here

with you," McLeary said coldly. "Now, you said you had somethin' to talk to me about. That's why you dragged me in here. I have other business to attend to, so if you have somethin' to say, get to it."

McGregor sat a moment, collecting his thoughts, and letting the anger sift down and away. Finally he said, "You know, everyone in town knows what you did here this morning."

"So?" McLeary stroked his mustache. He had still not touched his drink.

"It was the first time anyone around here's ever stood up to the Stoughtons' regulators. It was a—" he licked his lips, not sure how this would be taken—"brave thing to do."

McLeary shrugged, irritating the miner. After some silence, McLeary said sarcastically, "If you brought me in here to compliment me on my courage, thank you, Mister McGregor. I'll be going now."

"No, wait! I—" He stopped, anger and worry fighting for supremacy on his face. He cleared his throat, licked his lips again, and then tossed down another shot before saying, "We have been looking for someone like you, Mister McLeary. I . . . we . . . need someone like you to help us. To stand up to the Stoughtons. To help us—"

He stumbled to a stop, his face pink, flushed with embarrassment and anger at his inability to express himself properly. He was not this way with the miners. There he could speak, and speak well, swaying them, holding them in check whenever they got too out of hand. But here, talking to this drifting gunfighter, he was a stumbler over his words. It was not that he was afraid—at least not of having McLeary shoot him. But there was another kind of fear: the fear of doing something he didn't really want to do; the fear of having his request rejected; the fear of having to expose his troubles, and those of the other miners.

He took a deep breath. Firmly, he said, "We'd like you to side with us, Mister McLeary. Join with the new mine union—the Squaw Gulch Workingmen's Collective—in fighting the injustice of the owners. Side with those in the right."

"No," McLeary said flatly, stunning McGregor with the brevity of it. McGregor had expected the rejection, but not without some talk and maybe argument.

"But—"

"No buts, Mister McGregor. I told you and Mister Bowers earlier that I was not taking sides in this. That still holds."

"But what about this morning? You gunned down two regulators."

"So?" McLeary asked, his voice icy.

"Well, surely, the other regulators will be against you now. Surely, you will want to join with us after they have pulled guns on you—attacked you."

"Bullshit. Those boys were doin' a job. They were *supposed* to be doin' a job. Then they got it into their heads to take me on—not because they were hired by the Stoughtons to do so, but because they wanted to see if I was as good as my reputation. That showdown this mornin' had nothin' to do with this mine business. It was just two young punks feelin' their oats and lookin' to make their reputations."

McGregor sipped some whiskey. "But those others certainly will turn against you for killing their friends."

McLeary laughed. "Friends!" He chuckled. "Most of them'd be just as happy shootin' each other down as they would shootin' a handful of miners. I don't doubt that some of 'em actually are friends—"

"Like you and that hulking clod Bodie Wheeler?" McGregor interrupted, snarling angrily.

"Yes," McLeary said tightly, his own anger building. "There are times when some men like me and Bodie get to be friends. But it's rare. Men like us can't afford friends. The regulators, as the Stoughtons call 'em, are hired guns. No more, no less. They ain't gonna become bosom pardners just 'cause they hired on to the same outfit. Each and every one of 'em's headstrong, and has his own ways. For the most part, they're loners. Includin' me. Just 'cause me and Bodie are friends, doesn't mean we spend all our time together. Hell, I ain't seen him in two, three years. We had done some things together, and then drifted on our own ways. He knows I ever need him for somethin' important, I can call on him. He can do the same. But most men like me and those regulators ain't likely to call on help even from a friend, 'less it's *real* important."

McGregor sat silent for a few minutes, then said, "It's a sad life you lead, Mister McLeary."

McLeary looked a little surprised.

McGregor smiled wanly at him and said, "Not having friends

to speak of. Or families. I expect bein' so footloose and fancy free as men like you are is good sometimes. But"—he grew almost defiant—"there's nothin'—not money, not freedom, nothin'—that can replace the companionship of friends, a good woman, strong, helpful young 'uns."

"Too many troubles for me," McLeary said. He had always believed that, but at the moment he was not so sure.

"That might be, Mister McLeary, that might be. But all the troubles are worth it when you're lyin' in bed with your woman at your side; or when one of your children puts his little arms around you and says, 'I love you, Papa.' " He was almost misty eyed at it.

"That why you kowtow to people like the Stoughtons?" McLeary said harshly, angry, and not sure why he was.

"Goddammit," McGregor snapped, eyes flashing with heat, "my family's worth anything—includin' kissin' the ass of any of the Stoughton brothers. Or even dyin' for. But you wouldn't know that, would you?" It didn't require an answer, so McLeary said nothing.

"No you wouldn't," McGregor continued. "Long's you got your horse and your . . . gun, maybe a trollop now and then, you're happy. Men like you will never know the pleasures of a really good woman, or the pleasure of havin' young 'uns, or even the pleasures of doin' a good day's work and earnin' a good day's pay."

"Don't get carried away," McLeary snapped. "If you were gettin' a good day's pay for a good day's work, you wouldn't be tryin' to get this damn union off the ground and threatenin' to strike. I don't really reckon your life is so rosy as you'd like to think, boy. It was, you wouldn't be complaining so much about everything in it."

McGregor sat fuming, his face flushed with anger, his blue eyes flashing under the floppy felt hat he wore.

McLeary, sitting across the table from McGregor, could see Pete Bowers enter the Pick and Shovel. The miner stopped, letting his eyes adjust to the gloom. He spotted McGregor from the back, facing McLeary, who sat with the back of his chair against the wall at the far end of the room. The he moved forward, looking a little angry.

He stopped at the table, looming over the two seated men. McLeary glanced up, a bored expression in his eyes. McGregor viewed Bowers with a mild look of distaste.

The tall, skinny miner said nothing. Finally the short, powerful McGregor said from his chair, "Sit down, Pete." He paused, then said, "McLeary and I were just discussing the merits of his joinin' our cause."

Chapter 10

"I think Mister McGregor is talkin' through his hat," McLeary said mildly, but with no hint of humor.

"So," Bowers said as he sat, "you won't join with us against those oppressive sons of bitches, eh?"

"No, sir. I told that to Mister McGregor here. I also told that to the Stoughtons, and the head of their regulators. I also told them, and Mister McGregor, that I would not join their side, either. Now," he added, pushing back from the table, "since our business is done, I have other things I'd rather be doin'."

"Wait, please," McGregor said urgently.

"I doubt there is more to say to you, or you to me," McLeary said quietly.

"But you do not know the whole story," McGregor's eyes pleaded, and McLeary finally relaxed back into the chair a little.

"Thank you," the broad-chested miner said. "I tried," he said with a pallid smile, "before to convince you to throw in with us by trading on your sympathies. That obviously didn't work." He shook his head. "Perhaps the cold, hard facts will sway you."

"I doubt it, but go on and try. I'll listen."

"Nice of you," Bowers muttered, barely audibly.

McLeary gazed at him with icy eyes and raised eyebrows. Bowers quieted. McLeary was building up a considerable dislike for this tall, bony miner. Bowers had a poor attitude, and always seemed to have a chip on his shoulder.

On the other hand, McLeary did like the stumpy Duncan McGregor. The man had nerve, and was willing to fight for what he believed in; no matter what the consequences—or cost to himself. McLeary liked that in a man. He would not change his mind, but he would, at least, give McGregor the courtesy of listening to what he had to say.

McGregor stared at Bowers for a moment. Apparently,

McLeary thought, there was no love lost between these two, either. "Why ain't you in the shaft?" McGregor asked his companion suddenly.

"Lookin' for you," Bowers said with a nasty edge to his voice. "Folks was beginning to wonder where you was."

"The boys knew where I was goin'. They was the ones wanted me to talk to Mister McLeary here. And I told Brown and Courtland where I was headin'. There was no need for you to come lookin' for me." He was angry, and it showed on his dirty face.

"We thought maybe you left town," Bowers said in a dismal attempt at levity.

McGregor and McLeary stared at him. He held their gazes, flickering from one to the other, for a moment, before dropping his stare. He stayed silent.

McGregor shook his head and looked at McLeary. "It's like this, Mister McLeary," he said quietly, but with a tinge of urgency in his voice. "We been workin' them mines now almost four years. We started out makin' two dollars and seventy-five cents a day. You know what it's like workin' down in those shafts six days a week, ten hours a day?"

"Can't say I do." McLeary almost shuddered. It wasn't the thought of so much hard work, or the long hours or low pay that got to him. It was the idea of spending half your life in a deep, foreboding hole in the ground. That got to him.

"Didn't reckon so. But that's what we do. The goddamn Stoughton brothers pull out between sixty thousand and seventy thousand dollars a month from them mines. The miners' payroll is less than seven thousand a month. Even with the cost of extracting the silver through the smelter, payin' blacksmiths, firemen, the cost of the donkey engines and all, they're still makin' a profit of forty-five to fifty thousand a month. A *month!* And that's at the depressed prices on today's market. Hell, the first couple of years they were makin' a profit of more than ninety thousand a month."

"Seems like they're takin' a bigger loss than you are," McLeary said blandly, downing the first shot of whiskey, which had sat untouched all this time.

"You bastard," Bowers breathed.

"He's right," McGregor said through clenched teeth. He did not like to admit it, but it was true, and so he had to. "Still, Mister McLeary," he said gently, "that does not take away from the fact that we are bein' paid no more now than we were three and a half years ago. Yet prices for everything have gone up. Not that you'll understand what it means to raise a family," he jabbed, and McLeary accepted it as coming from an honorable man trying to protect his interests. "But most of the boys can't even make ends meet any more. I doubt you could say the same of the Stoughtons, even with their income cut in half the last six, eight months."

"No, I suppose," McLeary said sarcastically, "the Stoughtons have enough money stashed away to tide them over for a few weeks."

"I have no doubt," McGregor said dryly. "It costs us married men around thirty dollars a month just to feed our families. And that doesn't count the cost of housing, providin' coal or wood for the stoves, kerosene for lamps, things for the young uns' schoolin'. And"—he actually grinned—"money for such things as this." He raised the shot glass and poured the reddish-gold liquid down his throat.

"The single men pay close to thirty a month just for boarding, and it costs them between fifty and seventy-five cents for each meal. Hell, we just can't make it on what the Stoughtons are payin'. Not on sixty dollars a month."

McLeary was beginning to feel some sympathy for the miners. It was, he imagined, terribly hard work, for which they were paid a pittance. But, then again, most working men were paid far less than their worth, he figured. Still, the thought of those men working in that hole in the ground—and he almost shuddered again at that—for next to nothing tugged at him.

Then his father's face popped into his mind, with the words, "Don't ye go 'round bein' no goddamn fool, boy. Bein' foolish comes naturally to some. Let 'em keep such doin's to themselves. Ye don't need to go lookin' to throw in with 'em."

"You ain't the only boys who work hard, make almost nothin' and give the businessmen a comfortable livin'," he said, reassured by his father's "help."

"That's true, too, Mister McLeary." He paused, thinking of the next argument with which to mount an assault on this hard-edged gunfighter. He had been opposed from the beginning to trying to hire McLeary, but he had been talked into it by the miners. Now, however, he was beginning to like McLeary, despite the gunfighter's absolute—and so far unyielding—determination not to join in the miners' cause.

"Tell him the rest," Pete Bowers ordered.

McGregor snapped down another jolt of redeye. He was reluctant to do this. He did not feel this way personally; but nearly all the other men did, and it was an important point in their battle against the mine owners.

"Well," he said with distaste, "what I've already told you ain't the all of it. Ain't too many carpenters, wheelwrights, blacksmiths and undertakers and such that have to deal with the Chinese."

There, he thought, it was out, and he was done with it. But Bowers was not. "That's right, goddamn it. The company's been hiring heathen Chinese to work the mines. Them yellow bastards work for half what real men do, so the Stoughtons can make themselves a heap of money off 'em. They've imported twenty or so of 'em from other minin' towns. And we expect more in soon. Once they get some more, they'll probably cut a bunch of us loose.

"Goddamn it galls my ass to see them yellow heathens comin' in here and takin' over jobs from men who need 'em," Bowers ranted. "Damn, the only thing worse they could do is hire Negroes or maybe Injins." He shook with fury.

"You all feel that way?" McLeary asked.

"Yes," McGregor whispered shamefully, hanging his head briefly. And McLeary knew here was at least one who did not.

McLeary could see the sense of hiring Chinese labor for the mine, especially the way the market for silver was these days. He had seen the Chinese working on the railroads both during and after the Civil War, and he had seen them in a dozen towns throughout the West. They worked hard, twice as hard as Americans, it seemed, and the quality of their work was second to no one's. In addition, they worked cheap. It made them ideal employees of the profit-driven businesses of the West, ideal workers for men like the Stoughtons, who thought little of the men who worked for them and were only interested in how many greenbacks they could amass.

There was no easy answer to any of these questions. McLeary could not side with the bigoted miners, especially when they wanted more wages for less work. But he had less interest in siding with the mine owners, who would let their employees starve to death, or die of the diseases that ran rampant through mining camps and towns, or die in some filthy, unsafe hellhole in the ground.

No, he thought, if he was—and he wasn't, by God, he told himself firmly—going to take sides here, he would have to join the miners. He was, he knew, little more than a poor-stiff workingman himself. The miners might look on him as something special, since he carried a gun and gambled in his ability to use it every day, but what they did not realize was that he admired them—or any other working man. Like the sodbusters he had hired on with so recently. They worked ferociously hard for a pittance; they endured Indians, heat, cold, wild animals, starvation, sickness and loneliness, conditions that were far more unsafe—regularly—than almost anything McLeary would encounter. To him those men were special. Their courage in just making do every day, of fighting just to provide for their families, for making the country grow and progress filled him with awe.

That still did not mean he wanted to join them in their fight. He had no desire to face down two dozen or so hardened gunmen simply to get a handful of miners an extra dollar a day; or to preserve their jobs against the influx of Chinese, or Cornish miners or Scotsmen or Irish or any other group that the mine owners might bring in as cheap, effective labor.

The bigotry McLeary saw in these miners—and many others—bothered him deeply. He knew he had—though he did not know them—half brothers and half sisters who were half-breed Indians. He had seen the kind of antagonism people had for half-breeds, and it hurt him. He had become inured to it for the most part during his life, but he never liked seeing a people downtrodden because of their skin color or their parentage.

Well, he sighed, musing that there was little he could do to change men's thinking. And these men did have some reason to dislike the Chinese, he guessed.

He snapped back to attention as McGregor started speaking again. "Just keep it to yourself, Pete. Such a thing ain't Mister McLeary's problem."

"Like hell it ain't. We're gonna ask him to side with us, he's got to know all the reasons. If he's a real man"—and McLeary caught the implication, meaning a true white man by *their* standards—"he'll be as outraged by such actions as we are. Might help convince him." He stared insolently at McLeary.

McLeary ignored him, instead gazing with his pale blue eyes at McGregor.

The stubby miner sighed at his companion's boorishness. Then he said quietly, "The men have taken up a collection—union dues, I guess you could call it. We have decided to use that money to try to hire you to fight against the many and frequent injustices of the Stoughtons and their hired gunmen."

He paused, waiting for McLeary to say something, but the gunfighter kept his silence.

"It's almost three hundred dollars," McGregor said stiffly.

"And just what would you boys expect me to do for this magnificent sum?" McLeary asked cynically.

"Keep the regulators away from us. Send them packin', hopefully. You do that, and we can negotiate with the Stoughtons."

"And get rid of the goddamn Chinese," Bowers shot out.

"And how would you like me to do that?" McLeary asked coldly, turning icy blue eyes on the miner.

"Scare 'em off. Or kill 'em," Bowers said bluntly.

"Were you born this goddamn stupid?" McLeary asked in a voice as hard as one of the miner's drills. "Or have you had to work at it?"

Bowers' face was a study in rage. His nostrils were flared, and his lips clamped together in a bloodless line. His eyes were bloodshot and wide, and his hands bunched into white-knuckled fists. McLeary could see the fight going on inside the miner—the fight to control his anger. Despite not wearing a gun, Bowers was afraid of McLeary and wanted to get himself under control before he said or did something foolish. At the same time, his rage knew almost no bounds.

McLeary watched him for a few moments. Realizing he was in no danger from the man, he turned back to look at McGregor. "I'm afraid, Mister McGregor," he said—and not without some regret evident—"that I cannot join you in your efforts."

"But why? . . ."

" 'Cause he's a yellow-bellied coward, that's why," Bowers said, his fury overcoming what little sense he ever had. "Bastard ain't got the balls his reputation says he has. We'd do better hirin' one of the trollops over at Lucy's to hump all those regulators into submission. Shit, this man ain't—"

He never got to finish as McLeary's backhanded punch cracked against his jaw, knocking him sideways out of the chair and onto the floor.

McLeary stood up, his face carved of granite. McGregor leaped up from his chair, standing in between McLeary and the fallen miner. Bowers lay on the floor, rubbing his already discoloring jaw, and shaking his head.

McLeary smiled. McGregor might not like Bowers, but Pete was a fellow miner, and as such, McGregor would help him if he could. He nodded at McGregor and started unbuckling the gunbelt with the Smith and Wesson American.

McGregor's eyes widened in surprise, then he, too, smiled. He stepped out of the way as McLeary gently placed his gunbelt on the table.

Chapter 11

"You're supposed to be a hard-rock miner, boy," McLeary snarled. "Let's see just how tough you are." He moved around the table as Bowers stood with an effort.

Bowers wiped his hands on his filthy work pants, as the two other customers in the place looked up in interest. One bolted for the door, and McLeary could hear him yelling in the street: "Fight! Fight goin' on at the Pick and Shovel."

He was back quickly. Within two minutes of the fight's beginning, people were streaming in from outside.

Bowers grinned, the ringing gone from his head. He figured that while McLeary might be good with a pistol, he probably could not handle himself with his fists very well. Since boxing was one of the favorite diversions of the miners—and Bowers was one of the top boxers in Silver Canyon—he figured he could handle this cowardly gunman with ease.

Bowers' fists came up, knuckles facing the ceiling. His right hand was up almost near his chin; the left, the same height, but perhaps six inches forward of the right. Both elbows were even, down around the belly, protecting it.

McLeary was a little concerned. Apparently, he reasoned, Bowers knew how to box. Well, he could handle himself, too, with strength and agility, if not finesse.

He brought his own fists up as Bowers moved in on him throwing a flurry of punches. McLeary managed to either block or duck the flying fists; but it was hard work, and the miner's rocklike fists occasionally thumped on his shoulders and biceps, each blow smarting a little.

Bowers finally backed off a bit, and McLeary waded in, swinging roundhouse punches at a slippery and very elusive miner. Soon the gunfighter eased away, too, to allow himself to catch his breath, and to try to devise a new strategy.

But the miner gave him no time to think. Instead, Bowers charged in, fists ready, feinting and jabbing. McLeary did what he could to fend off the assault, but some of the punches began to hurt as they thumped on flesh, mostly of the arms and shoulders. A few got through to land on McLeary's chest. He was being driven back slowly as the blows began to take a toll.

Sweat poured off both men. McLeary swiped at his forehead with his left sleeve. Bowers, seeing that, drove in to pummel the gunfighter. Several punches landed hard on McLeary's shoulders, biceps, and then one on the left cheek. It hurt, and McLeary knew now that Bowers should not be taken lightly. The miner's hands felt like they were made of stone.

Another punch landed on McLeary's cheek, staggering him. But it also angered him. As he stumbled back, he saw Bowers stalking toward him, a gleam of triumph and vindication in his eyes.

McLeary caught himself, and as Bowers approached, McLeary kicked the miner in the right knee. The miner's eyelids popped wide in pain and shock. That was not fair! he thought.

But McLeary had no intention of playing fair. When he fought, it was for keeps, and he would do whatever he had to, to win. He pushed forward, his own rock-hard fists set.

Bowers took a step back with this left foot. Then with his right. But as his weight came down on the knee, he yelped in pain, and his fists dropped slightly.

It was the opportunity McLeary had been waiting for. Suddenly he was all over the miner, his strong fists flashing, each blow eliciting a grunt a fraction of a second after the audible splat of flesh on flesh.

Bowers sank down to his knees, trying to protect his head with his arms. McLeary stopped the flurry, dipped and swung his left hand as hard as he could. It went in under the protecting arms and slammed into Bowers' chin. The miner's head jerked back, and he toppled over, not unconscious, but he had no more fight left in him.

Bowers' eyes were hazy as McLeary bent over him. McLeary grabbed Bowers' shirt with his left hand and lifted the miner up a little. He cocked his right fist.

"Stop!"

McLeary turned to look at Duncan McGregor. The small miner was still standing by the table. His hands were on his hips. "Pete's had enough. You don't need to hit him any more."

McLeary hesitated. Then he dropped Bowers, whose head hit the dirt floor. With the adrenaline still rushing through him, McLeary's movements were sharp and a little jerky. But by the time he got to the table, he had recovered himself. He took up his gunbelt and strapped it on. He pulled a bandanna out and mopped his sweaty forehead. Then he dabbed at the blood seeping from the cut high on his cheek. He put the handkerchief away and pulled on his duster.

With a nod toward McGregor, he walked out of the saloon, keeping himself from smiling as men transferred money to others, the results of betting on the impromptu bout of fisticuffs.

Not wanting to go sit by himself in his room, McLeary wandered to the livery, where he checked on the cinnamon gelding. The horse was being well cared for, and, satisfied, McLeary moved back to the center of town. By now the adrenaline rush was over, and he felt tired, and a little sore. But he was hungry, too.

He went to Lankshire's. It was the only restaurant in town that he knew of, he told himself sternly. But he knew full well he went there in hopes of seeing Molly again. He was, therefore, rather disappointed when she was not there, though he knew he should not have been expecting it.

He ate with no particular rush, but with no dawdling either. The waiter—the same one as earlier—was much more effusive this time. After the meal of pork chops, stewed apples, boiled potatoes and peas, McLeary strolled outside.

The heat of the day was easing as the sun sank over the peaks of the western edge of the San Juan Mountains. It would be a nice night, now that the clouds and rain had scooted far to the east.

McLeary stopped at the Pick and Shovel and bought a bottle of whiskey from Lem Wilson. McLeary was glad the saloon was nearly empty; he really did not feel like meeting anyone just now. Then he went back to his room at the Casa de Plata Hotel. There he spent the night in drinking, puffing on cheroots, and finishing off the two city newspapers he had.

He was hung over and in a foul mood the next morning. So he bought some canned foods, saddled up the cinnamon and rode off into the mountains. He spent the day in recovering from his excesses of the previous day, resting in the shade of cottonwoods, napping, daydreaming, cleaning and oiling his weapons.

McLeary was much refreshed and in far better humor when he

rode back into Silver Canyon in the purplish dusk. He ate supper at Lankshire's, battling back the renewed bout of dejection he experienced at not seeing Molly again. Afterward, he went to the Pick and Shovel, where he spent the night gambling and drinking—the latter only moderately.

Back in his room, he told himself drowsily as he sank onto the soft bed that he would have to do something about Molly. He would have to find her, maybe find out about her. Something. But he had to get rid of this demon. He felt sure that if he saw her again, he would not feel so smitten, and that he would work out his emotions.

With that plan firm in his mind, he allowed himself to fall under slumber's spell.

Throughout the next day he made discrete inquiries around town about one beautiful, honey-blond, exquisite young woman. But no one seemed to know who he was talking about; no one seemed to know her, or even anyone named Molly. He thought it odd.

By day's end, he was frustrated and spent another evening at the Pick and Shovel, winning a few dollars from the miners. He saw McGregor, who nodded in greeting but did not stop at his table.

The next morning, McLeary started on his hunt for information again, with the same results.

Then he spotted her across the street.

"Molly!" he yelled, stepping off the sidewalk and walking in her direction. He had been wrong. The excitement at seeing her again had not diminished whatsoever from the earlier time, and his emotions went crazy. He had never felt like this before, and it was disconcerting.

The woman turned her head, saw him, snapped her head back forward, and started walking very fast. It was, McLeary thought, as if she did not want to see him and was trying mightily to avoid him.

"Molly!" he bellowed again, hurrying toward her. His long legs closed the gap rapidly, and as he neared her, he called her name again.

She glanced back, frightened. When she saw how close he was, she knew flight would do her no good. She stopped and waited, her face stricken.

"There something wrong?" he asked, reaching her.

"No," she mumbled. She looked up and down the street, afraid someone might see her.

"Then what is it?" he asked. "I can't think you'd not want to see me again."

"No," she said nervously. "No, that's not it."

"Then what?"

"Come," she said, turning. "Let's walk a bit."

She seemed to relax a little as they strolled. "I wanted to see you," she said hesitatingly. "But . . ."

"But what?" he demanded, though politely.

She stalled, then said, "I'm married."

"So?"

"That doesn't matter to you?"

"Should it?"

"But . . . I . . . he . . . if we . . . he . . ." she sputtered to a halt, thinking, *Why should it matter to him? Or to me either, come to think of it?* Her husband paid her too little attention; thought too little of her. Here was a man who wanted her. "I reckon it shouldn't," she finally said. "But if he were to find out . . ."

"Is he ten feet tall?"

"No," she said in surprise.

"Is he as big and nasty as a grizzly bear?"

"No." She smiled.

"Does he have three arms?" McLeary was smiling, too.

"No." Molly was giggling now.

"Then there's no reason I can see for me to be afraid of him, is there?"

She sobered immediately. "Well, he's . . ." She almost said the name, then stopped herself. "He's a powerful man in these parts," Molly said lamely.

"Don't matter. Besides," McLeary said with a handsome grin, "we ain't done nothin' for him to get in an uproar over. All we done is have lunch once, and now we're walkin' down the street, in bright daylight, innocent, mindin' our own business. We ain't harmin' no one."

"Still," Molly said a little nervously, "if someone were to see us—and then go tell him—I doubt he'd take it kindly. I know certain he wouldn't understand."

"If it worries you that much . . ." He started to leave.

"Wait!" She hissed it, rather than whisper it, conveying her sense of desire, but designed not to attract attention.

He turned back, a question in his eyes.

Molly looked away for a moment, before saying softly, "Let's walk a little more."

Molly was confused, and needed time to think. She could not explain her attraction to this man; she only knew that it was palpable. How could she, a woman of wealth and breeding, desire this man? she wondered. And there was no denying that she desired him; so much so that her legs almost trembled. The desire was shocking to her. It was not right—not *normal*—for a woman to have such feelings. To think of holding this man's naked body next to hers, to have him inside her. . . . She shuddered, both with desire and with shame at her lustful thoughts.

McLeary was glad for the respite, too. He was perplexed. He had never felt about any woman quite like he did about Molly. He had always shielded himself from that. Come to think of it, he was not even sure what he felt. Certainly there was lust—a man would have to be dead not to lust after this woman, he thought, a chuckle forming in his mind, if not on his lips. But could it be love? he wondered. He didn't think so, but there was far more to his feelings than only lust.

He shook his head and stroked his mustache. Then he said, "We can't walk all day, Miss Molly. What would you like to do?"

She shrugged, unsure, desire tempered by the fear of being found out.

"We could," he said, trying for a light tone, but not quite achieving it, "go to my hotel room." He left it hanging.

She looked quite shocked. "Just what kind of woman do you think I am, Mister McLeary?" Molly demanded, angry. She stopped and stared up at him.

"I think," he said, taken aback, "that you are a young, lusty, and incredibly beautiful one."

She lowered her eyes modestly, then raised them and looked full at him. Desire again smoldered in the soft hazel pupils. "What makes you think I would consider such a thing?" she asked softly.

"Because I think that you are a normal, healthy woman, with healthy needs and wants. I think—"

"I think you're *loco,*" she said, but the corners of her full lips twitched, trying to smile.

"That might be true." He grinned. "But I don't think so," he added seriously.

"Indeed." Molly turned and started walking again, still nervous, but losing some of the fear, since no one paid them much attention.

"And where is your room?" she asked so softly he was not sure he heard her. Perhaps, he thought for a moment, he was only *thinking* she said it, because he wanted it so much. Perhaps . . . but, no, she was now looking at him expectantly. God, how beautiful she was, he thought, with her perfect skin, her delicate features—now flushed with . . . what? Excitement? Desire? Fear? Shame?

She asked again, still softly, her mouth dry with nervousness.

"Casa de Plata," he finally said.

She stopped short, shock written all over her face.

"What's wrong?" he asked, worried.

"I couldn't go there," she muttered. "No, never."

"Why?"

"I just can't. I can't."

"It's all right," he said, still a bit worried. They began strolling again, both immersed in their own thoughts. At last he said, "I'm sorry I said anything, Miss Molly." He hesitated, then said with a sadness and heaviness he had never known, "I'll be goin' now, Miss Molly, and leave you in peace. You don't need to worry. I'll not bother you no more. I should've know that a fancy lady like you—"

"What?" she gasped, spinning to face him. "What?"

"I said I'd be leavin'," he mumbled. "I'll not—"

"I heard what you said. But I—"

"But what?" he asked, filled with hope.

"But I don't want you to go away." She gulped, and her face was flushed. "I want you to stay. I want to . . ." She was too embarrassed to finish.

McLeary felt a pleasurable warming and tightening in his groin.

"But I can't go with you to your room." She stood thinking as he watched expectantly. Then she said, excitement coloring her face and voice, "I have a friend whose house I . . . we . . . could use. Meet me there in one hour."

"All right. Where?"

"Routt Street. Two blocks east of the creek. The first street is Animas. The house is on the northwest corner of Routt Street and Sixth Street. Wood. Whitewashed, with green trimmings."

"All right." He was nervous now, eager to get away, more eager for the hour to pass.

"You have a watch?"

"Yep."

"Good," she said, seemingly all business now. "Meet me in one hour. No more than that, and certainly no less."

She disappeared into the bustling crowd. McLeary, whistling *I'll Take You Home Again Kathleen,* wandered down the street.

Chapter 12

Charlie McLeary couldn't help it, but he arrived at the house fifty-nine minutes after he had left Molly. She was on the wide front porch, waiting for him, her face a mix of fear, nervousness and desire.

Without a word, she took his hand after he mounted the three steps to the porch and led him inside. Her palms were damp with sweat.

McLeary had used his fifty-nine minutes well. He had taken another bath—the first time he could ever remember doing so twice in less than a week—and had another shave. He went to Markham's General Store and bought a new shirt and new pair of wool pants with finely woven stripes. He wore both now, and wished he had had enough money to have bought a new pair of boots, too.

Molly did not seem to mind. She tugged him hurriedly through the parlor, and then up a flight of carpeted steps. There were three rooms on the second floor: one set out as a woman's den; one filled with a jumble of objects, which probably was a storage room; and the other was a bedroom. It was into the latter room that Molly dragged McLeary, seemingly with urgency.

"You in a hurry?" he asked with a crooked smile.

"Yes," she whispered nervously.

He was not surprised. Knowing how apprehensive she was, he figured she wanted to get this over with before she changed her mind. Well, he would have to change her mind about that, he figured.

Molly stopped at the edge of the bed and released McLeary's hand. Still facing away from him, she unbuttoned her dress and let it drop to the floor. Then she peeled off her five petticoats, leaving her standing there in stockings, shoes and corset.

She climbed up on the huge, four-poster bed and lay there. With an almost detached look, she said, "Well, come on, then."

McLeary, who had taken off his hat, set it firmly back on his head, his sense of disappointment almost overwhelming. "Sorry, Molly." He turned and strode to the door.

"Charlie!" she wailed.

When he turned, he saw she was crying. It detracted from her beauty only a little.

"Come back," she pleaded.

He walked to the bed. Reaching out a finger, he brushed away one of her tears.

"Please, Charlie," she said.

"Not like this," he said gently.

"What's wrong?"

He realized with shock that this was probably all she knew: get half undressed and then let her husband have his way with her.

"You're supposed to enjoy this, too, Molly," he said quietly.

"But I . . . I don't . . . know . . ."

"Doesn't matter," he said. "Long's you're willin' to help, relax, take part, let yourself go."

"Yes," she whispered, her tears dwindling to a few. The remaining moisture made her hazel eyes sparkle. She pushed herself up on her elbows. "What do you want me to do?"

"Just relax for right now, Molly." He grinned. Without haste, he unbuckled his gunbelt and hung it over one of the bedposts. He peeled off his new blue shirt and the Colt Lightning in the shoulder holster. Sitting in a straight-backed chair, he pulled off his boots and socks. Feeling a little odd, he stripped his pants off, and then pulled off his long-handle underwear—under Molly's very intent gaze.

She gasped when he stood before her naked. "Oh, my," she muttered, feeling stirrings she had never felt before.

He climbed on the bed. Looming over her, he searched the beauty of her face for a moment before lowering his head to smother her mouth with his. Her eyes opened wide as his tongue probed for hers, and then shut dreamily as warmth gushed through her limbs.

He turned and unlaced her high-top button shoes and pulled them off. With a little effort, he peeled down her stockings. He rubbed her feet and her tiny toes, and she giggled joyfully.

Then McLeary went to work on the corset. Soon it was off, and McLeary began working at the drawstring on her drawers.

"What are you doing?" Molly gasped.

"What do you think?" he asked happily.

But she no longer cared, until he pulled her drawers off and she realized she was as naked as she had been on the day of her birth. "Oh, my," she muttered.

Then his lips and tongue were busy again, and she groaned, uncaring that she was naked, in bed with a man who was not her husband.

"Oh, Lord," she muttered. She could no longer think, since her brain was a jumbled mass of impressions. Nothing that had ever happened to her had felt this good.

There was a building inside her, a tension that rose and built and grew and took her over, until there was a brilliant flash and an explosion of pleasure that sent her mind reeling.

And then came a calmness and peace unlike any other she had experienced. "That was ni—" she started, then bit her lower lip as McLeary continued his ministrations. "Oh, my God," she moaned her head rolling from side to side on the pillow, almost in shock from the intensity of the pleasure she was feeling. And she fought for breath as he collapsed atop her.

It was a long time before she could talk. By then he had rolled off and was at her side. "That was . . ." she started, then stopped, not knowing the words.

"Was it?" he asked, smiling.

"Yes. It's," Molly added haltingly, "never like that with . . . I mean, my husband never . . ." Her face colored red.

"The man's a goddamn fool, whoever he is," McLeary said. It was strange. But never had he been happier.

"Why?" she wondered.

"Any man don't take the time to pleasure his woman is a fool. Especially when she's as flat-out beautiful as you. Is that the usual way of it?" he asked. "You get down to your corset and drawers and he just gets atop you for a couple minutes."

She flushed again, this time from shame. "Yes," she whispered, closing her eyes so she did not have to look deep into his pale blue eyes and see his ridicule.

When he said nothing, she opened her eyes again. McLeary was staring at her in concern. There was no hint of condescension there.

He smiled. "He's an even bigger fool than I thought," McLeary said. "A man don't take a heap of pleasure in lookin' as often as he can at somethin' like you has got to have somethin' wrong with him."

"You really think so?" she asked, full of hope and wonder.

"What do you think?" he countered.

"I think he's the biggest damn fool in the world," she said firmly, then laughed. "Can you do that again?" she asked, only slightly embarrassed. "I mean, with him . . . my husband . . . it's only one time, thank God. But when it feels this good . . ." She was afraid she was making a fool of herself.

McLeary smiled softly and pulled her close. "It takes a little while"—he paused, his turn to be a little embarrassed—"for me to build up my ammunition."

She laughed fully, her soft, yet still firm, breasts jiggling against his chest. He joined in. "Are you loaded yet?" she asked, with an embarrassed giggle.

"Not quite," he said firmly. But before long, Molly was muttering and groaning and moaning, her hands clutching at his back and shoulders.

Quietly afterward, McLeary slept a bit, as Molly lay awake, stroking his hair. It was wrong, she thought, all wrong to be here like this with a man. But how could something that felt so good be so wrong? McLeary had not used her, had not degraded her, had not taken his pleasure of her while leaving her laying there unsated, wanting. Her husband had done all those things. He seemed to get enjoyment from degrading her in small ways—talking down to her in front of the servants; taking himself off to Lucy's with more frequency than he partook of the hidden pleasures Molly offered; occasionally beating her.

No, she reasoned, she was not doing anything wrong here. Even if all the other women in town would be horrified by her actions, it did not matter. For the first time in her life, she was looking out for herself and her own joy.

Still, there remained a lingering fear that McLeary was just using her. She realized that she loved this hard-edged gunfighter. And she realized how foolish that was. There could be no life with him—drifting from town to town, always worried that this day might be the one when he met someone a fraction of a second faster or more accurate than he. There was no security in loving this man. There would be no home to always go to, no life of respectability such as she was used to, and certainly no life free from want.

Maybe she could, through her love, she thought, change him. But she knew immediately that such a thing was foolish, if not impossible. Even if she could change him, it would not work out. For if she changed him, he would no longer be the man she fell in love with. By changing him, she would lose him.

She shook her head, almost smiling. Then she realized she didn't much care what he was. Nothing she had thought of here changed what she felt for him.

She grabbed his hair lightly and shook his head with it, calling softly, "Charlie."

He awoke in an instant, alert. Realizing where he was, he grinned at her. He sat up, rubbing his face. "Was I out long?" he asked.

"Nope," she said, rubbing his arm. She was loathe to do what she had to do, so she delayed. She touched the cut surrounded by the discolored bruise on his cheek. "How'd you get this?" she asked.

"Disagreement with someone," he said with shrug.

There was a short silence, but Molly knew she could not put the inevitable off any longer. "We've got to go," she muttered.

"What?"

"We've got to go. My friend needs her house back, and I must get home. So as not to arouse suspicions."

"I don't give a damn about suspicions. Tell me who your husband is, and I'll go settle it with him—one way or another." The words surprised him. What was he saying, he wondered. But it was too late to take them back now—and he was not sure he wanted to anyway.

"Not now, Charlie. Please. Let's just leave it as it is for now."

"Am I gonna see you again?" he growled.

"Yes. I want that. Very much." She gazed steadily at him. "Two o'clock tomorrow. Meet me here again."

He finally nodded.

"Please get my clothes," she asked. "And turn away while I get dressed."

He looked at her with a question in his eyes.

She looked stern for a minute, before it cracked and she grinned. "Guess it doesn't matter much now, does it?"

"No, ma'am."

Without reservation, Molly tossed off the covers. She slid off the far side of the bed and walked around it, giving McLeary an eyeful, something for which he was most appreciative.

Chapter 13

Charlie McLeary sat in his hotel room, wondering, as he had been for the past several hours, just what he had gotten himself into with this woman he still knew only as Molly.

But finally he could sit here no more with the same questions burning through his brain—the same answerless questions. He was getting nowhere. He was, he felt fairly certain now, in love with the woman. But being so would only bring him no end of grief.

"Damn," he finally grumbled, standing and hooking on his gunbelt. He would have to put it from his mind until some things could be answered. Maybe they would be tomorrow when he met her again. But perhaps they would not.

Here I go again, he thought angrily. He had to get his mind off it. He did not feel like going to the Pick and Shovel again. He decided, as he left his room and headed down the stairs of Casa de Plata, that he would take Bodie Wheeler up on his invitation to visit the Silver Nugget. More than likely, his old friend would be able to take his mind off the whirling dervish of his thoughts.

He pushed into the saloon, and was dazzled by the lights. There were lanterns everywhere, as well as several crystal and silver chandeliers hanging from the ceilings. But that was far from the only difference between the opulent Silver Nugget and the simple Pick and Shovel.

For one thing, the Silver Nugget was two stories, the lower devoted to the long, long bar, and to gambling, tables for which were scattered through the huge saloon. The bar itself was of dark, expensive wood. Filagrees and curving lines were carved in it. A brass foot railing ran the length of the bar, behind which three paintings of lounging nudes hung. McLeary wasn't sure from this distance, but he thought one of them was Janie

May Dillon.

The floor also was wood, covered with a light coating of sawdust. Brass spittoons were plentiful, as were the painted, barely dressed women who roamed about drumming up business to take upstairs, or dealing cards or running some of the other games. A bored-looking man sat in one corner, playing popular tunes on a tinny piano. When McLeary entered, the piano player was coaxing his way through a lively version of *Home on the Range.*

Several men were playing billiards at the two tables to McLeary's left, in the space between the front wall of the building and the bar. One of the cigar-smoking players was Alva Stoughton.

A massive, gilded staircase curved up to the second floor from each side of the cavernous room at the back. A balcony, with rooms behind it, ran around three sides of the building on that floor. At each of the back corners sat a man holding a shotgun, watching over the saloon. As McLeary watched, a painted trollop came out of one of the rooms, a contented-looking townsman following her.

Stoughton stepped up to McLeary, hand out. "Welcome, Mister McLeary," he said in his booming voice. "Have you come to join us, then?"

"Nope," McLeary replied, shaking his hand. "Just visitin'. Had an invite from a friend."

"Oh?"

"I told him to come on over, Mister Stoughton," Bodie Wheeler grumbled, walking up.

"Ah, yes, I had forgotten you know this man. Well, Mister McLeary, enjoy yourself here in our poor establishment. I leave you in good hands."

"Thanks."

"Well, come on, boy," Wheeler said in his bass voice. "Let's go cut that dry in your throat." He grinned.

McLeary returned it. "Lead on, pard," he said.

They walked to the bar, and immediately there was a bartender waiting. "Two beers, Marsh, and a bottle," Wheeler rumbled.

The barkeep nodded and was back in record time. McLeary blew the foam off his beer and took a sip. He turned, leaning back against the bar to look out over the room. "Not a bad little place here, Bodie," he said. It was, he reckoned, the finest place he had ever been in.

"It'll do till somethin' better comes 'long," Wheeler growled. "Here, try this." He handed McLeary a shot glass brimming with golden-red liquid.

McLeary looked at it a moment, before putting the shot glass up to his lips and jolting its contents down in one swallow. It burned a little, but not much. "Fine. Very fine," he said appreciatively. Only twice before could he remember drinking whiskey that good. Usually he had to make do with some barely distilled rotgut.

"The Stoughtons import it straight from Kentucky," Wheeler said. "There are some definite benefits to workin' for them boys."

"I'm sure. But don't push me on it, Bodie. I gave you my answer the other day. I ain't changed it since."

"Sure, sure, Charlie." Wheeler set his shot glass down and leaned back against the bar like McLeary. He sipped his beer. "Heard you had a run-in with one of the miners the other day."

"Wasn't much of a run-in."

"Reckon not if you kicked his ass in for him as quick as I heard."

"Didn't take long." McLeary grinned.

"It was Pete Bowers, wasn't it?" When McLeary nodded, Wheeler said, "He's one of the worst of those miners, Charlie. Purely is. Goddamn agitator is all he is. Him and that short-legged little bastard Duncan McGregor."

McLeary shrugged. "Why ain't the Stoughtons fired those two, if they're so much trouble?"

"Hell, they're afraid that if McGregor and Bowers get fired, the other boys'll walk. Even without those two agitatin' leaders there, somebody'd be bound to take their place. The Stoughtons are hopin' to end this foolishness without losin' any profits. I'd just as soon shoot the both of 'em. That'd put an end to this bullshit about unionizin'. But I reckon the Stoughtons don't see it that way. Reckon it won't matter soon. The Stoughtons are tryin' to hire a heap of Chinamen from over in California. They get enough to fill the mines, they can boot all these union bastards out."

McLeary looked at Wheeler with disgust. "You've changed, Bodie, in the couple years since I seen you."

"All men change," he said harshly. "You don't, you'll die."

"Gonna die someday anyway. Besides, changin' to talk down about men workin' their asses off just to survive ain't your style, Bodie. Nor is talkin' poor about the Chinese. Not after you'n me helped those ones down in Tucson that time."

Wheeler shrugged. Then he said slowly, "Hell, Charlie, I ain't really changed all that much. Not about such things. But I was hired by the Stoughtons, not the miners. And it's to them that I owe my loyalty. As far as shootin' them two union leaders, hell, that's just frustration. Me and all these other guns been sittin' around with our hands up our asses for close to a month. I'm plumb tired of it."

He waved his beer mug, showing off the room. "All this here's fine. We get the best liquor, our choice of the girls, discounts if we want to go over to Lucy's, credit over to Taylor's Mercantile, good food, regular pay. But goddamn, am I bored," he added with feeling. "Hell, I ain't spent this much time in one place since I was sixteen.

"And as for the Chinese, damn, I'm just pickin' up bad habits from these idiots." He waved the mug around the room again. There were a substantial number of gunmen around.

"Those kind of habits'll get your ass shot full of holes."

"Hell, that'll be the day."

They drank in silence for a while, before Bodie muttered, "I see trouble comin'."

A gunfighter, having had more than his fill of whiskey, lurched up to them. "Well, well, well," he slurred, "if it ain't the great goddamn Charlie McLeary come to pay us a visit. Real goddamn nice of you." He stood weaving, his eyes bleary.

McLeary recognized the man as a vicious, unscrupulous gunslinger from southern Texas. The man had something of a reputation, but McLeary doubted he could hold his own with either him or Bodie. His name was Farren Peels.

"Go on back to your bottle, Farren," Bodie snapped. He was not angry—yet. Just annoyed.

"I ain't talkin' to you, you goddamn clod."

Bodie turned and set down his mug. He was about ready to slug the drunken gunfighter, but McLeary stopped him. "Let the man speak his piece, Bodie," McLeary said with some humor. "That way, when they lay him out, the mourners can't say he didn't have his last words."

Wheeler relaxed and grinned. He liked that kind of thinking.

Peels turned his bloodshot eyes back toward McLeary. It took a few moments before they fully focused. "I hear you're purty good with that goddamn Smith and Wesson. Stupid goddamn gun. Made for a bunch of stinkin' foreigners."

"This one's called the Smith and Wesson American," McLeary said calmly. "It is based on the .44-caliber pistol Smith and Wesson originally made for the Russians. Even those guns were made here. The Americans were too goddamn stupid to use a good pistol. The Russians saw the good in it and ordered a heap of 'em. Then they asked for some modifications, to better suit their uses. Finally, the Americans began to realize how good the Smith and Wesson .44 is. When they did that, they created enough demand so that Smith and Wesson began producin' the American model."

McLeary set down his beer. Then he lifted his pistol out of the holster and twirled it a few times on his finger. "Which is what this is," he said, sliding it back home. "Now, you got anything more to say?" He picked up his drink again.

Peels stood for some moments, trying to collect his drunken thoughts into some sort of order. "Hell," he finally spit out, slurring his words even more, "you should be usin' somethin' good, like this trusty old Colt."

He started to ease it from the holster to show it around, but froze with it halfway out of the holster as McLeary said, "You pull that piece out, Farren, and I'm gonna shove it up your butt before I fire it off four or five times."

Peels tried to focus his mind again. Then he muttered, "You don't scare me, McLeary." He resumed pulling his pistol.

McLeary grabbed Peels' gun hand with his left while still holding the beer mug in his right hand. He tossed the liquid into Peels' face. Then he brought the mug wide to his own right and smashed it as hard as he could into the side of the gunman's face.

Peels went down like a broken sack of corn, moaning once in his fall. He lay silent amid the shards of glass, his cheek bleeding.

Wheeler turned to the barman. "Get somebody out here *pronto* to clean up this glass, eh, Marsh. And Mister McLeary needs a fresh beer." He leaned over and grabbed a handful of Peels' shirt, then straightened, hauling Peels up in a sort of arch. He half dragged, half carried the gunfighter to the doors and then out, returning a moment later empty handed.

When he reached his friend, who already had a new mug filled in his hand, McLeary asked, "What'd you do with him?"

"Dumped him outside with the rest of the garbage." He drained his mug of beer. "Good," he muttered. "Well, pard, what say you and me join one of these games of chance here. Unless"—he grinned—"you wanna find some woman and head upstairs, or maybe head on over to Lucy's."

"Hell, I ain't got the money for any of it," McLeary said with a grin. "Like you said, jobs are hard to come by these days." He held up his hand, stopping Wheeler before the large man started. "I know what you're gonna say, but I ain't interested."

Wheeler shrugged. "Your business, Charlie." He paused, then said very quietly, "It really is good to see you, old friend. These others might be good with a gun and all, though I have my doubts about some of 'em, but there ain't a one of 'em I'd *want* to call a friend. Even if I could abide any of 'em."

McLeary nodded, grinning. "Hell, it's good to see you, too. And after what I been hearing from you, it's a good thing I showed up, too. Somebody's got to set you back on the right path."

Wheeler smiled, the gap prominent. "Yes, mother," he said, the sarcasm heavy. "Tell you what, I'll spot you a few dollars. You can pay me back sometime."

"I ain't of a mood for Lucy's," he said. His smile let Wheeler know that he had been satisfied recent enough. "But a good card game might be just the thing. Unless"—his eyebrows raised in a question—"there ain't no chance of winnin' here."

"The brothers told me the house ain't takin' advantage of any of the regulators." He winked. "Or their friends. Unless, of course, somebody starts winnin' real big, or the house gets cheated. From what I've seen, it's probably true."

"Then I'll let you stake me a bit. I ought to be able to win it back, and then some. I'll pay you back soon's I get enough winnin's."

"Reckon I can do that. I seem to recall a time you staked me."

"*A* time?" McLeary said with a laugh. "Hell, seems like every time we rode into some town somewhere, I had to stake you. Damn, I never saw anybody burn money the way you could."

Wheeler was laughing, too. McLeary had exaggerated some, but not all that much. Bodie Wheeler was a big man with big appetites, and a free hand with his cash. He was not one to put away for a rainy day. Nor was he beyond an occasional holdup—though he only picked on people he knew could afford to lose a couple hundred in cash—when times were particularly hard.

"Well, I got the stake now, and you ain't," Wheeler said, "so I wouldn't go rubbin' this old boy's nose in past doings. Too much." Chuckles still erupted from his ample stomach and bubbled up over his lips.

McLeary set down his glass. "Well, hell, what're we waitin' for?" he said, his humor restored.

Chapter 14

Charlie McLeary paced anxiously in his room at Casa de Plata. It was one o'clock. He had eaten lunch, and now only had to wait before heading for his rendezvous with Molly in the house on Routt Street. There was too much time for him to just sit; not enough time for him to accomplish anything.

So he paced, his mind going over and over and over the same questions he had about Molly, about their budding relationship, and about what to do. And, as he had the evening before, he got nowhere.

He tried focusing his thoughts on the night before. He and Bodie Wheeler had played stud poker for several hours, and McLeary had won enough not only to pay Wheeler back, but also to ease his worries over cash for at least a while.

He had also drank more than he had wanted to, but not so much that he had had to pay for it this morning. When he had rolled out of the Silver Nugget, feeling quite good about the world, Farren Peels was nowhere to be seen. McLeary had seen the gunfighter this morning, though, as McLeary was on his way to breakfast. Peels had looked pretty bad, with the left side of his face mottled purple, black and yellowish-blue. McLeary felt no sympathy for him.

He looked at his pocket watch. One thirty-two. Not much longer. Finally he snarled at himself and his unusual inability to turn off the useless thoughts that were plaguing him. He sat in the chair by the window, closed his eyes, and breathed evenly, deeply, forcing himself through will alone to calm his mind and to relax.

It worked after a few minutes, and it was with much more serenity that he waited the short while until it was time to leave. When he did, he walked leisurely up the main street to Fourth Street, down toward Animas Creek, then north on Routt Street to the house.

Molly was waiting for him on the porch again. She looked worried, her face sort of pinched. Until she saw him. Then her face brightened, and her breathing quickened.

Eagerly she grabbed his hand and practically hauled him up the stairs to the bedroom.

"Whoa, slow down, woman," McLeary said with a chuckle.

She laughed, but calmed herself. "Sorry. It's just that— Well, I . . ." She could not really bring herself to say that she hungered for his touch, his embrace, his kisses, his—

"I know," he said softly. "But we got time."

"You're right." She kissed him lightly on the chin, and had to stand on tiptoes to do that. Then she wrapped her arms around his waist. He could feel she was tight as a drum. But eventually she started to calm down.

"I was afraid you wouldn't come," she said into his shirt.

"You're lucky I wasn't here at eight this mornin'," he mumbled.

Her head snapped up, eyes searching his face. "You're not just sayin' that, are you?"

"No, Molly. No. I was up half the night, it seems, thinkin' over what we can do about us, but I never came up with any answers. But I'll tell you this, I never once thought of not coming over here this afternoon."

"I don't know what we're going to do, either. I've been worried about that. About everything . . ."

"It must be terribly hard on you."

"I think I'm strong enough to handle it."

"Reckon you are, Molly. Still . . ."

"Let's talk about this later, Charlie. I want you now, and I don't want to think about the rest."

"Yes, ma'am," he said, holding her at arm's length to take a look at her. The beauty of her face caught his breath in his throat.

She started unbuttoning her expensive, magenta satin dress, but he took her hands lightly in his. "Let me," he whispered.

She looked scared, but nodded. He smiled and started undoing the buttons, and then he gasped. She wore no corset today. "Didn't think I needed it," she muttered.

* * *

When their passion was spent, she said, "I still can't believe it can be that good."

McLeary sat up, swung his legs over the side of the bed and lit a cheroot. Then he said, "What are we going to do, Molly?"

"I don't know," she mumbled, saddened.

"We can't go on like this forever."

"It's only been two days."

"I know." He had realized—to his absolute horror—about an hour ago that there was no longer any doubt that he loved her. Hopelessly and totally. It was a shock to him, but he had come to accept it, as it was. Now it was time to use that knowledge and work with it. "But—" he hesitated, unsure whether he should say anything. He swallowed, took a puff on the cigar, blew out three smoke rings, and then said quickly, flatly, "I love you, Molly."

When she didn't say anything, McLeary figured he had finally gone too far. He stood up and said, "Sorry."

"Where are you going?" she croaked, her voice not working right from the surprise.

"Leavin'. I figure I just went and overstepped my bounds there."

She grabbed him. "You ain't goin' nowhere, mister."

He turned back to her, a query in his eyes.

"I love you, Charlie McLeary," she said, her face aglow.

"You never said."

"I was afraid to. I realized it right after we parted that first day we had lunch. I wanted to see you so bad. I wanted you so much, I was nearly crazy with it."

"Why'd you nearly run away when I saw you yesterday?"

"I was scared. I'm still scared. There's a lot of problems facing us. And I am still scared you might not love me—that you're just leadin' me on."

"Oh, I love you, all right."

"I'm glad."

"Me, too. But what are we going to do?"

"I'm not sure. I think I need some time to think about it."

"You know," he said, pointing the cheroot at her, "I don't even know your last name."

"You aren't going to know it, either, until I—or we—can figure out what we're going to do."

"I can fix it," he said with quiet menace.

"No," she breathed. "I can't allow that. No matter what he's done . . . I can't have his death hanging over me."

He nodded. "So what do we do?"

"Let's just go on like this a little bit. Please? Let's see what happens after a little while. We'll meet here every day. Same time. Take our pleasure, try to come up with a solution."

"I don't know," he said, unsure. He did not like this sneaking around, hiding from someone he didn't even know. He was a man used to action, a man who most often took the matter to hand and solved it—any way he could. He could see no solution to any problem in just sitting. Perhaps, he thought, he should make another effort to find out who Molly was. By knowing that, he could pay the husband a quiet visit and solve the problem—one way or another.

"It'll work out. I know it will," Molly insisted.

"I reckon," McLeary said, unappeased. It was difficult not to do *something*. But he did not know what, so he would have to sit and wait.

Molly came up close to him. She kissed his cheek, his ear. While her mouth was so close, she whispered, "While we bide our time, you can teach me some new things."

A grin spread across his face. He was a man of action, and here was action of the most gratifying sort. It would be, he deduced, a most satisfying way of passing the time.

Chapter 15

Their third afternoon together was even better than their first two, McLeary thought as he stretched out for sleep that night. They had not come any closer to solving their dilemma that afternoon than they had the one before, but that had detracted from their enjoyment only a little.

What had dampened his enthusiasm were the mottled bruises on Molly's body. She had been reluctant for him to strip her down, and he had thought that odd. But he persisted, and soon enough she was naked on the bed and panting under his skillful hands and mouth. She tensed when he stopped suddenly, knowing he had seen.

"What the hell's this?" he demanded, pointing angrily to the purplish-yellow contusion on her ribs. "And this?" He jabbed an accusing finger at another on the outside of her right thigh.

"What do you think?" she retorted, a mixture of fear and worry in her voice.

"Who did it?"

She did not answer. There were tears in her eyes, but she remained silent.

"Who, goddammit?" he demanded, grabbing her rather roughly by the arms.

He was shocked by the look of resignation in her eyes, and he laid her gently back down. That look would haunt him for some time, he thought—that look saying, "Go ahead, hit me. Others have done so, regularly. You can't hurt me any more."

He smothered her face with kisses, whispering, "It's all right, Molly. It's all right. I won't hurt you."

Eventually she calmed, responding to him eagerly, almost desperately.

Afterwards he said, "I've got to know."

"You know who did it," she replied.

"Yes and no. I know damn well it was your husband," he said tightly. "But I still don't know who that is. I want to know."

"No. You'll kill him."

"That's right." He had originally had no desire to kill the man, whoever he was. All he had wanted to do from the beginning was to tell the man to let Molly go free. But now, now there was no doubt about what he would do to the man when he caught him—not after what Molly's spouse had done to her.

"I don't want that on my conscience."

"But—"

"No, Charlie," she said softly, rolling onto her side so she could stroke his cheek. "It's not the first time he's done this. Might not be the last, either, but it'll be near the last. I'll leave him soon, Charlie. I promise. If you want me, that is. If I leave him, I've got to go with you, Charlie. Wherever you go. But if you don't want me, just say so. I'll—" Her hazel eyes were large, and very round.

"Oh, I want you, Molly," he interrupted, grinning in an attempt to ease her mind.

"I know you want me *that* way," she said seriously. "But do you want me by your side for all time?"

"Yes," McLeary answered solemnly, and he meant it.

"Then I'll leave him. But we have to wait a little longer."

"Why?"

She shrugged. She saw the anger color his face, and said, "I have to work a few things out, Charlie. That's all. A couple days is all I need."

"No. Tomorrow."

"Day after," she said firmly.

He accepted it, unhappily, and he remained angry. She smiled and crawled all over him, experimenting with the new things she had learned, and some she had dreamed up. His anger evaporated in the flood of passion.

Now, as he lay in his bed at Casa de Plata, drifting down the dark spiral to sleep, McLeary still had the desire to do something, to take some action. But, in deference to Molly, he would bide his time.

McLeary was a light sleeper, but even if he had not been, all the noise of clanging dinner triangles, pealing church bells and yelling would have woken him. He leaped up and went to the window. Even before he reached it, he knew what the trouble was. The orangish glow against his curtains was unmistakable. He pulled back the edge of the curtains. It looked to McLeary like several miners' homes up toward the mines were burning.

People rushed up Silver Street, many carrying buckets. There was, McLeary knew, no fire department, so it would have to be the people who handled it.

McLeary dressed as fast as he could and rushed out into the street. He joined the throng still running toward the fires. He slammed to a stop at a water trough that was the start of one of the bucket brigades. There was an old woman, about sixty, McLeary guessed, plump, white-haired, jerking the pump handle furiously up and down. She looked half-dead.

"I'll take over, woman," he growled.

She looked grateful and stepped aside.

McLeary grabbed the handle and jerked it up and down, not breaking the stride the woman had. Water sloshed into the trough in rhythmic spurts. From there, two men—one on each side of the trough—scooped up a bucket of water and passed it along. And down the line it went until the people farthest away tossed it onto the burning, crackling house.

As he pumped, McLeary took an occasional look around. He figured all this was futile, since these miners' shacks—like all the others he had ever seen—were made of rotted wood and canvas and tar paper, with maybe some tin for a roof. They would burn hot and fast.

But still he pumped. His arms began to ache, as did his shoulders and back. Sweat trickled down his chest, back and side, and rolled off his forehead from under his hat. He glanced up and noticed several regulators standing on the fringes of women and children who were watching. They looked unconcerned. Indeed, some even joked and laughed. McLeary saw Farren Peels, his head bandaged, whooping it up. The rest of the crowd—comprised mainly of miners' wives and children—was solemn, though the people were used to such things. It was an all too frequent occurrence in mining towns.

There was a blistering roar, and McLeary snapped his head up to watch the one house collapse in an eruption of sparks, flame and searing heat. McLeary stopped pumping and shielded his face for a few moments from the blast of hot air. When he dropped his hands, everyone was just standing, watching the collapsed house burn. There was no use in wasting more water—or energy—in trying to douse the flames.

Then came another rumbling bellow, and the second burning house—a hundred feet away—fell in on itself, sending up another flurry of sparks and heat.

Most of the people stood silent, stunned at the futility. Then someone yelled. Heads snapped up. Another miner's house was on fire, set ablaze by the drifting sparks. McLeary pumped again, feeling his muscles burn from overwork, but within seconds water was spurting and the buckets were moving. More men with buckets arrived from where they had been dealing with the other fire, and threw themselves furiously into helping.

The last blaze was small. Luckily someone had seen it just after it started, and so, with plenty of hard work, and hundreds of buckets of water, they put it out. There would be, someone said, little damage to that house.

Still, McLeary continued pumping, as several union leaders issued orders to soak down all the other homes within a hundred yard radius, so they would not be endangered by still-flying sparks.

By the time that was done, McLeary was in agony from his efforts. But no more houses had caught fire, and the two houses that had originally burned were down to smoldering piles of blackened wood, hot tin and twisted belongings.

People began drifting away, but McLeary stuck around, working his arms and shoulders in circles to ease the pain. He walked toward one of the houses, and looked sadly at the smoking ruins. He saw Duncan McGregor nearby, standing with a gray-haired, matronly looking woman and several tow-haired children.

"Mister McGregor," he said, walking up.

"Come to gloat?" McGregor asked sharply.

McLeary looked at him in surprise. The miner whispered something to his wife. The woman glanced sharply at McLeary, her gaze filled with hate. She left, shooing the children off ahead of her.

"You and your friends did a fine job this time," McGregor said, anger cluttering his voice.

"I have no idea what you're talkin' about, Mister McGregor."

"Do you think these fires were accidental?" McGregor demanded.

"I have no idea. I was asleep till I heard the alarm. I come down here and helped out where I could."

"You helped?" McGregor was surprised.

"Yep. This your place?"

"It was." Bitterness dripped from his voice.

"And you think the regulators had somethin' to do with this?"

"What the hell do you think?"

"Could've been an accident. Places like this burn easy."

"My house and Pete Bowers' burned down. We're separated by more than a hundred feet. Still think it was an accident?" He was so angry that he fairly shook.

"Reckon not. I'm sorry, Mister McGregor." The coincidence was too much. It had to be the Consolidated Silver and Mining Company's regulators behind it.

"I don't want your goddamn sympathy," McGregor snarled. He calmed a bit and said, "But see what we're up against. We can't fight this. Join us, Mister McLeary. Help us."

McLeary was tempted, but he could still hear his father's admonitions ringing in his head. "No, sir." Before McGregor could retort, McLeary added, "Look, I join you, one of those gunslingers is gonna back shoot me first chance he gets. You'll be in worse shape than you are now if that happens."

"Bah," McGregor spit.

McLeary shook his head and walked away. He was uncomfortable. He did not like such doings. And he wanted to help these men.

It took a little while for him to fall back to sleep again. And it seemed like only minutes before his slumber was shattered by the alarms again. The orangish glow against the curtains was brighter this time, and McLeary thought he could feel the heat.

"Goddamn," he snapped. He leaped up, dressed and raced out once more. As he hit the street, he felt a blast of hot, stifling air. "Goddamn," he mumbled again when he saw the Pick and Shovel in flames.

He ran over and thrust himself into one of the fire lines. He hurriedly passed full buckets one way and empty ones the other, all the while knowing it was useless. He was right. Within minutes, one side of the delapidated saloon fell in, and the roof crashed in on that side. Soon after, the other side followed.

The bucket brigade shifted efforts to wetting down nearby buildings, thankful that there was an empty lot on one side of the blazing Pick and Shovel and an alley between it and the next building on the other.

And then it was all over, small flames still snapping gently from the blackened timbers of the saloon. The people drifted off. McLeary was ready to head for his bed when he saw George Stoughton ride up on his buggy. He stopped next to where Lem Wilson and Duncan McGregor were talking. McLeary moved closer.

"Some bad things happening here," Stoughton said.

"Go on back home, goddammit," Wilson snapped.

"That's not a neighborly attitude," Stoughton said, sounding rather offended.

"You ain't my goddamn neighbor. Now haul your ass out of here before I wipe the street with it."

Three regulators who had been standing in the shadows nearby moved up to protect their boss, who sat smiling smugly at Wilson and McGregor.

McLeary, who was behind Stoughton, could not see the smugness, but he knew the man well enough to figure it. He unhooked the hammer of the Smith and Wesson before stepping into the path of the three regulators. They stopped, wary.

"Let's say you boys let your boss handle this one by himself, eh?" McLeary said softly, anger and menace thick in his voice.

The three looked uncertain. McLeary stood, right hand near

the ivory butt of the Smith and Wesson American, the other stroking his mustache. The three gunfighters had not been ready for this, and they also knew of McLeary's reputation. While they knew they would prevail, at least one of them, and most likely two, would be dead before McLeary died. None of the three wanted to be in that number.

Stoughton turned in the seat of his buggy and looked back. "What in hell are you doing here, McLeary?" he demanded.

"Keepin' the streets clean," McLeary said, not looking around. "Now suppose you do like Mister Wilson says and ride on home. You have no business here."

"You joining this riffraff?" Stoughton asked, incredulous.

"Nope."

"Then, what—"

"Just ride on home, Stoughton. Your boys have done enough damage tonight. Nobody needs you comin' 'round rubbin' these folks' noses in it. Now haul your ass home before I shoot down these three pissant punks and then put a bullet in you just for disturbin' my slumbers."

Stoughton seethed. He snapped the reins on his horse hard, and the buggy lurched forward.

"Your business is done here, too, boys," McLeary said to the three.

"We ain't gonna forget this, McLeary," one said. McLeary recognized him as a Colorado cowboy-turned-gunfighter named Mace Kenney. The other two were brothers—Alf and Arnie Bader—out of North Dakota Territory.

"We can settle it now, Mace." The words were cold. McLeary was hot, sweaty, tired and just plain, flat-out angrier than hell at all the things that were going on—not the least of them his situation with Molly. It all served to rile him. He wanted some action. This could be just the thing.

"Another time, McLeary," Kenney said with a sneer curling his scarred lip. Kenney had been shot in the face some years ago, and lived through it. It mutilated the one side of his face. It also gave him some sort of feeling of invincibility. But he knew when and where to pick his spots.

"Anytime." McLeary watched warily as the three turned and walked away. He waited until they had disappeared.

McLeary swiveled as he heard Wilson say, "Thanks, Charlie."

McLeary nodded. He almost smiled as he saw McGregor staring at him. He assumed the miner was amazed that he had held off the three gunfighters. "You figure the regulators did this, too?" he asked.

"Yeah," Wilson said.

"What're both of you gonna do?" McLeary asked.

"I'm gonna rebuild, Charlie. Damn sure I am," Wilson said angrily. "I'll have the Pick and Shovel open in a week. Less."

McGregor was defiant, too. "Well, they ain't gonna run me out, neither, that's for damn sure. They don't scare me."

"Things could get rough," McLeary said. "A lot rougher than they've been."

McGregor shrugged. "Don't matter. But, you know, you're gonna have to side with us sooner or later, Mister McLeary," McGregor said, still gazing at him. "Or get out of town. This is the second time I know of that you've gone against the Stoughtons' hired guns. They won't take kindly to it."

"Yes, Mister McLeary," Wilson added, "join the miners. They need someone like you. I'd like to see it for sure."

"We'll see," McLeary said noncommittally. "Well, good night, boys."

He walked away, knowing McGregor was right. Someone was going to force a decision on him—and soon. And he was beginning to think that someone already had.

Chapter 16

The next two days were filled with tension. The miners struck the mines all the day after the fires. The regulators poured out of their hotels, heading for the three mines in Squaw Gulch. Defiant miners stood around, fearful that the gunfighters might open fire, but ready to fight with what they had—a few rifles, some dynamite smuggled out of the shafts, picks, knives.

George Stoughton was ready to turn the gunmen loose on the miners, but his brother, Alva, managed to calm him down enough to make him see that if they killed any miners most of the others would flee and the mines would be shut down for lack of workers.

"Wait," he was overheard telling George, "till we get more of them Chinese up here. Then we can turn the regulators loose if the miners are still defiant."

The Stoughtons negotiated with Duncan McGregor, who was angry and obstinate; and Pete Bowers, who was quite subdued. He had disappeared right after his house burned down, and then showed up late in the afternoon the next day, just before the negotiating was about to start.

"Where've you been?" McGregor asked harshly. He was tense, understandably, with the situation as it was.

"Out," Bowers said vaguely, waving a hand in the general direction of the cottonwood-, aspen- and pine-covered hills around them.

"You with us, or not?" McGregor demanded. "If you ain't, get out of here. If you are, better get your mind back on what's got to be done."

"I'll be all right."

McGregor had no time to worry about it.

McLeary rode out to watch, after a disturbing session with

Molly. He had been tired and ill at ease; she nervous and seemingly frightened. They enjoyed the closeness and warmth the other brought to the clandestine rendezvous, but on this day there was hesitation and concern.

McLeary pulled up the cinnamon horse. It was the first time he had been near the mines themselves. There was only one entrance—a large hole in the side of the mountain, braced with thick wood beams. Thin railroad tracks ran from the smelter off to the left into the mine. Its small donkey engines were quiet today, the ore cars they pulled sitting idle.

Even the smelter was quiet, with just a small stream of smoke drifting from the stack. Evidently the Stoughtons were keeping the fires going, waiting.

A canvas canopy had been set up in the wide, dirt flat in front of the mine entrance, just past where the railroad tracks curved toward the smelter. Under the canopy was a table. At one side sat Duncan McGregor and Pete Bowers; at the other, George and Alva Stoughton.

Behind the two mine leaders stood nearly every miner that worked the Squaw Gulch mines. Only the Chinese were not there. They had been prevented from coming to work that morning, and so had returned to their homes in a small canyon off the main one.

In back of the Stoughtons, the regulators gathered. There were nineteen of them, McLeary counted. Most looked anxious for action, and McLeary understood the feeling.

Most of the townsfolk had turned out for the event. The people were quite interested, since nearly all of them depended on the operation of the Squaw Gulch mines for their livelihood in one way or another.

They stuck it out, though it was boring standing there in the heat, unable to see much or hear anything. Finally the four men at the table rose and shook hands. George Stoughton looked angry, his brother smug, Bowers glum and McGregor worried.

Alva climbed up onto an open buggy. Standing there, he bellowed, his deep, booming voice carrying well, "Friends, the strike is settled." He waited for the rumble of noise from the crowd to quiet. "The miners will be back at work tomorrow.

For our part, we will have Marshal Russell make a deep inquiry into the cause of last night's unfortunate fires. He will get to the bottom of this," Alva thundered indignantly.

He sat and waited for his brother to get into the carriage with him. They rode off, practically surrounded by regulators. The crowd began to disperse, leaving the miners to argue among themselves. McLeary rode up to McGregor and said, "Seems like a bad deal."

"Not that it's any of our concern, but, yes, I think so, too."

"Why'd you agree to it?"

"I was just tryin' to explain to the men. But they ain't interested in listenin'."

"Tell me."

"Simple. They said, 'Go back to work or we'll unleash the regulators.' I'm not about to risk the men's lives—not after last night—on something foolish. We've waited this long, we can wait a little longer."

McLeary nodded and rode back into town. If it wasn't for Molly, he would ride straight on out, and keep going. But tomorrow would be the day things would be settled. Tomorrow was the day she had promised to end it with her husband.

He stayed extra alert, even while he ate a hasty meal at Lankshire's. By the time he was finished, night had fallen, but the town had not seemed to relax any. Anyone who was on the street scurried from one place to another; most refused to look at the pile of burnt wood and metal, and melted glass that had been the Pick and Shovel.

McLeary strolled over to the Silver Nugget. He walked in boldly and strode to the bar.

"What'll it be, Mister McLeary?" the bartender Marsh asked.

"Beer. Bodie around?"

"Upstairs." He grinned. "But if it's important, I can have him fetched for you."

"How long's he been up there?"

"Ten minutes maybe."

"He'll be down anytime now," McLeary said with a chuckle.

Laughing, Marsh wandered away.

McLeary turned and leaned back against the bar. There were quite a few sets of eyes glittering his way—including those of

Mace Kenney, who rose and ambled toward McLeary. The place quieted some, as most of the customers watched.

"What're you doin' in here, McLeary?" Kenney asked, his damaged face twitching.

"None of your goddamn business."

"It's time to settle it, McLeary." He loosened his pistol. His face was fierce.

"I ain't of a mood, Mace. Maybe later." He grinned, though he felt no real humor.

"Goddammit, McLeary."

"Either shit or get off the pot," Bodie Wheeler growled from behind Mace.

Mace spun as laughter swelled up from the other gunfighters.

"Dammit, Bodie, this ain't your affair."

"You tellin' me to keep my nose out of it?" He had not moved, but his whole body seemed to suddenly emanate menace.

"Well, not exactly, Bodie," Mace muttered. "This is between him and me and—"

"Go sit down, boy, before you make me angry."

Mace skulked away, scarred face burning redly at the laughter that surrounded him. He angrily tossed down a shot.

"Best watch your back," McLeary said with a chuckle as Wheeler moved up to the bar.

"Hell, he don't concern me. Boy's got buffalo shit for brains and the balls of a chicken." He took the beer that Marsh brought him and drank half of it in one swallow.

"Well," Wheeler said, setting the glass down, "what brings you back to the Silver Nugget?" He seemed a little defensive.

"Want to talk to you, Bodie."

Wheeler's eyes widened, and he nodded. "So, come to join us finally, eh? Here's to you." He raised his glass, waiting for the corresponding action by McLeary. It never came.

"Afraid not, Bodie," McLeary said solemnly.

"Then what is it?" Wheeler growled, making a half turn to face McLeary. He leaned his right elbow on the bar.

McLeary mirrored the movement. "It's about the doin's of last night."

"What about 'em," Wheeler snapped, torn between anger, defiance, and a strong liking for the man he faced.

"Was you boys, wasn't it?"

"No."

"Don't hand me a line of shit, Bodie. We've rode together too many times for you to do that."

"So, if you know it was the boys here, why come askin' about it?" Wheeler was tense, frustrated, angry.

"Just makin' sure," he said, then added, "and to see what in hell's come over you of late."

Wheeler shrugged. "It's a job. The boss says burn a couple shacks, I send out some boys to burn a couple shacks. Hell, Charlie, they ain't worth but a few bucks each."

"That ain't the point, Bodie, and you goddamn well know it." He was angry now, furious with his old friend. Wheeler had never done anything like this. That, combined with the strange new feeling—love for Molly—he was experiencing, served to keep him tense.

Wheeler shrugged his great shoulders again, trying to look unconcerned. But he was failing. He was not comfortable with having done it, and now he had to live with that fact. But he did not need to have his friend call him down on it.

"Bodie," McLeary said, a mix of exasperation and fury in his voice, "they were people's homes. Folks lived there, goddammit. For Christ's sake, Bodie, there were women and young 'uns in those places. They could've been killed easy. You turned into a baby killer now?" The more he thought of it, the angrier he got.

"Hell no," Wheeler stormed. He grabbed a fistful of McLeary's shirt and yanked his friend so they were nose to nose. "Don't ever accuse me of somethin' like that, you son of a bitch." His face was red with anger and guilt.

"Take your goddamn hand off me, Bodie," McLeary snapped, almost as angry as Wheeler, but controlling it better.

Wheeler let go of McLeary's shirt and smoothed the garment with exaggerated moves. But his face was hard-set in defiance.

"Bothers you, too, does it?" McLeary asked.

"Goddamn, Charlie, you know me. And you know damn well I don't cotton to such things. Hell, I didn't mind settin' that pig sty of a saloon on fire, but it caught in my craw to have to order the boys to set them houses afire."

"Then why in hell did you do it? Do the Stoughtons have some kind of hold on you?"

Wheeler drained the rest of his beer. He took several minutes to collect himself. When he started talking, he was much calmer, though anger bubbled just below the surface. "I was in a fracas up in Deadwood last year. I'd done a job for some folks up that way, and was just driftin' through Deadwood, waitin' to see what would turn up next. Stopped in a saloon there. Some goddamn idiot started mouthin' off to me, and I coldcocked him."

Wheeler ordered another beer. He waited till it came, and then drank some. "I should've rode out then and there, but I didn't. He came back after a while, totin' a pistol. So I drilled him but good."

"What's the big deal?" McLeary asked, relaxing a little. "Seems pure self-defense."

"So it was, Charlie. But I didn't know when I shot that bastard that his old man was the town marshal. I found out soon enough, though, and hauled ass out of there. I heard later there was a warrant out for my arrest; so I drifted south, figurin' I'd spend some time down to Texas or New Mexico maybe."

"And," McLeary said with a crooked smile, "the Stoughtons learned of it, and when they hired you, they threatened to turn you over to the marshal up in Deadwood if you started kickin' up about anything they asked you to do. Right?"

"You hit that one plumb center, as your old man might've said."

McLeary smiled. "Why not ride out and just keep goin'? Head for Arizona or California. Or anyplace else."

His shoulders lifted in resignation. "That goddamn marshal up there in Deadwood put a price of a thousand dollars on my head. I run out now, the Stoughtons'll probably double that, which," he added with a sigh, "would be more than enough for this bunch of asses here to leave off this mine job temporarily to come a lookin' for me."

"They'd have to get together to catch you."

"That's true. But they'd do it. Besides, Charlie, I got enough goddamn enemies." He grinned his gap-toothed grin. "I don't need a couple dozen hungry gunslingers out after my ass just for a pocketful of cash."

"I reckon not." McLeary felt a little better about it, but not totally.

"If it'll make you feel any better, Charlie, I told the Stoughtons I'd not do no such thing again as burnin' down houses, or places where there might be women and kids. Hell, it don't mean shit to me if a couple miners get fried—or a couple mine owners, either," he added, smiling to take the edge off it. "But I sure as hell ain't no baby killer, and I'll shoot the eyes out of any son of a bitch that says so."

McLeary nodded. He believed his friend; he knew him too well and too long not to. It would, he thought, be interesting to see what would happen if the Stoughtons told him to burn down a few more miners' shacks. Interesting, but certainly not pleasant.

McLeary drained off his beer. "Well, Bodie, I reckon it's time for me to get some shut-eye. All the excitement of last night has me plumb tuckered out."

Chapter 17

Bodie Wheeler was waiting for McLeary in the lobby of Casa de Plata the next morning when McLeary came down. Both looked tired. It had been another rough night, what with alarms clanging three times to rouse the people to fight fires.

"Miners," Wheeler had snapped angrily the second time as McLeary took his place in the bucket line next to the big gunfighter. "It was the goddamn miners."

Unlike the first fire—at the Stoughton-owned Squaw Gulch Hotel—they managed to save Taylor's Mercantile from total destruction, but much of it was ruined, as was much of the merchandise inside.

"How can you be sure?" McLeary asked, feeling stupid as soon as he asked. He felt even more stupid when he saw the glare his friend shot at him.

"Well," McLeary mumbled, passing along a bucket brimming with water, "at least they picked places where no one was gonna get hurt."

"Ah, hell," Wheeler muttered back at him, passing on an empty wood pail. "They're takin' away a man's livelihood." He was tired, and that made him irritable.

McLeary felt the same. "Better than takin' a man's life, though. Or a child's."

Wheeler grunted. "Pass the bucket, boy," he snarled.

McLeary did as he was told.

But an hour later, they were out again. This time the fire was at the Silver Nugget itself, the gleaming gem of the places the Stoughton brothers owned in the town. But, the brothers, wary after the previous day's strike and the first two fires, had several men guarding the saloon. They did not see who had started the fire, nor were they able to prevent it; but they were able to sound the alarm early enough, and with the turnout from town, they saved the place, losing only the use of the four northwest corner rooms upstairs and part of a back storeroom downstairs.

"This is gonna set the cat to squallin'," Wheeler said to McLeary after they got that fire out.

"I reckon. But if there's another fire tonight, you can let the goddamn building burn to the ground without me. I'm plumb bushed."

"Me, too."

Fortunately, the rest of the night was peaceful, and they managed to get in several hours of sleep. McLeary walked downstairs tired, but with a sense of excitement. Today was the day that he and Molly would be able to put things together, to—

He spotted Bodie sitting in the lobby.

"Mornin'," Wheeler said, flashing the gap in his teeth. He seemed to McLeary to be forcing the jolliness.

McLeary only grunted.

"That's no way to greet your old friend," Wheeler said, still straining for humor and zest—and failing again.

"Bullshit. What do you want, Bodie?" He was too tired for any nonsense.

"Need to talk to you, Charlie," Wheeler said seriously.

"Then talk."

"Not here."

"Where?"

"Let's ride on up into the San Juans a ways. We'll get some breakfast, then head out."

"This important?"

Wheeler nodded. He looked a little sick, and McLeary began to worry some. It was not like Wheeler to seem so ill at ease, especially around McLeary.

"All right," McLeary said. "But I got to be back by two this afternoon. Got an appointment." He smiled wanly.

"Yeah," Wheeler grumbled, standing.

"I've got to go get the Henry," McLeary said. He would no sooner ride into the mountains without the rifle than he would without his pants or hat.

"Yeah," Wheeler mumbled again. "Just don't take all goddamn day about it."

On the way to his room, McLeary wondered what was bothering his big friend. But, he supposed, he would find out soon enough. Probably this trouble with the fires and all was sticking in Bodie's craw, and he wanted to jaw it out.

At Lankshire's, they ate eggs, ham, sausages, biscuits covered in thick gravy, and flapjacks lathered in heavy syrup. They polished off two pots of harsh black coffee. Done, McLeary leaned back and lit up a cigar.

"Let's go, Charlie," Wheeler said.

"But—"

"Now."

McLeary was surprised. He shrugged and followed Wheeler out. They walked quickly to the livery, Wheeler exhibiting the need for haste. They saddled up their horses and rode out at a trot, heading southward, more or less following Animas Creek.

Several miles outside of town, Wheeler pulled his horse into a copse of cottonwoods and willows. The river flowed smoothly by a few feet to their right. At this time of year, it was running heavy with water from runoff in the surrounding mountains. In amongst the trees, it was cool and shady, with a small clearing maybe fifty feet around. There was grass in abundance for the horses. The only drawback was the swarming gnats and mosquitoes.

"Light one of them cigars of yours, Charlie, would ya," Wheeler snapped, whacking at the buzzing insects.

"What for?"

"Keep these goddamn skeeters away from us." He was too annoyed to chuckle.

"I'm surprised they're botherin' you, Bodie," McLeary said in an attempt at lightness. "Seein' how you ain't had a bath since '76."

Wheeler only growled.

Both men dismounted and unsaddled their horses before hobbling them. Quickly they gathered up firewood and made a fire. Once it was going, they tossed on some leaves that soon began to smolder, filling the air with smoke.

"That ought to help," McLeary said, sitting.

"Should." Wheeler seemed distracted. He took his time rolling up a cigarette and lighting it. When he was finished with the smoke, he reached inside his shirt and pulled out a small bottle of redeye. He tossed it toward McLeary.

Charlie caught it. He held it, looking askance at Wheeler. "I don't reckon you dragged me all the way out here just for a couple swallows of this," he said very slowly, holding the bottle up. Slanted sunlight filtering through the tall canopy of cottonwood leaves dappled the shining bottle.

Wheeler nodded, but said nothing.

"Goddammit, Bodie!" McLeary exploded. "What in hell's wrong with you. You been actin' *loco* since I first saw you in Silver Canyon."

Wheeler stared at his friend for a moment before saying quietly, "What I got to talk to you about ain't easy for me. You're my friend, Charlie. Have been for a heap of time. Ain't many others'd take in an overgrowed lummox like me. But you and your pa did."

"Bodie, there can't be anything so bad you can say to me that should put you in humors like this. 'Less you brought me out here to tell me you're gonna kill me."

Wheeler snorted. He might be one of the best with a pistol, but he couldn't hold a candle to McLeary. And besides, to think that anything would make him want to kill his best—maybe only—friend was ridiculous.

McLeary pulled the cork from the bottle with his teeth and spit it to the side. He swallowed deeply, eyes watering as the cheap liquor blazed a path down his throat. He handed the bottle over to Wheeler. "Now, tell me, old friend, what you got to tell me."

Wheeler drank deeply, too. It was a few moments before he could speak right. "I hear tell you got yourself a lady friend. A real classy woman."

McLeary tensed. "Supposin' I do?" he questioned tightly. "It wouldn't be no concern of yours."

"Might be," Wheeler mumbled. He paused, then: "You know she's married?"

"Yep." Still tense.

"You know to who?"

"Nope." He was angry, as he was every time he thought of

that lack of knowledge.

Wheeler looked like he had swallowed the whiskey bottle, rather than the whiskey. He could only nod when McLeary questioned, "You know who it is?"

There was silence, except for the steaming of the leaves on the fires, the chirp of the birds, the crunching crop of grass by the horses, and the gurgling of the creek.

"Then tell me, goddammit," McLeary growled, feeling ready to snap from the strain.

Wheeler took a deep breath, then said, very fast, "George Stoughton."

McLeary sat very still, holding his breath without realizing it. Finally he expelled it in one explosive breath, the words coming with it. "You're lyin'."

Wheeler shook his head.

"Yes, you are, dammit." He leaped up and charged straight across the fire, barreling into Wheeler. The big man grunted as he went over backward, whiskey bottle flying out of his hand. But he had enough strength to toss McLeary off to the side.

"Come on, Charlie," Wheeler said as he pulled himself up. "You know I wouldn't come tellin' you stories about this. I—"

He stopped as McLeary plowed into him again. But standing, Wheeler had his balance, and he easily flung McLeary to the side.

"Dammit, Charlie. Listen to me!"

"No!" He charged again, but Wheeler was ready. He was a lot more agile than people usually gave him credit for. McLeary knew that, but was not thinking. Wheeler sidestepped him and shoved on McLeary's back as the smaller gunfighter went by.

McLeary fell face down, skidding in the grass and dirt. "Shit," he mumbled as he pushed himself up. He whirled and tried again.

Wheeler, trying to keep calm and feeling bad for having had to break it to his friend, was beginning to lose his temper. He grunted with surprise and sharp pain as McLeary, instead of trying to bowl the big man over again, stopped short just in front of him and jabbed Wheeler in the snout.

"Don't do that no more, Charlie," Wheeler said, wiping off

the trickle of blood with his hand.

"The hell with you." McLeary was enraged. He swung again, then twice more.

Wheeler ducked all three. "Don't," he warned as McLeary cocked his hand back again. When he knew McLeary was not going to stop, Wheeler hauled off and pounded him once in the jaw.

McLeary went down in a heap. He was aware of Wheeler kneeling over him, saying sadly, "I told ya, Charlie, I told ya."

McLeary was not completely out, but he was close to it. His ears rang, and there were stars and other astral objects swirling about before his eyes. It was so peaceful just to lay here, he thought.

It was some time before he decided to try to venture up. And when he finally did, it was not without a considerable thumping in his head.

"You calmed down now?" Wheeler asked, concerned for his friend.

"I reckon." McLeary stood shakily and then staggered to the creek. He waded in and ducked his head under the water. "Whoooo," he yelled, jerking his head back up. "Damn that's cold." But it helped clear his head some and ease the pounding.

He walked back to their smoky fire and sat. He was silent for a considerable time. He lit a cigar and smoked it down, tossing the butt in the fire. Then he said, "Was I as big a goddamn fool as I think I was?"

"Awful close."

"Goddamn," McLeary muttered. He stood and packed, kicking at pebbles and driftwood. "*Goddamn.* She had me flummoxed. Christ, to think I fell for her, when all she wanted was to . . ."

"Was to what?"

"I was going to say to keep me away from her husband, but that don't seem right. Then I started thinkin' that maybe she was tryin' to talk me into joinin' you and your boys. But she never, ever brought that up."

"You ever think maybe she just plain loves you?" Wheeler said gruffly. "I know that might be hard for other folks to understand, considerin' the look of you and all, but you never can tell just what's goin' on in a woman's mind."

McLeary actually grinned. "I'd like to think that."

"You care for her some, eh?" Wheeler smiled.

"Some ain't the word for it. I don't figure even my old man had a sayin' for this one."

"Hooked whole, are you?"

"Yep. No denyin'."

"Well, she loves you, too."

"The hell you say."

"I know what I'm talkin' about, son."

"How do you know all this?" McLeary asked, suspicions stabbing at his brain.

"Nothin' she's done or said, I can tell you. But I got my sources and my ways." He hesitated, then ventured on, "Now, I don't want you to take this the wrong way, my friend, but was I you, I'd ride back to town, gather up that little filly and ride for someplace else. Now. Today."

"I'll do some thinkin' on it." McLeary rubbed his jaw, which still hurt like blazes. "Damn," he muttered, "I hope you didn't mark me up too much."

"Hell, you get a little color on your jaw; it'll improve your looks a powerful lot, I'd say." Wheeler chuckled.

McLeary grinned wanly. He looked at his watch. Still only ten o'clock. He lay down with his head resting on a small log. "But I reckon I need some sleep first."

Wheeler kicked the bottom of McLeary's boots. "Rise and shine, there, lover," he said with a grin. "It's one o'clock and time you was ridin' off to your fair maiden."

"What in hell have you done, Bodie?" McLeary asked, sitting up and rubbing his eyes. "You go and read a book?"

Wheeler chuckled. "How you feelin'?" he asked as McLeary stood.

"Some better." He was glad to see that Wheeler had the fire out and the horses saddled. He took his canteen and opened it. Taking off his hat with one hand, he doused his head with water from the canteen. The coldness snapped him completely awake. "That's good," he said. "Ready?"

"Yep." Wheeler paused, then asked, "You ain't still mad at me, are you, Charlie?"

"Nope." McLeary smiled crookedly. "I was a fool for gettin' mad at you in the first place."

Wheeler smiled and touched his spurs to the horse. Half an hour later they were on the edge of town, where they heard gunshots, followed by screams and angry yelling. With a quick glance at each other, they kicked their horses into a run.

Chapter 18

As McLeary and Wheeler raced up Silver Street, they could see a seething mass of people, like a giant wave crashing onto the shore and then ebbing again. Several more gunshots shattered the thick, humid afternoon air.

"Damn," McLeary murmured. He yanked out the .44/40 Henry and fired several rounds high; but the heavy thud of the rifle was not heard over the noise of the melee, so no one paid it any heed.

"Damn," McLeary swore again as he jammed the rifle back into the scabbard.

He and Wheeler thundered smack into a swirling cacophony of screams, wailing, angry shouts and gunfire. Fearless, they charged their horses into the midst of the mob, separating the two factions—gun-wielding regulators, snarling and deadly on one side; angry, bellowing miners on the other.

McLeary saw at least two bodies, but he did not have time to look closely.

The gunplay stopped, but both sides still shouted oaths and taunts at each other.

"Shut up!" Wheeler bellowed, his amazingly deep bass cutting through all the noise.

Things began to quiet down, though the two friends knew that anything at all could set the two groups off again. Wheeler faced his horse toward the regulators; McLeary toward the miners. He noticed that there were women, and even some children, in the crowd, and he felt a nervous tightening in his belly.

"I don't know what in hell's goin' on here," Wheeler roared, "but it's goin' to stop. And now!"

"But, Bodie," one of the regulators said angrily, "them goddamn miners started this."

"Like hell," one miner yelled. From around him echoed a chorus of enraged shouts.

"The miners might be a lot of things, Creed," Wheeler snapped, "but they ain't so goddamn stupid as to go against a dozen gunmen when they're unarmed."

"Right!" a bunch of miners yelled.

"Shut up," McLeary snarled.

"Who put you boys up to this?" Wheeler demanded of the regulators. "Or did one of you idiots come up with the idea all to himself?"

"It was Mister Stoughton," Creed said.

"George?"

"Yep. And high goddamn time, too. We been sittin' here on our asses for a goddamn month while these peckerwood miners been doin' what they please. Mister Stoughton finally turned us loose."

"Christ!" Wheeler exploded. He paused, surveying his men. He shook his head in anger. "Go on back to the Silver Nugget," he finally commanded. "Don't stick your noses out the goddamn door till I give the say so."

"But what about Mister Stoughton?" one shouted.

"I'll deal with that pissant bastard soon enough. I've had enough of that little shit goin' behind my back, pullin' goddamn stunts like this. And when I get done with him, goddammit, I'll deal with the rest of you. Now go on! Move!"

"The hell with you, Wheeler," one shouted.

"You challenging me, Reid?" Wheeler asked savagely, his voice sounding something like a landslide.

"Might be. Seems you been gettin' awful high and mighty since we been here, Wheeler. Seems you ain't willin' to do nothin' but set down to the Silver Nugget all the day drinkin' and takin' the girls upstairs."

McLeary spun his horse, trusting to Duncan McGregor to keep his people in line for the time being. He had to, since he wanted to make sure he was in a position to back up his friend's play, should it be necessary.

Wheeler smiled, but there was no friendliness in it. "You got a better way of passin' the days, Reid? You ain't got the balls for sportin' with the women, eh? So you got to use your Colt, 'stead of your other piece?"

There were some chuckles, though it did little to lessen the overall tension.

"You son of a bitch," a red-eyed Reid snarled, hand darting for his Colt.

Wheeler snatched out the converted Walker and fired. Reid's head exploded as the bullet from the massive pistol smashed into his face just above the nose.

Creed made a move for his pistol, but the Smith and Wesson leaped into McLeary's hand and leveled at the offending party. The man pulled his hand away from the pistol butt very carefully and lifted both hands up to shoulder level.

"Anyone else want to test me?" Wheeler growled. When there was no answer, he said harshly, "Then get your asses back to the Silver Nugget. Now!" It sounded like the voice of doom.

The men backed away, shuffling, unwilling to turn their backs to either the two gunfighters or the still-angry miners.

Before they had gone ten feet, McLeary swung his horse back to face the miners. "You folks got nothing more to do here. Go on and leave. Go on back to work, where you belong."

"We're on strike," someone shouted.

"Again?" McLeary asked sharply. "I thought you settled that yesterday."

"Only thing settled was that the Stoughtons thought they had us by the balls," the same man said.

"Then go home," McLeary snapped. "You got no business here no more.

"The hell you say," another yelled. "It's a public street."

"You goddamn fool!" McLeary exclaimed, feeling the anger rise. He swiped a sleeve across his forehead, wiping away the sweat. "There's already two of you layin' here dead—"

"More'n that," someone shouted, and McLeary could feel the heat of anger emanating from the crowd.

A close-standing knot of determined, angry people moved, splitting like water around a rock. Their movement revealed a woman, her hair graying, her threadbare brown dress dirty and covered with blood. She was kneeling, her face a horrifying mask of grief. Tears poured down her cheeks, though she made no sound.

Cradled in her lap was child, a girl no more than six. A sea of blood coated the front of the child's linsey-woolsy dress.

Just beyond the woman, McLeary now saw another body—an old man laying in an odd, half-bent position.

"Jesus goddamn Christ Almighty," McLeary breathed. He holstered the Smith and Wesson and stepped down from the horse. "Goddamn! Bodie, come look."

The big, disheveled gunfighter swung his horse around. Pain crossed his face. "Sweet Lord," he whispered. He shoved the Walker into his holster and slid off the horse.

Both men knelt and looked at the girl's body. McLeary stared at her, rage searing through him. He glanced once at Bodie, whose face was hard with anger. Then McLeary looked at the mother, who had not changed her position.

McLeary surged up, shoving past Wheeler's bulk. "Help this woman!" he roared. "And see to the others. Then go home!"

No one argued this time, not after one look at McLeary's fury-etched face.

McLeary stood, tightly controlling his anger, as one man pulled the girl away from the grief-stricken mother. Several tugged the unyielding woman up and led her away. Still others lifted the old man's body and the bodies of the two slain miners. They straggled away until McLeary and Wheeler were standing alone in the street, with only Reid's corpse to keep them company.

The town was eerily quiet, until Wheeler's deep voice shattered the silence. "What now, Charlie?"

McLeary looked up at him ready with a retort. But it never reached his lips. He was startled to see his big friend—a man he had known as fearless, sometimes heartless, always unyielding—with tears in his eyes.

"I got an appointment to keep," McLeary said sharply, angry. He swung into his saddle and rode slowly toward the house. He had never felt this depth of rage before, and it was disconcerting.

Adding to that feeling was the utter fury he felt with himself for having been so stupid as to have stayed here. There had been no reason for him not to ride out the first day he arrived. He should have just had a beer, ate and left. At most, stayed the night in comfort at the hotel, then left.

But no, he had to tempt his luck. He had to stick around just to show he wouldn't be run off this time. Then, to top that off, he had to go and fall in love—with the wife of George Stoughton no less. Goddamn, he must've done something awful wrong along his life's trail to have brought such things down on his head.

His father's voice popped into his head: "When bad times—or Blackfeet—are nippin' at yer ass, boy, ye ain't got the time to choose yer trail. Jist ride whar yer horse brings ye, boy, and soon enough them Blackfeet—or hard doin's—will git tired of chasin' after ye and let ye be."

He was not cheered by the vision, but at least the frustration with his circumstances eased a bit.

He tied the horse to a hitching ring on a post outside the house. Molly Stoughton waited on the porch, like she had every day. With Henry rifle in hand, and saddlebags over his shoulder, he walked up the steps, heart heavy.

Molly wore a shimmering silk dress, gold-colored, with a trim of forest green and a high-necked white bodice. Her hair was freshly curled and gleamed in the summer sun that slanted in on the porch. A hat—concocted of flowers, lace and God knew what else—was perched at an angle on her head, and she held an open parasol that matched her outfit.

She looked, McLeary thought as he plodded up the steps, like a vision. As he neared her, he saw that she was pale and was gnawing nervously on her lower lip.

Molly kissed him lightly, but he hardly responded. Stepping back, she stared up at him quizzically. "What's wrong?" she asked.

"Nothin'," he mumbled.

"Don't you tell me that, Charlie McLeary. I know you better than that. Something's stuck in your craw, and you need to let it out."

He hesitated, aware of the buzzing insects, the soft sighing of the breeze, the noise of an active town, the sounds of the slowed but still working mine, of Molly's enticing perfume in the air, and of his own breathing.

He sighed. "There was a fracas between the miners and the regulators in town a little while ago. I was up in the hills; when I got back, I run smack into it."

"Are you all right?" she asked, alarmed.

"Yep."

She was relieved. "Anyone hurt?" she asked, almost not caring, as long as he was unscathed.

"A few killed." A vision of the little girl popped into his head, and the anger boiled in his veins.

She didn't know what to say, so she said nothing.

"That where you got this?" she asked, lightly touching his discolored jaw.

"No," he snapped, anger filling him to overflowing again.

Molly looked frightened, but kept mum.

After a long silence, she whispered, "We better go on inside." She still did not want to be seen.

McLeary followed her into the house and up the stairs. All the while, he got more and more confused. She could not be against him, no matter who she was married to, he thought. But surely if she was George Stoughton's wife, she must have some loyalty toward the mine owner.

Then he thought of the bruises he had seen on her body, and decided maybe she didn't have any loyalty. There were no quick answers. He had to go along and see what happened.

Molly was even more nervous than before when she turned to face him. She smiled, but it was an effort, since she was frightened. More frightened than she had ever been.

McLeary set down the rifle and tossed the saddlebags on the floor. He plopped into the chair.

"You sure you're all right?" she asked, her voice catching in her throat. She knew something was wrong, something more than he was saying. And she was deathly afraid that whatever it was would ruin what they had. She had made up her mind, and she prayed now silently and briefly that nothing would spoil things.

"Yep." He grinned, but there was none of the real Charlie McLeary in it, and both knew that.

She tried to force herself to brighten up and was at least

partially successful. She went and sat on his lap, planting small, nibbling kisses all over his face. His man smell and salty taste excited her, and she really began to feel better.

McLeary sat stiff, trying to force himself not to let himself be too affected by this tiny bundle of woman who was unlike any other woman he had ever known. It was difficult, and he slowly warmed, unfreezing his hard frame minutely.

"That's better," Molly whispered into his ear just before nipping the lobe playfully.

McLeary even grinned.

Molly stood and stepped toward the bed. She turned away from him so he would not see her fingers—fumbling in the excitement she felt growing in her—struggle with the buttons on her dress.

"You know," he said, his voice strangled with—and he had to admit it—fear and anxiety, "this ain't necessary no more, Missus Stoughton."

Chapter 19

Molly's face was as white as new snow when she turned to face McLeary. Her fingers were frozen on the buttons of her dress. "You know?" she asked in hushed tones.

"Yep." He spat out the single word.

"How?"

"I got ways."

"But—"

"It's too late, Molly. It's all over." He had a sick feeling in the pit of his stomach, and it was not pleasant. Indeed, it was the hardest thing he had ever done. Facing down a half-dozen angry gunfighters was a Sunday picnic compared with this.

"But . . . why?" Molly's voice trembled, and her hands fell helplessly at her sides.

"I don't like bein' lied to," McLeary said coldly. He felt he had to be harsh. To give her even the slightest warmth would be to melt himself.

"I never lied to you," Molly said seriously, gnawing at her lower lip.

"Well, what in hell do you—" He stopped, thinking. She *had* never lied to him, it was true; she had just never told him the name of her husband. She had not tried to hide the fact that she was married or that her husband was a rich and important man in town.

Molly swallowed her nervousness and approached him. She sat on his lap again, eyes searching his face. "You can't say that I lied," she told him again. "I might be some . . . bad . . . things, but a liar isn't one of them." There were tears in her soft hazel eyes, and she sniffled.

"I reckon not," McLeary said gruffly, trying to figure out why he was so mad at her. It did not matter who she was married to if she loved him now. That was it! he thought. He wondered if she really loved him, or if she was just using him somehow in a scheme to get him to help the Stoughton brothers against the miners.

Molly laid her head on his hard shoulder and wept quietly. McLeary sat in silence, trying to sort it all out. He realized that he was afraid—so afraid that it left an icy, dead feeling in his stomach—that she did not really love him. He had never let himself love—or be loved—until now. It was not a comfortable feeling, but he was willing to give himself up to it freely.

But to think that his love might not be returned after he bared his heart to this woman . . . well, it was too much for him to even contemplate. He'd rather wrestle a grizzly bear than have to deal with such a thing.

"I have to know," he croaked, hating himself for such unmanly behavior, "do you love me, Molly? Or were—are—you just usin' me?"

Molly's head snapped up, and she looked at him through red-speckled eyes. "Do you really think," she asked in a whisper, "that I would do the things we've done if I didn't love you?"

"Well . . ."

"Do you think that little of me?" she demanded, tears beginning again. "Do you think I'm some kind of trollop? Some kind of—"

"No," he said hastily, self-loathing growing. "No, Molly. No. It's just that I' . . . I . . ." He paused, pulling her close to him. She resisted briefly, then let herself be enclosed in his arms. McLeary rested his chin lightly on Molly's head. "I never loved no one before," McLeary said hoarsely. "I don't know. . . ." He growled, ashamed of letting his emotions get the better of him.

"How could you think I didn't love you?" Molly asked, pulling back so she could look at him again. She stroked his cheek with one soft, small hand.

"I don't know," he said with a shrug, thinking himself a fool. "I was afraid that maybe you were usin' me . . . tryin' to—"

"To what?" Molly asked, a touch of anger in her voice.

"To," he went on, knowing full well he was about to say the most stupid thing he had ever—or ever would—said, "get me to help your . . . husband against the miners."

"But how?" she asked. The surprise in her eyes was real.

With a catch in his throat, and a severe case of shamed embarrassment, he explained about Janie May Dillon. *Well,* he thought as he finished telling Molly, *I've killed any chance of regaining her love now.* He was certain of that.

Molly stared at him a few minutes. Then she burst into laughter, shocking them both. She was angry with him for thinking such a thing about her, but at the same time, the idea was so ludicrous that she could not help but laugh.

"You're not mad at me?" he asked, rather incredulously.

"A little," she admitted. "I'm angry that you think I'd let myself be used so badly, that I think so little of myself that I'd let a man get me to do that."

"But . . ."

"But what? I hate that man. Have you forgotten the bruises?"

"No," he snapped. "But why didn't you leave him right off?"

"Because I didn't know if you really loved *me,*" she said in exasperation. "How was I to know? You were—are—a gunfighter. A drifter. How was I to know you weren't just taking your pleasure where you could find it and planned to ride out soon's you got tired of me? I loved you from the very first time we came here, but Lord, how I was scared that I was being used. And degraded, too, maybe. You know, women aren't supposed to act like . . . to do the things we . . ."

"There's nothin' wrong in those things we did," McLeary said softly.

"I know," she muttered. "I think."

"Didn't you know I loved you, too?" he asked, thinking it strange to be saying such a thing. "I ain't usin' you, Molly Stoughton. It ain't easy for me to say such things, and I sure as hell ain't used to doin' so. But it's true, and there's no denyin' it. My old pa had a sayin' about it. He used to say, 'The truth is like findin' yourself surrounded by a heap of Injins. They might be friendly and ye'll have yerself some shinin' doin's; or they might be Blackfoot half-froze to raise hair. But thar ain't no gettin' away from the fact that ye be surrounded.' "

Molly giggled, and McLeary chuckled. Then he sobered and said, "But after you knew I loved you, you kept puttin' me off about leavin' your husband."

"I couldn't," she said, suppressing a shudder. "I might be good in bed"—she flushed with a combination of excitement and guilt and embarrassment—"but I ain't had to do much work bein' married to Geo—him. We've got servants and such to do most things around the house. You learn I maybe can't cook, or somethin', and you might want to get rid of me. Then what would I do?"

He grinned, trying to ease her fears. "We'd make out all right, Molly. You ain't a common woman, that's sure, and I figure you'd be able to overcome nearabout anything."

She beamed in pride, then said sadly, "It was you, too, though. Or, rather, your life. I don't want the life you live of drifting from one place to another. I want a home and"—once again a flush of embarrassment—"children."

"I reckon most women do," he said. "We'll work that out."

She grinned again, feeling better, catching the nuance. "Besides, a woman has got to have a dowry these days, if she expects a man to marry her."

"A dowry?" he asked, surprised.

"You hadn't thought of it?"

"No," he replied.

Molly could tell by the expression on his face that he was telling the truth. "Well," she said, "I have one now. It took a couple days to get my hands on some cash, sell some things I didn't need. George is mighty miserly when it comes to givin' me trinkets and such. But I have some money now. A dowry for you."

"I don't want it," he said seriously.

"Let's just call it a nest egg, then," she said happily.

He smiled and then kissed her hard.

"Everything's going to be all right," Molly whispered breathlessly after the kiss. "It'll work out. I've left him. What things I need are here. I've made arrangement with Alice—that's my friend—to stay here. She's not happy with the arrangement. Actually, she's horrified at my scandalous behavior. I'll get a divorce soon's I can. Then we can get married. I'd like to get out of Silver Canyon as soon as we can."

"I reckon," he muttered, suddenly distracted by the thought that had been growing in his mind for the past hour. "But it might be a spell yet."

She looked up, a worried question in her eyes.

"I'm throwin' in with the miners," he said bluntly.

"What?" she asked, eyes popping wide open.

"It's time."

"Tell me the truth, Charlie," she ordered.

"Remember I told you there was a set-to between the miners and the regulators before?" When she nodded, he said, "Well, I didn't tell you the whole story. It was your husband, George, who ordered the regulators to go out after the miners. They were striking again today because the deal made with the company was against them."

She started to argue, but he stopped her. "I don't agree fully with them, but let me finish. The regulators met the miners out on Silver Street and started shootin'. Maybe they had some provocation; maybe not. It don't matter. When the smoke cleared, two miners were dead, as was an old man"—he bit back the surge of fury—"and a little girl, maybe six years old. I—"

He stopped when he saw Molly crying. McLeary gathered her in his arms, holding her tight. "I can't bring that little girl back," he said quietly, fighting to keep the anger from overflowing into his voice, "but I can damn well try to make sure it don't ever happen again."

Chapter 20

Molly was frightened when she saw McLeary out the door the next morning. Since there was no longer any need for secrecy, there was no longer any need for them to leave in the afternoon.

They had talked and made love for much of the afternoon before moving off to another room on the top floor—one that the day before had been a storeroom.

"This is my room now," Molly said, somewhat proudly, somewhat guiltily.

"What's your friend think of all this?"

"Alice thinks I'm quite the shameless thing," Molly said, with a half-giggle, half-sigh. "She does not, I can assure you, approve of my activities of late."

"What does her husband think?"

"She's a widow. Three years ago."

"Can't she find another? She old or ugly or something?"

Molly laughed. "Good Lord, no," she said. "She's only a year older than I, and much more attractive. She just don't know what I know now." She winked with friendly lust. "If only she did." She got serious for a moment. "But then, there's few men take the time and effort like you do, Charlie."

Later that afternoon they had heard Alice return. An hour after that, Alice called in a stiff, serious voice for them to have their supper. When McLeary walked down the stairs with Molly, he saw that his woman was right—Alice was attractive. She was more full-busted than Molly, and several inches taller. But she had a pinched-face look that was not appealing to McLeary.

"She needs a man—a good man," McLeary said later, when he and Molly were back up in her room.

She squinted up at him. "You ain't volunteering, are you?"

"No, ma'am," he said, meaning it.

"Good thing," she whispered before falling asleep with her head on his broad, muscular chest.

Now she stood in the doorway, the sun shining brightly onto the porch, watching as he shoved the Henry rifle into the scabbard. He left the saddlebags in Molly's room, not figuring he would need them for a while.

Molly gasped when she saw the large, disheveled man heading toward McLeary. "Charlie!" she yelled.

He spun, right hand snaking toward the Smith and Wesson American. Then he straightened, relaxing, when he saw Bodie Wheeler standing there, McLeary's gunny sack in his hand.

"Thought you might be needin' this," Wheeler said, holding out the bag that contained McLeary's extra shirt and few other clothes and belongings.

"What gave you that idea, Bodie?" McLeary asked, taking the bag. He turned and walked toward steps leading up to the house, Wheeler at his side.

"Seems like you been asked to leave the Casa de Plata," Wheeler said with a gap-toothed grin.

"By who?"

"The management." His grin widened. "Seems like the feller who owns that fancy-assed hotel somehow all to a sudden took a serious dislikin' to a certain skinny feller that carries a Smith and Wesson American and a Henry rifle."

"I don't know nobody like that." McLeary chuckled.

They were at the door now, and McLeary introduced his woman to his friend. Molly was wary, tense, knowing that this tall, powerful-looking misfit was the leader of the regulators. It made her uneasy that he was here, and even more so knowing that he was McLeary's friend.

"Take this up with you, please, Molly," McLeary said, holding out the bag.

Her eyes widened, and he said, "I need a place to stay. Bodie here tells me your husband don't want me in his fancy hotel no more. While I'm out, I'll look for another place, but I don't feel like haulin' that bag all over with me."

"You can stay here," she whispered, embarrassed and defiant in saying it in front of Wheeler.

Bodie just grinned and looked up at the porch ceiling innocently.

McLeary was rather stunned, but he recovered quickly. "Well, I'll have to think about that, Molly," he said disarmingly. "I ain't sure, you know. People will talk about me and . . ."

Wheeler sputtered with barely suppressed laughter, and McLeary could contain himself no longer. He burst into laughter and swept Molly up off her feet and swung her around. "Sure I'll stay here, Molly darlin'."

"Put me down, you big oaf," she shrieked, but she was laughing all the while.

He set her down. "Well," he said, growing serious, "I got to go take care of some business."

She nodded, instantly unhappy. While she agreed with what he was going to do, she was frightened beyond belief for his safety.

"Well," Wheeler said gruffly, "I'll let you two young folks say your good-byes in peace." He turned and thumped his way heavily down the steps.

"You be careful, boy, you hear me," Molly said sharply to McLeary. "I just found you. I sure as all get out don't want to lose you already."

"I'll be all right," he said confidently.

"Don't be smug with me, Charlie McLeary," she snapped. "You were to go and get yourself killed, I'd be in a powerful poor spot."

He had not thought of that. He had only thought of himself, and what he had to do, and what it meant to him. But not once had he thought of what his going off like this would do to her. "I'm sorry," he said quietly. "I'll watch out for myself."

"All right." She nodded. Then she kissed him.

He turned then and walked down the steps toward his cinnamon horse. He did not see the fear that kept Molly's face pale as death. He was only one man. A very good man, she knew, but still, he would be alone against all—

She slammed the door shut and leaned back against it, fighting to keep her tears contained.

McLeary settled his hat more firmly on his head before pulling himself up onto the horse. He was not afraid, that he knew, but he felt a nagging sense of discomfort. It was quite a new feeling for him, and he knew for sure that he did not care for it. Well, he sighed as he clucked the horse into moving, he probably would have to get used to it.

There was a knock on the door, and Molly hurried to answer it, figuring McLeary would not want to just enter. She swung the door open, and an icy chill stabbed her belly. "What do you want?" she asked.

"I forgot to give this to Charlie," Bodie Wheeler said, stepping inside and holding out a small book.

"Thank you," Molly said, frightened beyond all belief. What would this hulking giant of a man do to her now that he had wormed his way in here?

"You're welcome," he said, and pleasantly enough, she thought.

Maybe he was not so bad as she had imagined, then again . . .

"Why'd you come back, really?" she demanded, anger dulling the edge of the fear some.

"To see you."

"Oh, Lord," she muttered, an even deeper fright spreading up from her stomach into her chest. Molly found it hard to breathe. "What do you want?" she asked, fear making her voice come out in a tremulous squeak.

"To talk to you."

Molly thought she might pass out. She felt her knees buckle. She was dimly aware of Wheeler moving, faster than she would have expected. Then she knew that he had caught her. She struggled against him, her senses returning.

"You all right now, ma'am?" he asked softly, trying his best not to frighten her any more. But he knew that with his deep, reverberating voice and wild looks, it was hopeless.

"Yes." It was in a tiny voice, one that sounded like it was coming from very far away.

As Wheeler set Molly down, she made up her mind to not be

so weak again. She stood firmly. "Well, go on," she said, chin raised in defiance.

"Go on what?" he asked. He appeared to Molly to be truly befuddled.

"You mean you ain't going to . . . you don't want to . . . you . . ."

Wheeler burst into laughter, the sounds booming loudly off the walls. "I'd purely *like* to. . . ." He winked at her, but not in a lecherous way. "And if you wasn't my friend's woman, I just might try. But not with force."

"But you said . . ."

"I said I wanted to see you. So I could talk to you."

"You never said you wanted to talk."

"Yes I did, but you wasn't payin' no attention."

"Oh." She felt mightily relieved. "Well," she said with a sigh, "what did you want to say?"

He took his hat off and twirled it in his hands, all of a sudden uneasy. "Well, ma'am, it's like this. I ain't quite sure what you think about Charlie. But I know he likes you a powerful lot. A *powerful* lot. And since he's the best friend this old hoss ever had, I'd sure hate to see him bein' hurt."

Anger flashed in Molly's hazel eyes. She gazed up at his six-foot-four frame towering above her. "And what gives you to think I'd do anything to hurt Charlie?" she demanded.

"I didn't say I thought you would, Miz Stoughton. Just tellin' you I'd hate to see such a thing happen."

"Well it won't, Mister Wheeler," she said in frigid tones. "Now, if you would please leave." She tried to step around him to get to the door handle, but he was a formidably sized object to get around. She failed and stared up at him, enraged.

"I'll be leavin' soon's I had my full say, Miz Stoughton."

"Don't call me that," she demanded with an angry shake of her head.

"It's who you are."

"Not much longer."

"All right Miz . . . Molly. I know who your husband is, and it occurred to me that you might try to take advantage of Charlie to help him for some kind of purpose."

"You're not much given to thinking, are you, Mister

Wheeler?" she asked sharply.

"No, ma'am. I—"

"Then you should not do it at all, if you are going to abuse it in such a way. I will tell you this only one time, so clean out your ears so you might listen properly. I love Charlie McLeary more than anything in this world. Perhaps you don't understand that, Mister Wheeler, but it is true.

"I have left my husband for this man, risking scandal and ridicule. I have left a fine mansion with servants and a full social life. And I did so because I love Charlie McLeary. I am willing to give up the mansion and live on the back of a horse, if that's what my man wants. I am willing to do without servants, to cook for my man—and do it over an open fire if that's what is necessary.

"I will sit here with my heart beating in my throat from fear because he is going to join the miners against a horde of men my husband hired to kill the miners. I might be dying of fright, but he is my man, and this is something he has to do; therefore, I will abide it as best I can. I . . ."

Wheeler stood there looking abashed, head down. "All right, ma'am," he finally managed to edge into her torrent of words. It took a few more sentences; but she finally realized what he had said, and she screeched to a halt.

"Well . . ." she said.

"I just wanted to make sure your feelin's were true for him is all, ma'am."

"And if they hadn't been?"

Wheeler's great, shaggy head came up. "You would've had to answer to me, Miz Molly," he said firmly.

"You really like him, don't you?" she asked, surprised. Then she was ashamed of herself for being surprised. Why would he not have a friend, just because of his looks and his profession?

"Yes, ma'am." He twirled the hat a few more times, trying to come up with the words. "It ain't often a man of my sort can find a friend—or a woman." He smiled ruefully. "I'm a gunfighter, and make no excuses about it. Turns most people away from me. But more than that, ma'am, take a look at me—my great, mashed-flat nose, a couple teeth missin'. I'm too big and messy. Nothin' but a big, dumb, shufflin' bear of a feller."

He shrugged. "Well, anyway, ma'am, when someone takes to bein' friendly with me, I either do the same back—or I get mighty suspicious. And once I'm a friend, I'm a damn good one. Oops, excuse my language, ma'am."

"It's all right." She reached up a tiny hand and touched his cheek. It was quite a stretch. "Well, I like you just fine, Mister Wheeler. And I give you my promise I'll not ever do anything to hurt Charlie."

Wheeler was grinning when the door hit him in the back. He slouched out of the way as a woman stepped in. "Alice," Molly said, "this is Mister Wheeler. Bodie, Alice Van Leuewen."

"Pleased to meet you, ma'am," Wheeler said, bobbing his large, thatch-covered head.

Van Leuewen looked at him with disdain, or so he thought of her glance. She sort of sniffed and walked away.

It was some moments before Wheeler was able to speak. He had never met quite such a woman as this. He scratched his head. "See what I mean," he said, half-sadly, half-angrily. He paused and shrugged. Then, clapping his rattlesnake-skin-adorned Boss Stetson, he said, "Well, I reckon I'd best be goin', ma'am."

"Mister Wheeler," Molly called. When he turned away from the door to face her, she said, a soft, pleading tone in her voice, "Please help him, if you can."

"I aim to, ma'am." Then he was gone, clumping down the stairs.

Chapter 21

McLeary could hear the services long before he actually reached the church set between the mine and the town. It was a typical church—small, made of plank wood, whitewashed, with a tall spire that listed to the east a few feet. Inside the spire hung a bell which announced the births and deaths and the ever increasing emergencies the miners and their families faced.

McLeary entered the open door and leaned against a back wall of the church, in the shadows. He knew he had been seen entering, but still he wanted to keep as much out of the crowd's eyes as he could. It was stifling hot inside the church.

The church was filled with hard-eyed, dirty miners, and worn, crying women. The preacher stood at the front, facing the congregation, eulogizing the poor girl who had died, and railing against big corporations that stepped on the rights and the lives of the little men and women of the world, those by whose sweat and labor the mine owners could make their millions and live in the mansions and . . .

McLeary shut him out after a while. It was a sin, he thought, that a man of the cloth should use such an unfortunate situation as the girl's funeral to breath his fire and brimstone against big business. It was, McLeary thought, neither the time nor the place for such goings on.

The preacher ranted on, but even the girl's parents were beginning to look bored and a little annoyed that they should be subjected to such long-winded nonsense at their daughter's funeral. Either the preacher realized it, or someone whispered to him from the front row, because he finally began winding down.

At last the reviling ended, and a final prayer closed the services. McLeary turned and slipped out the door. Standing to the side, he waited. A few moments later, people began filing mostly silently out of the church. Duncan McGregor and several other men stopped near McLeary and waited as the others left, ending with the pallbearers carrying the small, simple pine casket. They curled around the building toward the small cemetery alongside the church.

When they had done so, McGregor turned to McLeary. "What are you doing here, Mister McLeary?" he demanded, his tone unfriendly.

"Come to talk," McLeary said, unconcerned by the three men bunched up behind him. His right thumb was hooked into his gunbelt, not far from the butt of the Smith and Wesson, which was not secured in the holster. His other hand stroked the luxuriant mustache.

"It's too goddamn late for talkin'," McGregor snarled, anger stamped on his face.

"It's never too late for talkin'." Before McGregor could say anything, McLeary snapped, "And you better tell this idiot creepin' up on me that if he touches me I'll break his arm."

McGregor waved a hand, and out of the corner of his eye, McLeary could see the miner back off a few steps. "Suppose it ain't too late for talkin'. What do you suggest?"

"This ain't the place for such talk, eh? Let's you and me—alone—go down to Lem's place and talk a spell."

McGregor thought for a minute, his face reflecting both the rage and the uncertainty he felt. Then he nodded once, curtly. "All right. But I have to see little Martha off to her last rest." His lower lip quivered.

"I understand. I'll wait for you there."

"Shouldn't be more than thirty minutes. Probably less."

McLeary rode to Lem Wilson's new "saloon." It was a huge canvas tent set up in the empty lot next to where the Pick and Shovel had stood. Some of the rubble from the original saloon had been removed, but not all of it, and smoke still spiraled up in thin streams from what was left.

McLeary entered the tent. A bar, much like the last one—several planks on some old casks—was set up to his left. There were a half-dozen hastily built tables, and that was it.

"I'll have a beer, Lem," McLeary said, leaning on the make-shift bar.

"Got none," Wilson said. "All I got's redeye. Take it or leave it."

"I'll take it. Where'd you get the supplies?"

"None of your business." He grinned a little to take the edge off. "Trade secret. But I got enough to last, if I'm careful, till the next full shipment arrives."

"Plannin' on stayin' around, then eh?" McLeary asked.

"Yes, sir. I ain't lettin' no goddamn bunch of gunslingin' punks—" He looked at McLeary oddly. "Sorry," he mumbled.

"Quite all right."

"Anyway, I ain't lettin' them regulators, or whatever the hell you want to call 'em, run me out."

"That's the spirit," McLeary said, not knowing what else to say.

"Yeah." Wilson did not seem happy.

It was not long before McGregor arrived. He still looked confused, worried and filled with rage. When Lem saw the miner, he brought over a glass and poured him a drink from the bottle in front of McLeary.

"Want to take a seat?" McLeary asked after McGregor had swallowed the shot in one quick gulp.

"This'll do." He poured another drink.

Over McGregor's shoulder, McLeary saw three regulators enter the tent and start heading his way. McGregor noticed McLeary's eyes and hardened jaw, and he spun.

He whirled back. "You goddamn son of a bitch," he snarled, raising a fist.

"Just calm down," McLeary said harshly.

"You told me to come over here alone, just so you could have these bastards help you rough me up, goddamn it." He was purple with fury.

"Bullshit." Then he shut up as the three gunmen arrived.

"Well, well, well," Mace Kenney said with a smirk on his ravaged face. "What've we got here? The big, bad gunfighter gettin' all chummy with the stinkin' union man. Must be concoctin' a plot against the Consolidated Silver and Mining

Company. What do you boys think?"

Alf Bader and his brother Arnie agreed.

"I didn't think you knew that many words, Mace," McLeary said nastily.

Kenney stood sputtering for a few moments, then said, "I ain't here to talk to you anyway, McLeary. I come to talk with this runty little union bastard."

"You have nothing to say here, Mace, except maybe *adios,*" McLeary said. "Now get, before I get all fired up."

"If he's got something to say to me," McGregor said softly, "then I want to hear it."

"You do, eh?" McLeary said. "I'll tell you what he's going to say. He's going to tell you, Mister McGregor, to get your miners back to work before he turns the regulators loose on you."

"They've tried that—"

"They ain't tried nothin' yet," McLeary snapped. "Two miners killed is all. And a girl and an old man done in by stray bullets. A few places been burned down. George Stoughton lets animals like the Baders and this sputtering idiot here loose, and there's going to be dead bodies all over this damn town. I get that about right, Mace?"

"Yeah. I'm supposed to make sure . . . union man here got the message." He reached for his pistol.

As the weapon cleared leather, McLeary moved. With a wary eye on the Baders, McLeary's hand darted forward, catching Kenney's gun hand. Then he yanked forward and spun. Kenney stumbled and fell, his pistol landing a few feet away.

Before Kenney hit the ground, McLeary had his Smith and Wesson out and leveled at the Baders. Neither of the German brothers was as stupid as Kenney, and so both stood stoically.

In the corner of his eye, McLeary could see Kenney sliding along the ground toward his Colt. McLeary smiled savagely, spun, took two steps, and then stomped down as hard as he could with a boot heel on Kenney's gunhand.

The regulator screamed as bones snapped.

McLeary whirled and crouched, facing the Baders. Both the

Germans stood, hands at their sides. Standing between them, with an arm around each of their necks, was Bodie Wheeler. He was grinning, and in his right hand was his old Walker pistol. The Baders looked angry, and even a little fearful.

"Thought you might need a hand," Wheeler said with a smile.

"Oh, you did, did you?" McLeary straightened, grinning.

"Yep." He stepped back a little. "Now suppose you Bader boys pick up your playmate over yonder and get the hell out of here. Might be a good idea if you was to get out of town, too. You tell McGregor yet, Charlie?"

"Tell him what?"

"Yes, tell me what?" McGregor demanded, confused by the whirl of events in the past few minutes.

"No, I haven't, Bodie," McLeary said carefully, playing along until he could figure out what Bodie meant.

"You gonna do so?"

"I was plannin' to before these three broke up the party."

"All right," Wheeler said sharply. "You three have had your fun. Now get out. And you can tell George Stoughton that the days of the regulators are over. Right, Charlie?"

"I reckon," McLeary said slowly, unsure of what exactly was happening.

"I reckon your old man would've said somethin' like, 'When starvin' times are settin' heavy on ye, boy, don't go overlookin' a buffler even if'n he is a poor ole bull.' " He grinned as wide as he ever had.

A smile crawled slowly across McLeary's face.

The Baders helped a cursing Mace Kenney up and boosted him along as they headed out of the saloon.

McGregor spun and gulped down a shot. He turned back and said, "What in hell's going on here?"

"You wanted a hired gun to help you, Mister McGregor? Now you have two of the best."

"We . . . I . . ." He circled around, facing the bar, taking a shot and then facing the two gunmen again. "But he's the leader of the regulators," McGregor said, pointing to Wheeler.

"No more," Wheeler growled.

"But why?"

"I might be slow to learn, Mister McGregor," Wheeler said fervently, "but once I catch on to somethin', I've got it good. I just couldn't see what side to be on for a while. Now I know."

"You trust this man, Mister McLeary?" McGregor asked.

"With my life."

"But can I trust you, Mister McLeary?"

"With your life."

Chapter 22

Pete Bowers stormed into the tent saloon, his eyes blazing hotly. Stalking directly up to McLeary, Wheeler and McGregor, he demanded, without preliminary, "What in hell are you doin' talkin' to these two, Duncan?"

McGregor looked at the skinny miner with surprise. "The men wanted us to hire—"

"Not these two." Bowers was livid.

"Why?" McGregor asked confused. "We had talked about it. A few days ago—"

"A few days ago, I didn't know these two were friends. Unless you forget," he added with pointed sarcasm, "this big clod"—he pointed to Wheeler—"leads the regulators."

"But he—"

"And the other one," Bowers plunged on, heedless of McGregor's protestations, "has turned us down several times, beat hell out of me one time—while you were watchin'—and didn't do nothin' to stop the regulators from burnin' down our houses."

"I've listened to your gibberish long enough," McGregor snapped, visibly annoyed. "I don't even know what you're saying any more. I don't think even you know what you're saying. These men have come over to our way of thinkin'. They have said so, and goddammit, I believe 'em. I ain't sure exactly why I believe 'em; I just do. Now, if you'd like to argue with that, I'm ready." McGregor hitched up his pants, waiting.

When Bowers stood, tightly controlling his anger, McGregor said, "Or if you'd rather, you can go to the union council—or straight to the men for all I goddamn care—and discuss it. They want to override my decision, I'll abide by that. But I'll also leave the workingmen's collective if that happens. If the men don't trust my judgment any more, I don't want nothin' to do with 'em."

Then the small miner turned back to the bar and, with an air of unconcern, poured himself a shot of whiskey and drank it in two short gulps.

Bowers stood for a few moments, face blotchy with anger, before spinning on the worn heels of his work boots to stalk out of the canvas saloon.

McGregor turned back to face his two hired guns. "Damn, that man is exasperating," he said with feeling. "I don't know what's come over him lately. He used to be like the rest of us. We might not've agreed all the time, but when things got bad, we always stood together. Very puzzling."

"Naw it ain't," Wheeler growled.

Both McLeary and McGregor snapped their heads around to stare at him. The big man grinned, then said, "He's double crossin' you, and all the others."

"What?" McGregor exploded.

"He's took to sidin' with the Consolidated Silver and Mining Company."

"But that can't be," McGregor said, stunned and trying to recover from the shock of the news. "He's always been one of us. I don't understand. How? When?"

"Just after they burned his house down. That was about all he could take. He was afraid for himself—and his family."

"But—"

"Look, Bowers was scared half to death. The company knew you'd be a hard man to break but Bowers was easy. He was always scared of the regulators. Then they burned his house down, letting him know they could kill him—or anyone in his family—any time they chose. That broke him."

Wheeler took a moment to pour a shot and pour it slowly down his throat, savoring it. "Right after the fire, he went to George Stoughton and asked if there was anything he could do to set things straight."

"But what can he do for Stoughton?" McLeary asked.

"Give him information, mostly. One of the first things he went and told Stoughton was that you was foolin' around with his wife—Molly."

"How in hell did he know that?" McLeary asked, anger rebuilding.

Wheeler shrugged. "Hell if I know. It didn't make Stoughton none too happy, of course, but once he knew it, he was grateful for Bowers tellin' him."

"Even still . . ."

"Even still what, Mister McGregor? You think that wasn't so bad?"

"Well." He shrugged.

"He went on to tell Stoughton just after that, that you miners were not plannin' on goin' back to work the next day like you'd agreed to. He even told the boss man that you miners were gonna march through town. That's why the regulators were there to greet you. You didn't think that was an accident, did you?"

"Actually, I had." McGregor looked disgruntled, and ill at ease.

"Well, it wasn't true. The regulators was ready and waitin' for you. And where was Bowers that day, eh? He was nowhere to be found, was he?"

"No," McGregor said sourly.

"Couldn't you have stopped them?" McLeary asked, uneasy for some reason, but not sure why.

Wheeler growled. "It's another reason I'm throwin' in with the miners now. Right after Bowers told Stoughton about the march, Stoughton sent me off to check on some things. I found out after that ruckus in the street—when I was talkin' to some of the regulators—that Stoughton didn't trust me any more. Because of us bein' friends and all, Charlie. So he got Mace Kenney to bring the regulators out into the street to meet the miners. Behind my back." Wheeler was enraged, thinking on it.

"Well, I'll be damned and cast into the pit," McGregor said, his voice a mix of amazement, anger and shame at having been duped.

"Most likely," Wheeler said tightly. "But you ain't gonna be lonesome."

There was silence for a while, as each man wrestled with his own thoughts.

Finally McGregor sighed, and said, "Well, are you two men still willing to join our cause?"

Wheeler nodded. McLeary said, "Yep. I heard you say you boys had raised up three hundred dollars for such aid as can be rendered?"

"Yes," McGregor gulped. "But that's all we have. We can't afford three hundred dollars each. We have families, we need to buy food and . . ." He trailed off.

"What do you say, Bodie?" McLeary asked with a wink. "Think we can take care of an insect problem for a hundred and fifty each?"

"Sounds fair. Aftr all, shouldn't take a hell of a lot of effort."

"Well, Mister McGregor," McLeary said, holding out his hand, "looks like you've hired your own regulators. And at a damn good discount, too, I might add."

McGregor beamed. He was happy, though he knew that the situation was far from being resolved and despite knowing that bloodshed was almost sure to follow. But at least now he and his miners could fight back. He grasped McLeary's hand and shook it vigorously, then did the same with Wheeler's. He started to leave, but McLeary stopped him.

When he turned back, McLeary said, "There's still a few things to settle."

"Like what, Mister McLeary?"

"Like your men."

"What about the men?" McGregor questioned.

"Me and Bodie are gonna be a mite busy the next few days. We don't need your men makin' matters worse."

"What do you want us to do?"

"Nothin' but work."

"But we're on strike," McGregor said adamantly.

"Not no more you ain't."

"Yes, we are. Especially after what was done to Mackey's little girl yesterday. Hell, she ain't even cold in the ground yet."

"I know that. But I want you boys back to work in the mines tomorrow."

"No. Why the hell should we—with the sweat of our brows—supply the Stoughtons with the money to buy regulators to shoot our children down and Chinese to take our jobs?"

"Because this situation ain't gonna be resolved overnight. It's gonna take a little time for Bodie and me to do what needs to be done. In the meantime, you miners have got to eat; you've got to clothe yourselves and your families. You ain't gonna have any money comin' in if you ain't workin'. And it'll keep you out of trouble. That'll do two things: It'll let me and Bodie do our jobs, and it'll keep the regulators off guard. That'll be to our advantage."

McGregor thought for some minutes, before saying slowly, "I think that can be arranged."

"What about Pete Bowers?"

"What about him?"

"Won't he go runnin' off to your council, or whatever, and talk down about you to 'em? He does that, they might not listen to you."

"I'll see to that son of a bitch, don't you fret."

McLeary nodded, then said, "One more thing."

"Yes."

"No more fires. No more marches. No more nothin' but workin'."

"We'll do our part, Mister McLeary. You two had better do yours, though." He turned and walked out of the saloon.

"Tough little bastard, ain't he?" Wheeler said with a grin and reached for the whiskey bottle.

Chapter 23

"Oh, shit," McLeary snapped suddenly, an icicle of fear slicing into his innards.

Wheeler froze, bottle in hand wavering in the air. "What?" he asked, startled.

"Damn, I never thought."

"What, goddammit?"

"Bowers was some steamed when he roared out of here."

"Yep. So?"

"He's the one told George Stoughton about me and Molly."

"So what?"

"So, if he was that angry, he'd head straight off to tell Stoughton that I—and you—joined up with the miners. Stoughton ain't got the guts to come against me head on, even with all his damn regulators. But he sure as hell could make a play against Molly, if he has any notion where she is. . . ."

"Jesus Christ!" Wheeler dropped the bottle. He and McLeary ran.

Outside, they jumped into their saddles and slapped the reins on the horses' necks. They thundered down Silver Street to Sixth, swinging right so hard that both horses almost fell. The same happened when they spun south onto Routt Street.

As they neared Alice Van Leuewen's house, Wheeler yelled, "Slow down, Charlie!"

McLeary yanked hard on the cinnamon's reins and slowed the horse, finally stopping, both man and beast breathing hard. "What?" he asked as Wheeler stopped beside him.

The big gunfighter patted the side of his horse's neck. "I ain't so involved in all this as you are, so maybe I can think a little clearer about it. But if Stoughton has made a play against Molly, it would be plumb goddamn foolish for us to go chargin' straight up to the house like this, out in the open.

Don't you think?"

"Yep." He nodded, but he was angry with himself. So intent was he on getting back here that he almost rode into a trap—if there was anyone waiting. A stupid, foolish, and usually fatal mistake, he told himself.

McLeary pointed to an alley on the west side of the street. "That alley leads around to another one down to Sixth Street, doesn't it?" he asked.

"Yep. Across Seventh, it goes on a bit farther. We can come in from the back of Miz Van Leuewen's house."

McLeary nodded again and turned his horse's head in that direction. They rode up the foul, garbage-strewn alley, to the one that cut off at right angles north. Across Eighth Street, just past where the house would be a little to the east, they tied their horses and walked up a narrow, barely shoulder-width path between two houses.

At the end of those two houses was a yard. Abutting it was the back yard of Alice Van Leuewen's house. Four horses were tied to the massive oak tree in the woman's yard near the house.

McLeary and Wheeler stopped behind a large chokecherry bush across the yard from the house.

"Them horses belong to four mean *hombres* who do most of their ridin' in the Injun Territories north of Texas. Von Neery is more or less their leader. The others are Carlos O' Keefe, Dave Claymore, and the worst of the lot, a full-breed Choctaw who tried to live white most of his life. Real friendly cuss named Red Moccasin, though he often goes by the name Billy Jefferson," Wheeler whispered.

McLeary looked at Wheeler a little oddly, but said nothing. McLeary scanned the area around the house, fixing it in his mind.

"I reckon it's best," he said after a few minutes, "if we go down the south side there, keepin' behind those cottonwoods. We'll be hidden mostly, and it'll get us up close to the house. We can climb up on the porch and get to the front door."

"Let's go," Wheeler said. His eyes were bright with eager anticipation.

Carefully, but quickly, the two men made their way under the shadowy canopy of tall cottonwoods. In a spot that would be blind to anyone inside, they dashed across the ten feet of open ground and flattened themselves back against the wall of the house.

Sliding along, they reached the porch. McLeary took a quick look around the corner, and saw no one. He reached up and grasped the rough wood that braced the railing. He hauled himself up. As Wheeler followed him, McLeary glanced toward the large window in the front of the house. He nodded and then whispered, "Curtains are closed."

They were heavy brocaded drapes, so it would be impossible for anyone inside to see out through them. McLeary knelt and undid his spurs, laying them quietly aside. He looked back and saw that Wheeler had done the same. Then McLeary undid several shirt buttons, so he could reach the small Colt Lightning, if need be.

McLeary and Wheeler moved silently toward the door, guns drawn but not cocked. Sweating from heat and tension, McLeary tried the door knob. It turned easily and without a sound. He cracked it open and peered inside.

He saw no one, so he shoved the door fully open and leaped inside, off to his left. Wheeler was right on his heels, jumping to the right. There was no one in the room.

McLeary brushed his left sleeve across his forehead to mop off the sweat. Sounds came from the kitchen at the back of the house.

The parlor was spread out before him, the wall on his left only wide enough to accommodate the window. The room was wide to his right. There was a rug spread in the middle of the floor, and a fireplace in the far wall on his right. Almost directly across from him was the short hallway leading to the pantry and kitchen. Next to the hallway on the left was the staircase, and on the right was a short wall forming part of the hallway. A few feet to the right of that was a wood-frame sofa with plush, brocade back and seat. Two matching chairs were against the wall directly behind Wheeler, a hassock in front of one chair, and a small table next to each.

There was a movement through the hallway. With deceptive speed, Wheeler was up and moving. He flattened back against the short wall of the hallway, hidden from the hallway. McLeary backed outside, holding the door open just a crack so that he could see.

A sallow, skinny, consumptive-looking man walked out of the hallway, shoving Alice Van Leuewen before him. The woman looked pale, frightened half to death, and almost numb from shock.

As the man entered the parlor, McLeary shoved the door open and stepped inside. The man was fast; McLeary had to give him credit for that. Before McLeary could get off a clear shot—since Alice was in the way—the man had his pistol out and cocked, pressed up against Alice's temple. His left arm had snaked up at the same time and grabbed Van Leuewen. He pulled her against him, his hand on her satin-covered, corseted breast.

"You must be McLeary," the man said, his voice like an ungreased axle squealing.

"And you?"

"Dave Claymore."

"Can't say as I'm pleased to meet you. Now what say you let the lady go."

"You make one more move, you stupid son of a bitch, and the woman's gonna have her brains splattered all over the wall."

Van Leuewen whimpered. She almost fell, but Claymore was a lot stronger than he looked, and held her up.

McLeary thumbed back the hammer of the Smith and Wesson American and took aim. "You kill her, you dumb bastard, and you're gonna be standin' there just ripe for the pluckin'."

"We got company, boys!" Claymore roared in his high, tinny voice. "It's four to one, punk. You might get me if you get real lucky, but the others'll—"

He never finished. Wheeler moved like lightning, stepping out from his hiding spot. In one step he was directly behind Claymore, his Walker Colt back in the holster. He reached around and jammed the length of his right thumb into the space between the cocked hammer and the chamber of Claymore's pistol. The rest of his beefy hand wrapped around the cylinder.

Claymore did not hesitate, firing instantly. The Remington's hammer slammed down on Wheeler's flesh, and McLeary winced at seeing it. It must have hurt like hell, he thought, but Wheeler never even flinched.

Wheeler snapped his left hand up and grasped Claymore under the chin. He yanked the man's head to the side.

Claymore fell, releasing Van Leuewen, but leaving his pistol locked onto Wheeler's hand. Van Leuewen screamed and fell sideways. But she managed to twist her body a little so she did not fall atop Claymore.

Three men burst through the hallway. McLeary snapped the Smith and Wesson up and fired all five rounds he kept in the weapon. The three men fell in a tangled, bloody heap, spilling out of the hallway and into the parlor. McLeary dropped the Smith and Wesson on the floor and snatched out his small Colt. He heard a thundering boom that slammed from wall to wall.

Glancing up, he saw that Wheeler had flung Claymore's pistol off his hand, drew the Walker and calmly shot Claymore, whose face blew apart when the .44 caliber bullet plowed into it just below the nose.

Spinning back, still ready, McLeary slowly approached the heap of bodies. Two of the men were dead, the third would not linger much longer. He grabbed that man by the hair and pulled his head up. "Where's Molly?" he demanded.

"Up," the man whispered. His eyes rolled oddly, then stopped moving, staring out at nothing.

"Take care of Alice," McLeary roared as he charged up the stairs. His heart pounded in fear for his woman. He found her, hogtied and gagged, on the bed in her room—their room now, he reminded himself.

Heart still thumping with worry and the pulsing of adrenaline, he pulled the gag down off Molly's mouth. "You all right?" he asked breathlessly.

She nodded, her mouth too dry to speak properly.

With some relief, he pulled out his knife and cut the bonds from her ankles and wrists. She sat up, seemingly a little dazed, and rubbed life back into her arms. He knelt at the side of the bed and did the same service for her legs.

She grinned at him after a few moments. "We ain't got time for that now," she whispered, then giggled.

He laughed, much relieved. "You sure you're all right?" he asked, still a dart of worry pricking him.

"Yes."

"Did they? . . ." He couldn't finish it. Suddenly his mouth was arid, and a new fear clutched him.

"No," she breathed. "I don't understand why, though. They were going to take Alice. I could hear them talking about it. But they wanted her to make them some food first." She blinked back tears.

"It's all right," he said, "George knows you left him for me. He also knows me and Bodie have thrown in with the miners. He thought to get at me through you, I figure. It would also get you back. I reckon those men were told they could do what they wanted to Alice, but they were to leave you alone."

"Why didn't they take me right back to the mansion?" she asked, still worried, but growing stronger by the minute.

"Waitin' for me, I reckon. I can't say for sure, but I would expect. They were to have their fun with Alice. When I came in, they were supposed to kill me, then take you back to George."

"How's Alice?" Molly asked, suddenly frightened for her friend.

"Alive. Bodie's with her."

"She won't be pleased to be left in his care," Molly said with the barest hint of a smile. "She met him this morning. . . ." When she saw McLeary's blank look, she very briefly explained Bodie's visit that morning. "Anyway, she wasn't too fond of meeting him."

"It wasn't for him, she'd be layin' down on the parlor floor with half her head gone," McLeary said harshly. Molly blanched. "But I reckon we ought to go see how they're gettin' on," he added.

He stood and held out his hand. She took it and let him pull her to her feet. For a moment, she stood and rested her head on McLeary's bicep. Then she lifted her head and smiled. "I'm glad you're here," she said, kissing him on the cheek.

He felt a strange, warm glow starting in his middle and spreading outward. It was, he thought, rather disconcerting. Molly linked her arm through his, and together they walked down the stairs.

Van Leuewen was sitting on the sofa, crying and sobbing into the broad crook of Wheeler's arm and shoulder. Bodie sat next to her, one huge arm draped uneasily across her shoulders.

McLeary burst into laughter at the look of discomfort on Bodie's face. The big gunfighter tried to look angry with him, but it didn't work. As McLeary went to retrieve his Smith and Wesson, Molly sat on the other side of her friend, trying to console her.

A relieved look drifted across Wheeler's face, and he started to move his arm from around Van Leuewen's shoulders.

"Don't leave me," Alice moaned.

"But I'm here, Alice," Molly said, shocked.

"I want him to stay," Alice sniffled into Wheeler's shirt.

McLeary, reloading the Smith and Wesson, grinned at his large friend. He received a fierce scowl in return.

Chapter 24

It was an unusual council of war, but it was necessary that they all be there. It was early evening, and McLeary, Wheeler, Molly Stoughton and Alice Van Leuewen were gathered around the long wooden table in the kitchen at the back of the house. Dirty dishes and pots—the remains of supper—were scattered on the table. All four sat with coffee cups in front of them.

"This coffee's good, ma'am," Wheeler said, lifting his cup toward Molly. "But," he added in a whisper to McLeary, "I sure as hell wish I had somethin' to put in it."

Alice, looking wan, but better than she did before, stood and went to the pantry. She returned in a moment with an almost-full bottle of whiskey. She set it on the table. "There's times when such 'medicine' comes in handy of an evening."

Wheeler grinned widely. "Thank you, ma'am," he said joyfully, pulling the cork from the bottle and pouring himself a liberal portion into the coffee cup.

"Call me Alice. I told you that."

"Yes, ma'am."

Earlier, Molly had finally persuaded Alice to go upstairs with her for a while. Alice had shuddered as she passed the pile of bodies. The two women had been gone a long time, during which McLeary and Wheeler had discussed their options.

"We can't leave these women alone no more, you know," Wheeler growled.

"Yep. And that's gonna make our job a heap harder."

"Sure is. You gonna clean your piece?"

"Eventually."

Wheeler went around back and brought both his and McLeary's horses up to the back yard of the house. He came back into the parlor, carrying the necessities for cleaning his pistol. He performed the task as he and McLeary spoke.

"I reckon the best thing is for us to take turns paying visits around town," McLeary said.

"Good. When do we start?"

"Tomorrow, I reckon. I want to make sure Molly and Alice are all right. And, I figure we're gonna have to take turns stayin' up the night just to make sure Stoughton doesn't pull anything overnight."

"You worried about fires, Charlie?"

"Worried about everything. Tell you the truth, Bodie, these are strange times for me. I never had a woman to care about before, and goddamn if it don't put a different light on things."

"Reckon it does," Wheeler said with a chuckle. "Should've never got yourself hobbled, boy."

"Bah. Too late for that now." McLeary saw that Wheeler was finished cleaning his pistol and had reloaded it. He took the gear and began working on the Smith and Wesson.

"What're we gonna do with our friends here?" Wheeler asked, waving a hand at the four bodies.

McLeary shrugged. "We sure as hell can't leave 'em here much longer."

"That's a fact, Charlie. I say we load 'em up on their horses and take 'em over and leave 'em in front of the Silver Nugget."

McLeary thought about that for a few minutes as he worked. Then he grinned. "I like that notion." Then the grin dropped. "But it's too damned dangerous."

"How so?" Wheeler demanded, unafraid of anyone or anything.

"Well, we can't leave the women here alone, and it ain't too wise goin' down there just one of us alone. Either of us. We'd be shot down sure as hell. And if we both went to watch over each other, half the regulators would head here directly."

"Christ, Charlie, you take the fun and excitement out of everything."

McLeary grinned. "What we could do, though," he said slowly, thinking as he went along, "is to load 'em on their horses. Then ride straight down Sixth Street till we hit Silver

Street. Then we can send those horses—and the packages—racing down the street toward the Silver Nugget. We'll be back here in five minutes—not enough time for anybody to do anything."

"Unless they're watchin'."

"One of us'll stay a block back, keep an eye on the house. We'll be covered all ways."

"Goddamn, you just put the fun back into this," Wheeler said with a wide grin.

McLeary finished cleaning the Smith and Wesson, and reloaded. Done, he and Wheeler dragged the stiffening bodies out into the backyard. They flung the corpses onto the four horses that had been tied back there. As Wheeler mounted his horse, McLeary went back into the house. "We'll be back in a few minutes," McLeary yelled up the stairs.

Wheeler was waiting for him out in front. McLeary pulled himself into the saddle. "I'd like to do the last part of this trip," Wheeler said with a grin.

McLeary nodded.

The plan worked to perfection, and they were back at the house a few minutes later, laughing at the consternation their little surprise had wrought along the main street of town.

Soon after, Molly and Alice returned from upstairs. Alice looked much better. After McLeary and Wheeler had laughingly told the two women what they had just done, Molly said sweetly, "I need to see you for a few minutes, Charlie."

She seemed a little nervous, so McLeary assented right away. They climbed the stairs and went into her room. She kicked the door shut and then came to him. "I need you, Charlie," she said, almost panting with desire.

"Now?" he asked, surprised.

"Yes."

"Where are you going?" Molly asked dreamily, as McLeary started to get dressed again.

"Back downstairs. We've got some things—"

"No."

"What?"

"No."

"Would you mind tellin' me what the hell's going on around here?" he asked, exasperated.

"Alice wanted some time to be with Bodie," she said with a winning smile.

McLeary was momentarily too stunned for words. Then he said haltingly, in disbelief, "She *wanted* to spend time with him?"

"Uh-huh. Now come back here. *I* want to spend time with *you.*"

"But she doesn't like . . . she was . . . before . . . the regulators . . . you told me . . . she . . ."

"You're jabberin', Charlie, and making no sense at all."

"But . . ." He gave it up and did as he was told.

Two hours later, McLeary and Molly ventured cautiously downstairs. Wheeler and Alice Van Leuewen were sitting on the sofa, looking mightily pleased with themselves. Indeed, McLeary thought, Alice fairly glowed.

"Perhaps we ought to get supper going, Alice," Molly said.

The two women headed into the kitchen. When they were out of earshot, McLeary started laughing.

"What in hell you laughin' at, boy?" Wheeler asked, a surly note curling around the edges of his words.

"I do believe, old friend, that you done went and got yourself hobbled this afternoon." He chuckled some more. Wheeler's obvious discomfort only made him all the more gleeful.

"I ain't done no such thing," Wheeler argued, not at all convincingly.

"Don't bullshit me, Bodie," McLeary said with another guffaw.

A grin started tweaking the corners of Wheeler's mouth. It grew and spread slowly until it seemed to cover the entire bottom half of his face. "Well, shit," he mumbled, "what do you expect? A fine woman like that needs my help and my comfort—" He almost choked on the unfamiliar words.

"What in hell does she see in you?" McLeary asked, fighting off another wave of laughter.

"Honest to Christ, Charlie, I got no idea. I really ain't." He looked almost frightened, the first time McLeary had ever seen that in Wheeler.

"Well, you'll get used to it, I reckon." McLeary grew serious. "She seems to be takin' the day's events pretty calm."

"She told me Molly talked to her a lot before. She might look like some fragile little thing, but she's some stronger inside than she lets on."

"Reckon so. Well . . ."

Molly called them from the kitchen for supper.

So they sat after the meal, the two men outlining what few plans they were able to make considering their situation. The women did not like it, of course, that each man would go out by himself, but there was little they—or the men—could do about it.

McLeary took the watch that night, allowing Wheeler to go upstairs to the big bedroom and learn about his new woman—and she about him. McLeary and Molly spent some time together, but then he ordered her to go to sleep, telling her that she was too distracting for him to keep a proper watch over the house.

He prowled the house—and the grounds front and rear—throughout the night. It was perhaps an hour before dawn when a shadow moving out in the backyard caught his attention through a window. He raced upstairs and into Alice's room.

"Bodie!" he hissed, not wanting to wake the woman.

The big man rolled over, his Walker pointing at McLeary's nose. "Trouble?" he asked, setting the pistol down and swinging his legs off the bed.

"Might be. I saw something—someone—out back. I'm gonna go take a looksee, but I want you up and around in case there's more than one, or if it's a decoy while others come through the front."

Wheeler was already dressed. "Go," he said.

McLeary disappeared down the stairs. He slipped out the front door, and down off the porch. He carefully went around the side of the house, moving slowly, quietly. Though he had retrieved his spurs, he had not bothered to put them back on.

At the southwest corner of the house, he stopped and waited, silent as the shadows around him. He ignored the mosquitoes that buzzed around his head. He caught a movement again—a shadow somewhat more substantial than the others around him. And he knew someone was at the back door of the house.

McLeary stayed where he was for another minute, eyes searching all around to see if this one man had not come alone. When he was as certain as he could be that the man was by himself, McLeary slid around the corner and moved quickly toward the intruder.

The man—who McLeary did not know by name, but who he had seen in the Silver Nugget—heard the soft snick of the Smith and Wesson's hammer as McLeary cocked the pistol. He raised his hands slowly and started turning languidly. When he was a quarter of the way around, he leaped off the stair, grabbing for his revolver as he did.

McLeary fired once, then again. He was not sure if he hit the man the first time, but he was certain the second. Even in the darkness of the night—broken only by the wide carpet of stars and the quarter moon—he could see the snapping back of the man's head.

The man rolled several times and then lay still. Cautiously, McLeary moved up and checked. Sure enough, he was dead.

"Charlie, you all right?" Wheeler called from inside the house.

"Yep."

"Get somethin'?"

"Yep. Short, fat bastard."

"He wearin' a gold vest and look like quite the dandy?"

"Best I can tell."

"That'd be Chas Stiggerson. A useless little shit."

From outside, McLeary could hear both Molly's and Alice's voices questioning Wheeler. Then Bodie shouted, "What're you gonna do with him?"

"Reckon I'll take him over and drop him off in front of the Silver Nugget. You be all right here?"

"Yep."

He was back in a quarter hour, and chuckling with Bodie, Molly and Alice over the surprise the regulators would get shortly when the sun was full up.

"Now what?" Wheeler asked as the four sat to a breakfast of eggs and ham, biscuits and gravy.

"I reckon," McLeary said, heaping up his plate and accepting with a nod the cup of coffee Molly set before him, "that we will take the fight to them, instead of just waiting for them to come at us."

"One of us at a time?"

"Yep, unless you know some folks who'd like to come over here and set with these two fine young ladies while we're out shootin' up the town."

"It took me all these years to land me a woman like Alice," Wheeler said proudly. "I am damn certain not going to let her into the clutches of some other man's twice as handsome as me."

"The second ugliest man in Colorado is twice as handsome as you," McLeary chuckled. He ducked as Wheeler threw a biscuit at him.

The two women looked at each other and shrugged, as if there was nothing they could do about these two overgrown children.

"I reckon I'll be the first to go?" Wheeler said. He framed it as a question, but there was no denying it was a statement.

"Yep," McLeary said easily. "I had my fun last night. And I need some sleep." But he wondered whether they were doing the right thing. He remembered his father once telling him, "Don't go kickin' some griz in the ass just to git his attention, boy. Ye may not like the consequences of such doin's."

Chapter 25

McLeary woke shortly after noon. He was still mighty tired, and he rubbed the weariness from his eyes. Bodie Wheeler was not back yet, and McLeary was a bit alarmed, but not too much.

"Where could he be?" Alice Van Leuewen asked, fear and worry catching her words in her throat.

"Anywhere," McLeary said in some irritation, the tiredness and his own worry for his friend making him irritable. "But Bodie can take care of himself."

"But—"

"I said he can take care of himself," McLeary snapped.

Alice turned, sniffing unhappily and skittered upstairs to her room. McLeary and Molly, sitting at the table in the kitchen finishing off some coffee, heard the slamming of Van Leuewen's door.

"You were awfully rude to Alice," Molly said with some heat.

McLeary shrugged, not wanting to discuss it.

"I think you should go up and apologize to her."

"No." He drained off the coffee and stood. Walking to the sink, he set the cup down on the sideboard next to the pump.

"But—"

"You can go up and join her," McLeary snapped, "if you're of a mind to pester."

Molly's eyes widened in surprise, and an icy finger of fear—fear that McLeary might be tiring of her already—lanced into her insides.

"I'm tired, Molly," McLeary said a little contritely. "And I'm worried about Bodie, too. I figured he'd be back by now. I ain't real worried, since he's probably pickin' his own time and spot to harass the regulators. But, still, it's a little worrisome."

He paused, taking a few deep breaths, hoping it would somehow lighten his mood. It didn't work. "And I'm worried about you and Alice—havin' to watch over you both all the time. I don't *mind* doin' it," he added before she could protest. "It's just that it ain't easy bein' on guard all the time, havin' to watch four sides of the house, not bein' able to go out with Bodie and do some damage to the enemy together.

"If me and Bodie could ride together, without havin' to worry about leavin' you two here by yourselves and in danger, we could take the fight to the regulators, and get it over with quick."

She came up to him and reached up to stroke his cheek. "You need a shave," she said with a smile.

"Later," he answered, absent-mindedly.

"I understand," Molly said quietly, and he finally really looked at her, struck again by her beauty.

"That doesn't help matters," he said, smiling a little to let her know he was not angry about it.

"Reckon not," Molly said, dropping her head. She leaned against him, her head resting on his chest. McLeary wrapped his strong arms around her slim shoulders, still surprised at just how small she really was.

"What's with Alice?" he asked.

"What do you mean?" she responded, not moving her head. She quite enjoyed standing here like this, her right ear over his heart, listening to the strong, rhythmic thumping.

"Well, you told me she hated Bodie at first. Hell, you told me she didn't even like what you and me were doin' here. So right after she almost gets raped, she comes down here. Next thing I know she's in love with a man she couldn't stand a day before. And that night she drags him up to her bed. It doesn't make any sense."

She released him and pushed through his arms so she was standing back a step, gazing at him. "Some of that was my doing," she said seriously. "Alice has always been—like I was—stifled when it came to . . . to . . ." She hesitated. Then she went on. "Anyway, nothing did happen yesterday with those . . . men. Nothing happened because of Bodie. She thought she ought to show she was gratified. She *wanted to.* So I had to talk her into that. Which I managed to do when we went upstairs so long."

Molly wandered around the room a minute, straightening things that didn't really need straightening. She came back to McLeary. "You remember how I was at first?" she asked.

McLeary nodded. "Sure, not knowin' nothin' about love-makin' and such. But"—he grinned—"you was sure some willin' to learn."

Molly did not smile back. "Alice was much the same. She'd been treated poorly by her husband—not because he was a bastard—" she said, shocking herself, and McLeary—"like George, but because he didn't know better. Anyway, Alice always wanted to be more free with herself . . . that way. But she couldn't. And she thought she was *supposed* to look down on others who acted that way—like me. It seems everybody else does.

"All that made her terribly guilty that she even had those feelings, and it made her terribly lonely, since she thought that if she found a man, she might one day let those feelings out and embarrass herself and shock her man."

"That still don't explain why a day after she ignored Bodie she gives herself freely to him. And now she claims to love."

"Oh, she does love him," Molly said firmly. "She did from the first, but she thought she *shouldn't.* After all, he was a regulator, and a gunfighter, and a drifter. Kind of the way I treated you that very first time we met—at the door of the store. Remember."

McLeary nodded.

"When we went up to talk, Alice was quite upset—horrified by what had almost happened."

"That's understandable."

"Yes, it is. And she was about to let it ruin her forever. But worse, Alice let it slip that she had taken a liking to Bodie. A big liking. But she was going to let him walk out of her life, too, because she wasn't *supposed* to fall in love with a man like that.

"But I managed to talk her out of such foolishness. I just

kept hammering into her head that nothing had happened. True, she was terrorized some, and all, but still, she never had it as bad as me. With the way George"—she spit out her husband's name—"treated me, every time he took me to our bed, it was like being raped, especially when he would beat me sometimes."

McLeary's face hardened. There was one problem that would have to be resolved for certain before he left this town and started a real life with Molly Stoughton.

"So I told her that she didn't have it so bad, except that she wouldn't let herself be free in bed—or in letting the man she was attracted to know she was interested in him that way. She was quite shocked by that, of course. And it took a lot of talking to convince her. I managed to get through to her, and then started in on convincing her that if she really cared for Bodie, she should let him know in the only real way she could. It would make it clear to him, and—and Lordy, I was never really sure it would work—get the demons of that restriction out of her mind. I just prayed that Bodie was as gentle and thoughtful a lover as you."

McLeary grinned. "That big, clumsy ox can be quite carin' when he's of a mind to."

"So she told me this morning. I reckon it's all worked out, though I can tell by looking at Alice that she's still feeling guilty about it all."

"I reckon that Bodie will help her ease that over time," McLeary said softly.

"Ummm," Molly murmured, coming back to lean against him.

He was acutely aware of her body pressed against him. But he finally pushed her away. "Time for me to take a look around," he said.

She nodded sadly and stepped back. He patrolled the house, checking all the doors. He stood to the side of each window, staring out until he was certain no one was trying to sneak up on the house.

It took some time, but at last McLeary was satisfied. He sat in one of the plush chairs in the parlor, out of any line of fire through the front windows, to wait.

Molly, who had gone upstairs, came back down with Alice in tow. Van Leuewen looked much better, and McLeary expected that she had taken a nap. She smiled at McLeary, and he returned it, feeling better himself. Nothing was said about the morning's harsh words.

"We were thinking," Molly said, plopping herself down in McLeary's lap, "that we might have a solution to our problem."

"What problem?" he asked. Their problems were numerous, he thought.

"Of you and Bodie havin' to watch over us all the time, instead of being able to face the regulators together."

"Oh?" he asked, skeptical.

"Alice's aunt lives in a small place a few blocks from here. Over on Third Street down near the river. It ain't much, but she won't let Alice help her out any with money or anything. Alice is sure she'll let us stay there a few days."

McLeary thought for some moments. Then he heard a noise. He stood, dumping Molly unceremoniously off his lap and onto the floor. "Get upstairs!" he ordered, drawing the Smith and Wesson.

Both women scampered up the stairs, knowing better than to argue.

McLeary quickly looked through the front window nearest him. The sound had come from the back, but he just wanted to make sure the sounds at the back were not just to decoy him. He saw no one.

He hurried through the hallway into the dining room, and then into the kitchen. Through one of the windows, he saw a furtive movement in the backyard. He stepped into the pantry and cocked the Smith and Wesson, aiming it at the door. And he waited, sweating.

He saw a shadow move toward the door, and he tensed. Then he heard Wheeler's growling deep voice, "Charlie, it's me, Bodie, comin' in."

McLeary relaxed and uncocked the pistol. "Come ahead," he shouted.

A moment later, Wheeler was inside the house, grinning and pouring himself a cup of coffee from the large pot that simmered on the cookstove.

Molly and Alice ran into the room, Molly stopping next to McLeary. But Alice charged headlong at Wheeler. He had barely enough time to set the coffee cup down on the counter nearby before she was on him, practically climbing up his huge frame, kissing him and whimpering at the same time.

McLeary chuckled at both the activity and the abashed look on his big friend's face. Wheeler endured it for a while before growling, "I been busy, woman, and I'm hungry."

She looked afraid, thinking he was angry with her. "I ain't mad, darlin'," he said in as soft a voice as his deep bass could provide, "but I ain't plannin' on bein' a spectacle for those two"—he pointed at Molly and McLeary, who were laughing—"no longer. And, by God, I *am* hungry. So rustle me up some grub."

Soon enough, Wheeler was doing serious damage to a large plate of beans and a huge chunk of buttered cornbread.

As his friend ate, McLeary asked, "Well, how'd it go?"

"Well, there was two dozen regulators to start with, but the Stoughtons went and hired four more. You and me killed them four yesterday, and you the one last night. That's twenty-three left." He slurped down some coffee. "Now there's twenty-one." He grinned.

"Only two?" McLeary asked with a laugh. "You been gone for hours. Hell, I thought you were gonna take care of the whole damned lot of them."

"Thought of it," Wheeler said around a mouthful of cornbread. "But it ain't gonna be easy with one of us havin' to stay here the whole while."

"We were just talkin' about that before you come back. The ladies think they have a solution."

"Oh?" Wheeler asked, eyebrows raised. He spooned more beans into his mouth.

They brought him up to date. Then Alice said, "If we can get there without nobody seein' us, we'll be safe. Then you two could go about your business." She shuddered with a combination of fear and worry.

"Won't somebody be suspicious?" Wheeler asked.

"No," Van Leuewen said. "Aunt Cara is quite eccentric, and stays mostly to herself. She keeps the curtains drawn tight most times and doesn't go out much. Nobody will be able to see me and Molly, and George doesn't know that Cara is my aunt. It'll never occur to him to look there."

"How are we gonna get you there without bein' seen?" Wheeler asked.

"Tonight," McLeary answered. "Just past dark."

"It'll be dangerous, Charlie."

"Might be, Bodie. But I reckon we got to take the chance. We can't just keep sittin' here waitin' for them to come at us, or takin' the fight to them one at a time."

"Reckon you're right. I wonder why they ain't come at us all at once already." Wheeler shoved his plate away and leaned back with a cigarette and his cup of coffee.

"I reckon the Stoughtons don't want to make that much of a disturbance. They try havin' twenty men storm some widow's house, and that'll anger a heap of folks they don't want to anger. However," he added slowly, "that don't mean they wouldn't like to see this place burn down. Accidental like, you know."

"They'd do that?" Molly asked, horrified.

"Yep. George wanted you back, and to punish me. That failed, so he might not give a damn about you any more. This place catches on fire, it'll either kill us or chase us out. That happens, his men could gun us down and haul us away before too many other people arrive."

"That son of a bitch!" Molly gasped in shock.

"You really think they'd try that, Charlie?" Wheeler asked.

"Yep."

"Me too. When you think they'll try?"

"Could be as soon as tonight. Maybe next week. Maybe never."

"We got to get these ladies out of here."

"Yep."

"You sure your aunt will take you and Molly in like this?"

Wheeler asked uncertainly, realizing for the first time how much he cared for Alice Van Leuewen, and feeling strangely about it.

"No. But I reckon she will. I've got to get her a note somehow."

"You go write your note," McLeary ordered. "Me and Bodie will figure out how to get it to her."

Chapter 26

McLeary and Wheeler took turns napping throughout the afternoon. In one of his waking periods, McLeary slipped out the back and meandered the streets. He told a boy he would give him a quarter to deliver a message. The boy's eyes gleamed as he accepted the note, and directions.

"I'll meet you back here in an hour, boy," McLeary said, scaring the boy a little with the harshness of his voice. "You bring me back a message and you'll get your quarter."

The ten-year-old nodded and scooted off. McLeary turned to make his way back to the house, and spotted Mace Kenney. The regulator had his thickly bandaged gun arm in a sling. McLeary grinned grimly. " 'Lo, Mace," he said, no sign of friendliness in his voice.

The hate that colored Kenney's face was total and unyielding. "You son of a bitch!" he snarled, the enmity thick in his tone.

"How's the arm?" McLeary asked, almost innocently. There was something satisfying even now about the remembrance of Kenney's hand bones breaking under McLeary's boot.

Kenney was wearing his Colt butt facing forward on his left hip. He scrabbled for it now with his left hand, but was neither ambidextrous nor well practiced with his left hand.

"You pull that pistol, Mace," McLeary warned, "and I'll break your other hand for you. It'll be awfully hard to piss when you got both hands bound up in slings."

"You son of a bitch!" He kept trying to grab the pistol.

"You're repeatin' yourself, Mace." McLeary grinned. He stepped up to Kenney. Slapping Mace's hand out of the way, he grabbed the man's gun out. "This what you're lookin' for?" he asked with a smile. He flipped it in the air. It twirled several times before McLeary caught it by the barrel.

Kenney's eyes widened in fright, and a bead of sweat wound down his left cheek.

McLeary swung the pistol up and then down, thunking Kenny on the forehead, using the butt of the pistol like the head of a hammer. Kenney grunted and fell back a step. His knees wobbled and he swayed. Finally he steadied some, though his eyes looked a little funny, and there was a purplish knot growing.

"I want you to take a message back to the regulators," McLeary said airily. "I want you to tell those boys that me and Bodie already took care of seven of you. I could real easy make it eight right here and now. But we're gonna give you boys one more chance. You ain't seen nothin' yet, but if each and all of you idiot bastards ain't gone by tomorrow night, me and Bodie will bury the whole goddamn lot of you. Got that?"

Kenney nodded painfully.

McLeary stuck Mace's Colt into the back of his own gun-belt, saying, "I reckon you won't be needin' it. Now go on, get. And give those boys my message."

When Kenney was gone, McLeary mounted the cinnamon and dropped Kenney's Colt into his saddlebags. It clunked against the one he had taken from the cattlemen's "detective" a while back. It seemed, he thought wryly, that he was making a habit of collecting Colts these days.

He went back to the house, easing his way in, and had a cup of coffee before slipping back out for his rendezvous with the boy. The youth was waiting anxiously, figuring he would not get his quarter, a right tidy sum with which he could greatly impress his friends. And stuffed into one pocket of his grimy overalls was a return note from the crazy lady in the small, neat house over on Third Street.

But McLeary arrived soon, and the boy gave him the note. The youth waited impatiently while McLeary read the note. Then he smiled and gave the boy two quarters.

"Thanks, mister," the boy said, eyes bright at the sight of his booty.

"Thank you, boy." McLeary climbed into the saddle and

hurried back to the house.

"Well?" Alice demanded as he stepped into the kitchen.

"It's all set."

"Thank God," the woman breathed.

McLeary and Wheeler caught up on sleep, with the women awakening them just after dusk. They all sat to a meal of baked chicken, bread stuffing, biscuits, potatoes, peas and carrots. Afterward there was coffee laced with sugar and—for the two men—a whopping dollop of whiskey.

While McLeary had an after-supper cigar, Molly and Alice cleaned up the plates and pots, and Wheeler left. When he returned in a half-hour, slipping into the back door, the women were finished and waiting.

"Rainin' hard?" McLeary asked.

"Just a drizzle. No lightin'. A little thunder, but not much."

"You get what we need?" McLeary asked. When Wheeler nodded, he asked, "Ready, ladies?"

The two women nodded. They were dressed in men's pants, shirts and boots, all legacies of Van Leuewen's late husband. They had found some old caps, and stuffed their hair up into them. On close inspection, they would fool no one, but at night, from a distance, in the rain, they could pass for boys.

"Let's go, then," McLeary said.

They all filed out the back door, Wheeler first, pistol ready. McLeary's and Wheeler's horses were saddled and waiting, as were two other horses.

"Where'd you get 'em, Bodie?" McLeary asked.

"Back of the Silver Nugget," Wheeler said with a wide grin.

"Sounds fittin'."

"You can ride astride, can't you, Alice?" Wheeler asked as he helped his woman into the saddle.

"Not well," she admitted, frightened. "But we're not going very far or very fast. I should be all right."

"You, Molly?" McLeary asked.

"I've done it before."

They rode down the path between the two houses and out onto Animas Street. They turned south, not riding fast. It was raining a little harder, but not bad, though the ground was already a thick soup of mud. In less than ten minutes they were at Alice's Aunt Cara's house.

McLeary pulled back when Molly tried to kiss him. "No," he snapped. "Someone might see. Go."

Unhappy, Molly slid down off the horse. Grabbing the canvas sack with the few possessions McLeary had allowed her to bring, she and Alice stepped toward the house. McLeary and Wheeler waited in the rain until the women were safely inside. Then each man grabbed the reins of one of the horses and headed toward the Silver Nugget.

In back of the saloon, they tied the two horses off. Then McLeary grinned and said, "Hell, let's give these boys a little surprise while we're here."

Wheeler nodded, smiling, enthused—as he always was—by the possibility of action.

The crept up the back stairs to the second-story porch that ran around the entire building. With the heat of the summer, all the windows were open. McLeary and Wheeler walked silently along the balcony until they came on a room from which they heard no noise. McLeary went in first, Smith and Wesson in hand. Wheeler was right behind. There was no one else in the room.

They crossed quickly to the door, and McLeary cracked it open. He looked out, first left, then right. They were about in the middle of the landing that ran around three sides of the saloon. To each side of McLeary, at the corners, was a shotgun-toting guard to watch over the place.

McLeary shut the door a moment. "The guards?" he asked.

"Yep."

"We keep it quiet?" he asked.

"Don't matter. They're gonna know we're here soon enough. Gettin' out's gonna be a problem."

"We'll make it."

"Reckon so. Just go through the door directly behind you—they're never locked—out the window and down the stairs." Wheeler looked through the door. I'll take the one on the right. He's bigger. More my size."

McLeary nodded. He pulled open the door and stepped out,

walking silently, back pressed against the wall, toward the guard. Wheeler went the other way. He was closer, and got there first.

The powerful, large fingers of his left hand locked around the guard's throat, and the shotgun-holding guard was lifted up off his chair. Wheeler grabbed the shotgun and tossed it behind him. Then he pulled the chair out from under the guard and tossed it aside. The man struggled and almost broke loose enough to scream, but Wheeler squeezed all the harder, shutting off the man's air. The guard went mostly limp. Leaving his left hand tight around the guard's throat, Wheeler used his right hand to grab the guard by the belt in the back.

Lifting the big guard up, almost over his head, Wheeler tossed him over the railing. Half-unconscious from the lack of oxygen, the guard made no sound—until his body landed on the base of his back, square on the edge of the bar. His spine snapped, and glasses and bottles broke.

Then Wheeler spun and slipped through the door behind him. It was one of the rooms damaged in the fire several nights ago. Wheeler bulled his way through the half-open window, shattering glass.

At the same time Wheeler was locking his fingers around the one guard's neck, McLeary had reached the watchman on his side. He already had the Smith and Wesson cocked, and he placed the muzzle against the back of the guard's head. "Hand me up that scattergun," he ordered.

The guard, sweating from the heat in the oppressively hot saloon—and this sudden danger—did as he was told.

"Now, stand."

The man did so. McLeary uncocked the Smith and Wesson and slid it into the holster. He hefted the heavy, 12-gauge shotgun in his two hands—left on the twin barrels, right on the stock.

"Goodbye," he muttered. He swung the shotgun up, barrels over his left shoulder. Just as the other guard was flying to his death, McLeary smashed the butt of the shotgun as hard as he could against the nape of the guard's neck.

The guard grunted with the sudden, sharp pain as he

pitched forward over the railing. McLeary took a quick look over, seeing that the guard had landed atop a gunfighter playing cards below.

The card player screamed, and there was a crashing of the table. Chips scattered and men yelled.

McLeary dropped the shotgun, whirled and plunged through the door behind him. A woman screamed, and as he dove through the window, a gunshot rang out behind him. He landed heavily on the wet planks of the balcony. Then he was up and running, feet slipping a little. He could hear Wheeler's heavy footsteps thumping behind him as he headed down the stairs.

McLeary whipped out his knife and, as he ran, slashed all the reins of regulators horses tied on the hitching posts. Wheeler, behind him, yelled and hollered and flapped his arms, scaring the horses into running away through the mud, whinnying in their fright.

Wheeler and McLeary got to their horses and were in the saddles as the first of the regulators skidded around the corner of the saloon building. As the two men whipped their horses into a run with the ends of the reins, several regulators fired after them.

It was not long before McLeary and Wheeler were back at Van Leuewen's house. They tied their horses in the small stable in back and then ran into the house. McLeary expected a full assault from the regulators soon.

As they entered the house, McLeary noticed some blood dripping on the floor.

"You hit, Bodie?" McLeary asked, worried.

"Ain't sure." He became aware of a burning sensation on his side. He pulled off his soaking wet shirt and looked. "Just a scratch," he said, relieved. "One of those fools must've just nipped me." Then Wheeler started laughing. "That was one hell of a stupid thing we did, Charlie, you know that, don't you?"

"Do now. Sounded like a good time when we thought of it."

"Reckon it wasn't all bad," Wheeler said, still laughing. They headed up the stairs for some dry clothes. "We took care of two more of those bastards."

"Maybe three," McLeary said.

"Eh?"

"When I sent that guard over the rail, he landed on one of the regulators. If both of 'em ain't dead. I reckon neither is gonna be able to come against us for a good spell."

"Think the rest will be coming after us tonight?"

"Ain't sure. I think so, but . . ." He tore up a sheet into some strips, which he wrapped around Wheeler's midsection, bandaging the wound. "You get some sleep, Bodie," McLeary said. "I'll keep watch over things. I need help, I'll holler. And I'll wake you after a spell so I can get some rest."

Wheeler nodded, grateful.

Chapter 27

"Somebody's comin'," Wheeler yelled. He was at the back of the house, watching over the alley and backyard from the kitchen.

"This way, too," McLeary answered. He was stationed in the parlor.

It was almost dawn. McLeary had let Wheeler sleep for several hours after their escapade at the Silver Nugget, before waking the big gunfighter. Wearily, McLeary got some rest. Both men had figured that if the regulators were planning to raid the house they would need a little time to organize. They also would want to do it near dawn since they would assume that McLeary and Wheeler would stay awake throughout the night on guard and thus would be drowsy and less alert at that time.

It had stopped raining sometime during the night, and the cloud cover had drifted over the mountain peaks to the east. The moon shone brightly, and there was a fine display of stars twinkling in the early July sky. It was dark in the house, relieved only by a small lantern in the parlor and one in the kitchen. Neither was bright enough to give the enemy a good shot at McLeary or Wheeler, but provided enough light for the two men to be able to reload without fumbling.

"How many?" McLeary yelled.

"Four I can see. How about up front?"

"Six. No, wait, seven. Two of 'em's carryin' cans of kerosene."

"I got one doin' so back here."

There was no more to say, so McLeary said nothing more. He levered a shell into the chamber of his Henry rifle and stuck the barrel out the open window, taking aim at one of the men carrying a can. All seven men were across the street, hiding in the shadows of the buildings there.

From south down Routt Street came the sound of a wagon driven fast. It grew louder and louder. As the driver reached Alice Van Leuewen's house, he yanked hard on the reins and pulled the horses to the right as hard as he could. The animals squealed and skidded in the mud, turning tightly. The driver leaped as the flat supply wagon teetered on its two left wheels, then fell over with a resounding crash. It lay on its side, perpendicular to Van Leuewen's house, its top two wheels still spinning.

The driver sprinted through the mud toward the safety of the small path between two houses, as the horses raced away down Eighth Street toward the center of town.

McLeary heard another wagon coming fast from the south, up Routt Street, and he swung the barrel of the Henry around and waited. The wagon came into sight under the bright quarter moon. McLeary waited until he was sure it was being driven by a regulator. Then he fired.

The driver's arms flung outward, and he tumbled back onto the flat bed of the wagon, where he bounced as the horses ran unchecked. Just before passing Van Leuewen's house, the dead driver flopped off and landed with a splat in the mud as the driverless wagon raced headlong up the street and into the night.

It had been the regulators' plan, McLeary realized, as he snapped the Henry's lever down and then back up, to get two, maybe three wagons overturned in the street in front of the house and use them as protection as they moved up to the building.

Wheeler heard the crash of the wagon from out front, and then the shot. He grinned. McLeary's Henry had a distinctive sound, and he figured that his friend had scored a hit. Wheeler steadied his Winchester, aimed at the man with a can of kerosene in hand.

The four in back moved, splitting like wagon spokes as they ran out of the slim alley. One swung far south, heading for the line of cottonwood trees; one did the same northward, heading for the corner of the house. The other two came almost straight on, separating a little as they headed for the back of the house.

Wheeler fired three shots as fast as he could work the lever, all aimed at the one heading for the trees on the south. The man screamed and fell sidelong, at least two of the .44-caliber slugs in his chest.

But Wheeler did not wait to see. He knew he had hit the man, and didn't much care at the moment if he had killed the regulator or not. He whipped around and fired four times at the man on the north. The regulator was spun around and flung sideways by the impact of the lead. He yelped once as he tumbled on a heap in the muddy ground.

Wheeler nodded when he heard the heavy thump of McLeary's Henry from the front of the building, and some shouts of pain.

The other two regulators hesitated briefly, still running, but more slowly. They had not counted on this.

Wheeler smiled ruthlessly and took careful aim. He fired three more times. He was not sure which bullet did it, but suddenly the can of kerosene in the one regulator's hand burst into flames, spraying the man with a bath of blazing kerosene. The man screamed hideously as the flames spread all over him and began avidly consuming his flesh.

The last regulator tried to stop and skidded in the mud. He fell with a plop. It took some moments of frantic scrambling before he was up. Then he ran, stumbling, slipping, lurching, for the alley.

Wheeler had no remorse at all as he placed a bullet from his Winchester square in the man's back. The regulator was slammed forward, arms widespread, and he landed nose down in the mud.

The entire episode had taken only seconds. Wheeler could still hear the regular boom of McLeary's Henry. He took as close a look as he could from where he was at the first two men he had shot. Neither had moved—other than the meager twitching of muscles dying. He nodded at a job well done. Then he spun and ran toward the front of the house, yelling, "I'm comin', Charlie," so that his friend would not shoot him by mistake.

As soon as the first shot had come from the back of the house, the seven men across the street from McLeary in front moved. They poured a hail of lead at the window at which McLeary had been earlier, and ran as they did, heading for the overturned wagon.

McLeary had—just after killing the driver of the second wagon—grabbed his saddlebags, which contained the two confiscated pistols and all his ammunition, and rolled to one of the other windows. He sat waiting now, rifle ready, watching the wood and glass fly from where he had been. He smiled.

The regulators sent up another fusillade at the window where he had been. Three of them burst from behind the wagon, firing as they ran. They spread out a little, but all three headed toward the front door. The one in the center carried a can of kerosene.

It was he that McLeary took out first. He fired twice, both bullets from the big old Henry ripping into the man's chest. The regulator never even had time to scream, as the bullets stopped him cold and knocked him over on his back.

The others were shocked—not so much that their companion had died—but that they had been firing uselessly at the window where they had last seen McLeary.

The other two who had been running skidded to a stop and spun, boots having trouble gaining friction on the slick mud, but then they were heading back to the safety of the wagon.

McLeary dropped one of them with two well-placed slugs in the back—one high, one low. He whipped the rifle around and fired again, but missed as the man had reached the wagon.

That regulator stayed behind the wagon—regaining his breath, McLeary supposed—as the other four came out, two to a side. Three of the four fired at McLeary's window. The other carried two sputtering sticks of dynamite—one in each hand.

McLeary ducked below the sill and then rolled back to where he had been originally. He popped up, firing the Henry. He nailed one of the four men twice in the head, and then drilled the one not shooting, but not before the man had thrown both sticks of dynamite toward the front door.

He heard Wheeler yelling, "I'm comin', Charlie," as he ducked below the window ledge.

"Stay out!" he roared.

But it was too late. Wheeler flew into the room. He was halfway across when both sticks of dynamite exploded just outside the door. Glass and wood scattered around the room, and Wheeler was knocked backward by the concussion of the blast, landing flat on his back.

"Bodie!" McLeary hollered, looking worriedly back over his shoulder.

Wheeler moaned and then was silent.

"You sons of bitches!" McLeary screamed. He snapped himself up so he was kneeling. He brought the Henry up and fired as fast as he could work the lever and pull the trigger.

Finally the Henry was snapping uselessly, empty. But the last two of the four men who had charged the house were back behind the overturned wagon, safe.

Breathing heavily from anger and fear for his friend, McLeary called back over his shoulder, "Bodie? You all right, Bodie?" He was certain his friend was dead, but he could not really bring himself to believe that. Still, there was no answer. He glanced back quickly, and saw Wheeler's great chest rising and falling slowly.

McLeary pulled a box of shells from out of his saddlebags and began jamming them into the tubular magazine of the Henry rifle. Done, he glanced back at Wheeler again, and was a little reassured when he saw him still breathing.

McLeary knelt up again and shouted out the window, "Come on out, you bastards! Show yourselves, you chickenshit punks!"

There was silence. The three men who were left charged out, two firing rapidly, the third running hellbent with a can of kerosene in his hand.

McLeary smiled fiercely as he levered a round into the chamber of the Henry. He applied a little pressure to the trigger. Then he flinched as he felt fire sizzle along his upper shoulder, inches from his carotid artery. He fired wildly.

Surprised, he looked up and around frantically. He saw nothing. He moved a few inches to the side and then whipped the Henry up and fired twice. There was some satisfaction as he saw the man carrying the kerosene go down in a tangle of arms and legs.

There was another shot from above that thunked into the windowsill. But he had caught the muzzle flash this time. He sighted down the Henry's barrel and waited. When he saw the movement of shadow on the roof of a house across the street, he aimed, waiting.

The shadow resolved and become more firm, until it was a man—a regulator—with a single-shot Sharps rifle. The regulator raised himself up a little to take a shot, and McLeary fired. Though McLeary could not see it, he knew he had sent a bullet through the man's head.

McLeary whipped around, looking for a shot at either of the two other regulators who had been running toward the house. But they were not to be seen.

"Shit," McLeary muttered. They would be hard to find now, coming into the house in the dark. He grabbed one of the Colts he had appropriated and jammed it in the back of his gun belt. He ran to the lantern and turned it up as high as the wick would go. The room was flooded with light. He hurried toward the kitchen, taking a brief look at Wheeler as he leaped over his friend. Bodie was still breathing.

McLeary raced into the kitchen. Leaving the lantern low, he jumped into the pantry, letting the door remain open just a crack. He waited, sweat gathering under his hat and seeping down onto his face. He was not sure how long it was, but he heard sounds coming from front and back. He prayed that if one of the two regulators came in the front he would ignore Wheeler laying there.

The back door creaked open just a bit, then more, then fully. But no one was there—the gunman wisely standing to the side. Finally a pistol barrel and the edge of a dirty Stetson poked around the door jamb. It was followed by the rest of the gunslinger dressed in blue jeans rolled up several times over dirty, worn boots, and a sweat-stained gray shirt.

The man edged into the room, nervous. He moved toward the parlor. As he passed the pantry door, McLeary stepped out, Smith and Wesson cocked. He set the muzzle against the man's head, just over the right ear. "Ease the hammer of that Colt down and drop it."

The man did as he was told.

"Where's your friend?" McLeary growled, tension evident.

"Out front."

"Where?"

"Don't know." The man was sweating profusely, and smelled of it and dirt and mud and whiskey. "He was gonna come in the front; I was gonna come in the back. Try to catch you between us."

"What's in it for you?"

"An extra five hundred if we took you. Same for Bodie."

"You ain't gonna collect, you son of a bitch." McLeary calmly pulled the trigger.

McLeary ran for the back door, and was out and down the few steps quickly. He headed around the north side of the house and along the wall. He slowed as he neared the corner of the front, and then stopped. He peered around and saw a gunman racing across the street. McLeary snapped off two quick shots, but missed at the distance.

Then the last of the regulators who had attacked the house was gone around the corner of another building. McLeary took a careful look around the outside of the house, making sure no one else was there. He found the ashes of the man burned by the kerosene. Then he went back into the house.

Wheeler was sitting up, groaning, holding his head in his hands. For the first time tonight, McLeary smiled.

Chapter 28

Wheeler had not been hurt much by the double blast of aynamite; just knocked unconscious. He was, however, covered across his face and chest with small cuts from flying shards. "Take more'n a bit of dynamite to kill me, dammit. You ought to know that, Charlie."

"Should by now. Goddamn, Bodie, you had me scared the way you went down like that. Then laid there lookin' dead."

"I was just foolin' you, Charlie," Wheeler said with a laugh. "I was tired and needed a nap. I figured you could handle whatever come up after that."

"Oh, I see," McLeary said, chuckling, "you weren't really hurt much—just gettin' old and need a nap of an evening, eh?"

"Hell," Wheeler growled, grinning.

The sun was up, and already the heat was fierce. The muddy street steamed as water evaporated in the hot sun. Birds chirped joyfully, unaware—or unconcerned—of the signs of carnage around the once stately house.

"You know how to cook any?" Wheeler asked.

"You've ate my cookin' before," McLeary replied

"Yeah, reckon so," Wheeler said with a grimace of remembrance. "I been tryin' to forget all these years."

"Hell, you're still alive, ain't you?"

"I reckon." He grinned. Like always, it made him seem much younger and much less vicious. "But I'm still hurtin' some, so perhaps you could see to makin' us some breakfast."

"Hurtin' my ass," McLeary growled in mock ferocity. "You're just lazier than a twenty-year-old hound." It was true. Wheeler was the better cook of the two—though that by no means meant he was a gourmet chef. But he was lazy, and it usually took a lot to convince him to use his culinary skills, such as they were.

But, McLeary knew, Wheeler must be hurting for real, as much as he didn't show it. The blast had really rocked the house, and Wheeler's head must be pounding even now.

"All right, you lazy, old coot. I'll do it. But I want to check outside first. See what damage has been done."

They heard several wagons pull up. Alert, both grabbed their rifles. Wheeler headed back for the kitchen; McLeary, for one of the nearby windows of the parlor.

Several workmen—they were not regulators by any means—had driven up and a hopped off a large flatbed wagon in front of the house. Several others headed around the side of the house toward the back.

The ones in the front picked up the bodies from the muddy ground and tossed them onto the wagon. That done, they grunted together and shoved the other wagon—the one brought during the dark of the night for protection—onto its wheels.

The men came from the back of the house carrying the other three dead men. McLeary could hear one of them say, "There ain't nothin' left of the other but a pile of bones and some ashes blowing around in the breeze." They seemed unconcerned about it all.

The driver pulled the loaded wagon up. Then they attached the one shot with holes to the back. The men climbed up on the back wagon bed, and the driver clucked to the two massive Belgian draft horses. Without effort the huge animals pulled both wagons and the grisly cargo away.

McLeary strolled into the kitchen.

"Nice of the city to clean up the litter so well," Wheeler commented.

"Yep. Well, let's go see the damage."

They went outside. The back was fine, and the yard held few traces of the fight from several hours earlier; the almost gone pile of ashes and jumble of blackened bones, that had once been a man, and several splotches of blood on the drying mud.

The front of the house was another story, though. All the windows were blown or broken out. Two of the three window frames were blasted to pieces by the fusillade of bullets. One corner of the porch was blown away by the dynamite; the wood of the house, nearly blasted all the way through. The painted siding was singed and scorched.

"Christ, Alice is gonna be madder'n hell," Wheeler said, worried.

"Hell, a little of your tender ministrations, and she'll forget all about the house," McLeary chuckled.

"I ain't foolin'," Wheeler insisted. It was the first time McLeary had ever seen him so worried.

"She'll be fine. She'll be glad just to have you back alive. And with all them cuts and stuff on your face, she'll be gettin' back an improved lookin' Bodie Wheeler."

"Shit. Let's go eat."

As they walked into the house, Wheeler wondered aloud, "Why in hell didn't they just use the dynamite in the first place?"

"Just wanted to fire the place, I reckon," McLeary answered. "Keep it quiet, if they could. But, hell, I figure once they saw things was goin' bad for 'em, they threw caution out and tried blastin'. I'm glad they held off, though."

McLeary rustled them up some bacon and eggs. He was not about to attempt biscuits. But the eggs and fatty meat filled them. They drank coffee.

"What're we gonna do now, Charlie?" Wheeler asked as he leaned back in his chair to light a cigar. The chair protested with a squeak.

McLeary pulled the last cheroot he had from his shirt pocket and fired it up. "Get some sleep soon's I finish my coffee and this here cheroot."

"Think it's safe?"

"Sure. We burned their asses real good last night, Bodie. How many of them can there be left?"

Wheeler stuck his large cigar in his teeth and counted on his fingers. "Five? Maybe six, I reckon. Yeah, six, if you count Mace Kenney, who ain't got a gun arm no more, thanks to you." He grinned.

McLeary returned it. "You think the six of 'em will come

for us?"

"Nope. Not today anyway. I reckon they're gonna lie low for a few days, see if they can come up with a better plan—or until the Stoughtons can hire some new guns and get 'em here."

"I was thinkin' the same. I reckon we'll be safe."

Wheeler nodded. He puffed awhile, sipped some coffee, then said softly, "I'd purely love to see Alice."

"This from the boy told me he'd never get hobbled to no woman?" McLeary joked.

Wheeler only snarled.

"We can go over and see her and Molly this afternoon. I reckon it'll be safe enough, long's we make sure no one's keepin' a watch over us."

Alertness was ingrained in both men. McLeary didn't know where Wheeler had learned it, but McLeary had gotten it from his father, who had once told him, "Best thing ye can do, boy, is to be on yer toes ever' minute of the day—and night. I mind the time me and one of my *companeros* thought we was safe there winterin' by a big Shoshone camp up in the Wind Rivers. So we didn't put out no horse guards. Goddamn if some Blackfeet didn't come along and steal us blind, plews, horses, everything. Took us captive, too. Rode us off a heap of distance, stripped me and him down to what God give us when we was born, and set us to runnin'. Freezin' yer balls half off in a mountain winter will do a heap toward teachin' ye to be ever watchful, boy."

"That'll do, I reckon," Wheeler said. "Then what?"

"I think," McLeary said, stabbing out the end of the cheroot on a breakfast plate, "that we'll be goin' over to the Silver Nugget for another visit."

"In the back again?" Wheeler asked with a chuckle.

"Nope. Right in the front door. I reckon between the two of us, we can manage to convince the last of the regulators to be on their way—either out of town, or down to hell."

"I said it before, Charlie, and I'll say it again, I like the way you think most times." Wheeler was a man of direct action, and liked it best when he could do something straightforward.

Great battle plans were not his forte.

"Good. Well," McLeary said, standing, "it's time for this old boy to get some shuteye."

It was still light when McLeary awoke, hungry but refreshed. His shoulder hurt only a little where the bullet had creased it. McLeary rubbed his face and walked downstairs. He made a circuit of the inside of the house, checking the pantry and all to make sure no one had snuck in while he and Wheeler had slept. He didn't think so, since both he and Wheeler were light sleepers. He also checked all sides of the house through the windows. He saw nothing untoward.

He drank a cup of coffee that had been sitting on the cast-iron stove all day. It was thick enough to float a horseshoe, and so just about right. Then he set about cooking up some beans, more bacon and some cornbread. He found the bottle of whiskey in the pantry and set it on the table. There was little left in the bottle; but it was all they had, and it would be enough to wet their throats.

Wheeler came down a few minutes later. "Smells good," he said, grabbing a tin mug and filling it with thick coffee.

"Be done in a minute."

They ate quickly, leaving the remains of the meal's dishes alongside those from that morning on the table. They cleaned, oiled and reloaded their pistols and rifles. Done with that, they took turns washing up in the sink as best they could.

It was dark by now, and cooler, as they headed out of the house, across the back yard. They saddled their horses and rode slowly down to Alice's Aunt Cara's house.

McLeary and Wheeler sat chatting uncomfortably with Alice and Molly for a hour under the watchful eye of Aunt Cara. With great trepidation, Wheeler told Alice of the damage to the house. It was quite humorous to McLeary to see the actual fright in the big man's eyes—fear that this beautiful, cultured woman who had come to love him would drop him because of what had happened.

When he had told it, Alice came over and stood in front of Wheeler. She grasped his great, wild-thatched head in her small, soft hands—and kissed him full on the lips, ignoring the gasp of shocked indignation by Aunt Cara.

She finished the kiss, and with her face an inch from his, their lips still almost touching, she said, "I don't give a good goddamn"—another gasp from Aunt Cara—"about that house. As long as you're all right. Another house I can always get, but you, my big man, are one of a kind."

She went and sat back under the reproachful eyes of her aunt, but not caring about it. McLeary thought perhaps Wheeler would explode, so bursting with pride and good fortune was he.

"Can we go home, then?" Molly asked after a little while.

"Not yet," McLeary said, growing serious. "Me and Bodie have a few more things to do tonight. We should have everything squared away by tomorrow. Come on, Bodie, let's go." He stood and set his hat firmly on his head.

Wheeler was reluctant to leave, but he knew there was nothing he and Alice could do here together with the old aunt watching like a hawk over them. So he stood.

The two men said quiet private good-byes to their women and then rode off without looking back. The streets were quiet, and McLeary figured it was because of the excitement of the night before. The people, he thought, must be nervous and afraid that it would happen again.

They rode past where the Pick and Shovel had been. The rubble had been cleared away, and a new log saloon was almost complete. The saloon next to it was going loudly.

McLeary and Wheeler stopped in front of the Silver Nugget and tied their horses to the railing outside. The place was bright with candle and lantern light, but much more quiet than McLeary had remembered it.

"Ready, Bodie?" McLeary asked.

"Yep." His face was set in determination.

They shoved through the swinging half-doors together. The piano player played on, and men shot billiards to their left. Several men danced with painted women. There were only three card games going, and there were no guards stationed on the second story.

The silence grew slowly, but caught on quickly, until it was total. The bartender moved cautiously, and Wheeler transfixed him with a stare. "You best bring them hands up flat onto the bar, Marsh," he said stonily.

The bartender did as he was told.

"Now hop up onto the bar and then off on this side."

Once again Marsh did as he was told.

"What can we do for you gentlemen?" Alva Stoughton asked, stepping up to them. He was nervous, licking his lips. There was a slight twitch on the outside of his left eye.

"You can get the hell out of the way, Alva," Wheeler snapped.

"Now, boys—"

"It's over, Stoughton," McLeary said. "You're gonna have to talk to the miners. And you're gonna have to give in to them—at least to some extent."

Stoughton bobbed his head. "Yes, yes, I know." There was some regret there, but more resignation.

"Good. Now move out of the way. Me and Bodie have some unfinished business with a few of your customers."

The men who were not regulators began edging toward the walls, hoping to slip around the two gunmen by the door and bolt for freedom. McLeary and Wheeler paid them no heed. Most were businessmen from town, and not armed and therefore no danger.

Mace Kenney and three others who McLeary did not know stood from their tables, facing Wheeler and McLeary.

"You see the Bader brothers, Bodie?" McLeary asked.

"Saw a couple boys headin' for the back door a minute ago. Might've been them."

McLeary nodded. "You four boys got one chance, and one chance only: You can ride out of here now, and never come back. . . ."

"Or?" one said.

Kenney was the first to move, his good left hand going for the new Colt he carried backward in the holster.

Chapter 29

McLeary was fractionally faster than Wheeler, and the bullet from his .44-caliber Smith and Wesson American punched a bloody hole in Mace Kenney's lungs moments before one from Wheeler's converted Walker Colt punctured Kenney's heart.

The power of the bullets, fired from twenty feet away, almost lifted Kenney off his feet, knocking him onto his back on one of the tables. Money and cards flew into the air, and then drifted lazily down, some to land on Kenney's twitching body; most, onto the hardwood floor of the Silver Nugget. His pistol was still in his holster, his left arm twisted around, the dying fingers still grasping the revolver's butt.

But neither McLeary nor Wheeler saw Kenney land. Both were occupied in trying to sight down on the three other gunmen. Those three fired, two after diving in opposite directions. The third stood his ground.

McLeary winced as a bullet burned a blazing trail across the outside of his right thigh. The leg started to buckle as he emptied the Smith and Wesson at the gunman standing in front of a table. Three slugs slammed into the man's chest and stomach, kicking him back a step with each blow.

As McLeary fell on the weakened leg, he saw Wheeler gasp as a splatter of blood came from his gun arm. McLeary pushed himself up and behind a table, favoring the leg. He shoved the Smith and Wesson into the holster with his right hand, at the same time ripping open his shirt to free up the smaller Colt Lightning. He yanked the .38 out, ready. But it was not needed.

Wheeler had growled after the initial shock of the wound, and he poured lead from the five-pound Walker, the heavy weapon bucking in his huge right hand.

It was over in seconds, as slugs from Wheeler's Walker

pounded the remaining two gunmen. One's head burst into a erupting volcano of blood, bone and brains; the other had only a momentary awareness of his heart and lungs rupturing, sending out a spray of blood, from the force of bullets.

Wheeler sank into a nearby chair, clutching his right arm. McLeary looked around the room warily, but there was no one left to do him and his friend any harm.

There was utter silence, except for the pitter-pat of liquor dripping off the table on which Kenney's body lay. Then people began to move, coming out from their hiding places behind tables or posts. A few ran pellmell for the door.

The bartender, Marsh, had jumped over the bar and hid behind it. He came up now, cautiously, with a shotgun in his hand. McLeary, angry, a little scared, and hurting from the leg wound, yelled, "Drop the scattergun, Marsh!"

The bartender hesitated only a moment and, in doing so, sealed his fate. McLeary snapped the Colt Lightning up and fired only once. The bullet burrowed into Marsh's brain, smack through the center of the bartender's forehead. His head and body snapped back, smashing the mirror and several bottles behind him before he sank out of sight behind the bar.

"You all right, Bodie?" McLeary asked nervously.

"Sprightly," Wheeler said, annoyed, as he always was when he took a slug. It hadn't happened too many times before, but this wasn't the first time. "You?"

McLeary had been shot before, too, and knew this one was not too bad. There had been two other times when he thought he might die from it, but had managed to survive. Compared to those times, this was but a scratch. "I'll make do. Load your pistol while I keep an eye on things."

Wheeler's arm was stiffening up on him some, but he quickly ejected the spent shells from his Walker and inserted new ones. "Done," he said, still holding the pistol at the ready.

Wheeler nodded and shoved the small Colt into the shoulder holster. He then emptied the Smith and Wesson and reloaded it. He spotted Alva Stoughton still cowering behind the billiard table, and gestured to him. Stoughton, frightened, mopping sweat from his chubby face, moved closer. He was absolutely certain that he was about to be killed.

"It's over, Stoughton," McLeary said harshly. "You are gonna go and negotiate with the union tomorrow morning. I don't much give a damn what you get—or don't get—out of the talks. But talk you will. You and your brother can deal with Duncan McGregor and try to work out the deal that'll satisfy you all as much as possible. But you'll be doin' your negotiatin' without an army of regulators at your back. Got it?"

"Yes," Stoughton mumbled through his dry mouth.

Pain was starting to flood McLeary's leg, and he was distinctly uncomfortable. But he would not give anyone else the satisfaction of seeing him show it. "There's only two regulators left, far's I know—the Bader brothers. That right?"

"Yes." Stoughton was too frightened to lie.

"You get word to those two hardcase German bastards that they either ride out of town tonight and keep goin'—or they meet me just after first light tomorrow mornin'."

"I won't see them. I won't—"

"Don't bullshit me, Stoughton."

"Where will you meet them?" Stoughton said, brushing dust from his fine brown suit.

"Six-Gun Mine. Out front."

"If I see them, I'll tell them," Stoughton said more strongly. He was feeling rather relieved since it had become apparent that McLeary was not going to kill him.

"Good. Now fetch me a bottle of your best whiskey."

"I ain't no—"

The Smith and Wesson came up, cocked, with the muzzle brushing the underside of Stoughton's nose. He began to sweat again. Just because McLeary wanted him to deliver a message did not mean the gunman wouldn't kill him here and now.

"Yes, sir," he whispered. He breathed in relief as the gun was moved away. He hurried behind the bar and grabbed a bottle of whiskey.

"Make it two," Wheeler growled.

Stoughton grabbed a second bottle and brought them to McLeary. The gunfighter took them both in his left hand, fingers entwined around the necks of the bottles.

"You ready, Bodie?"

"Yep." Wheeler shoved up, Walker in his right hand, left hand still wrapped around the oozing wound on his right bicep.

"In case you—or your idiot brother—got any ideas of goin' against Miss Van Leuewen's house again, best drop them."

Stoughton knew when he was beaten. "You will have no more trouble from us—me, anyway—Mister McLeary," he said firmly. "Most of this was his idea anyway."

"Figured."

"He would like to take over the business for himself," Stoughton said with a wan smile. "Our oldest brother, Tom, has little to do with the running of it. That has been left to me. However"—he raised his hands as if to say, 'What can I do?'—"George disagrees with nearly everything I do. This was mostly his doing. Perhaps, when he sees how miserably it has turned out, he will ease off. I doubt that, though." He sighed, a businessman beset by business problems. No matter that over two dozen people had died, houses had been burned down and more.

"It would be wise," McLeary said sarcastically.

Wheeler walked toward the swinging doors, watchful, while McLeary started backing toward the exit. Thus they were covered on all sides. McLeary jammed the two bottles of whiskey in his saddlebags. It was awkward for the two men to mount their horses, but they managed it, and rode slowly down Silver Street.

"Where to, Charlie?" Wheeler asked.

"Aunt Cara's first. Then back to the house."

Wheeler grinned. "I was hopin' you'd say that, *amigo*. I feel the need to have Alice carin' for me."

They got Molly and Alice and, with their women on the horses behind them, rode slowly toward the house. The women bandaged up their wounds after determining that neither would require the services of a doctor. McLeary's wound was superficial, though painful. Wheeler's was somewhat worse, but still not really bad. It would, however, affect his shooting for a while.

After taking care of their men, the women took the two horses to the small shed and cared for them, making sure they were curried, watered and had plenty of feed handy.

McLeary was up before dawn. His leg stung a bit, and he limped a little; but it would not hamper him too much. He quietly drank some coffee, and then made himself breakfast.

He was just finishing the meal when Molly came downstairs. She padded into the kitchen on bare feet. Even in her shapeless nightshift, her eyes still red with sleep and her hair mussed, she looked great to McLeary. He wondered again at his good fortune.

"You're up early," she said, kissing him on the forehead as she headed for the coffeepot. "How do you feel?"

"I've been better. But, I been worse, too."

Molly poured some coffee and came to sit across the table from him. "Why are you up so early?" she asked, only her hazel eyes visible over the rim of her coffee cup through the steam.

"I have business."

A chill ran through her. "I thought that was all done."

"Might be," he said noncomittally.

"What's left?" Molly asked, setting the cup down. Her eyes reflected the concern she felt deep inside.

"There's two regulators unaccounted for. I told Alva Stoughton to tell them to get out of town—or meet me at the mines today."

"Do you think they'll show up?"

McLeary shrugged and popped the last of his bacon into his mouth. "I'm hopin'," he said, "that they've rode on."

"When are you goin'?" Molly asked, a sinking feeling in her stomach. Last night was the first night they had really spent together without a cloud over them—or so she had thought. Now there was this.

"Soon's I finish my coffee."

"What about Bodie?"

"What about him?"

"Aren't you going to take him with you?"

"No." It was said flatly. He stroked his mustache.

"But why?" Molly was truly surprised—and even more worried.

"He's given all he needs to give here. And with that wound, he ain't up to snuff."

"You've been wounded, too," Molly said, eyes wide with fear.

"Not in my gun arm."

"Stay here, Charlie," Molly pleaded. "Let some others handle it now. You've done more than your share, too. The miners can take care of themselves, even if the last two regulators show up."

"The Baders are real hardcases, Molly," McLeary explained calmly.

"So a few miners will die. They die regular in the mines anyhow. You've put your life on the line for them a dozen times already. So's Bodie. It's enough." She was close to tears, and that made her all the more angry.

"Don't make this any harder, Molly," McLeary said softly. "It's somethin' that's got to be done. Lord willin', maybe the Baders will have rode on, and then there'll be no more problem."

He stood and carried his plate and coffee cup to the sink and set them in. He pumped out some water and splashed it on his face. Drying himself with a towel, he turned. Molly was still sitting at the table, face set, back stiff.

"I'm goin' now, Molly," he said very softly.

Molly didn't move, and McLeary thought that she might not have heard him. He started to repeat himself, then decided not to. She had heard him, he realized, but was ignoring him, as if by doing so the problem would disappear. He headed for the door.

Molly leaped up and fairly flew toward him, clutching him. She said nothing, nor did she cry. She only clung to him—almost desperately—for a few minutes. Then she pulled his head down and kissed him hard and longingly. "Remember," she breathed when she pulled away, "that's what you have to come back to."

"I'll remember," he said, the scent of her lingering in his nostrils; the taste of her still on his mouth as he headed out to the shed.

He nearly had the cinnamon gelding saddled when Wheeler rumbled in. The big man was even more rumpled than usual, having just woken up. His shirt was not tucked in, and his eyes were puffy. "Goin' somewhere without me?" he grumbled.

"Yep."

"Seein' to the Bader brothers?"

"If the need arises."

"I'm goin' with you."

"No you ain't."

"Yes I am," he growled. He was not happy with his arm bandaged and in a sling. Making it worse was knowing that he could not help as much as he wanted to. He felt useless, old, unwanted.

"No you ain't."

"Why?"

"You know that as well as I."

"Shit. I can still outshoot most folks."

"Not the Baders." McLeary faced his friend, leaning against his horse. "Bodie, I know you got no give-up in you. But you know these Baders. They're bad asses for sure. I don't want to be responsible for you gettin' killed. Besides, I don't really even expect them to show up."

"But—"

"Bodie, the women need you here. You ever think that maybe the Baders might try comin' here if they figure we're both down at the mines?"

"Bah," Wheeler growled, "you're just tryin' to make me feel better about sittin' here on my ass doin' nothin' while you're out takin' care of things."

McLeary said nothing.

"Well, all right then, Charlie," Wheeler rumbled, still not happy, but knowing that it would be foolish—and dangerous—to go with McLeary.

McLeary pulled himself into the saddle. " 'Course," Wheeler said, almost grinning, "you realize I'm gonna be terrible upset you go and get yourself killed, not to say what Molly will be thinkin'—or feelin'—about it."

McLeary nodded and spurred the horse into movement.

Chapter 30

The miners were outside, talking in small groups, some still drinking coffee, waiting for the day's shift to begin. Most carried heavy sledge hammers, or hard, steel drills. Others checked over their fuses and dynamite. All were dressed in dirty work clothes, and most wore cloth coats since it was cold down in the lower reaches of the mines.

McLeary found Duncan McGregor standing with one group near the smelter and told him what had transpired, ending, "So I reckon the Stoughtons, or at least Alva, will be along shortly to start talks. I'm here to make sure they go off as well as can be expected."

"Thank you, Mister McLeary," McGregor said earnestly. "We've won. We've really won!"

McLeary shrugged. "Don't gloat in your victory, Mister McGregor, especially before it's done and said," McLeary warned seriously. "My father had a sayin' about doin' that. He once told me, 'Boy, don't ary start yer war dancin' afore the enemy's done and dead. Ye do that and sure's hell they'll come back to kick you in the ass.' "

McLeary paused, then said, "When you negotiate with the Stoughtons, you can do so from a position of strength now. But don't go in thinkin' they're beaten, and that you can make unreasonable demands."

McGregor shook his head. "Yes, yes, of course," he muttered, as if he had not heard a word. Then he sobered some. "You are right, of course," he said. "It's just that . . . well . . ."

"I understand."

Someone in the group of workmen shouted, "Look!"

McLeary and McGregor turned to watch three carriages coming toward them—each containing one of the Stoughton brothers. Flanking the first carriage, in which Tom, the oldest of the Stoughton brothers rode, were Alf and Arnie Bader.

"Looks like the party's about set to begin, Mister McGregor."

"Duncan. Call me Duncan." He looked worried. "Well," he said slowly, wiping suddenly sweaty palms on his grimy pants, "reckon I best get on over there."

"I'll be right behind you."

McGregor stopped and stared up at McLeary with a question in his eyes. He was pleased, but surprised.

"The Stoughtons got their hired guns with 'em. As leader of the Silver Canyon Workingmen's Collective, you deserve at least one." He shrugged, grinning. The grin dropped. "Besides, I set a challenge for the Baders last night. I expect they're here to accept it."

"The who?"

"The two gunslingers. Alf and Arnie Bader. They're the last of the regulators. I told Alva Stoughton last night that if they didn't ride out of town right off, I'd meet 'em here today. Since they've showed up, I figure they aim to take me down—if they can."

"Go," McGregor ordered. "Get out of here. There's no reason to face these men down here and get yourself killed. You've already been wounded," he added, pointing to the dried blood on McLeary's pants.

McLeary laughed. He was loose for the first time in a while. Facing down only two men—even if they were the Baders—wasn't so bad, when the odds had been twelve or more to one. "Just set your mind to negotiatin' with the Stoughtons. That's your job. The Baders are mine."

The wagons had stopped abreast, and the Stoughtons sat waiting. McLeary and McGregor walked toward them. As they did, the Baders dismounted and walked in front of the carriages, pulling off their gloves. McLeary's eyes hardened. He reached out a hand and stopped McGregor. "Stay," he ordered.

He moved forward a little more on his own, conscious that the great open area directly in front of the main mine—the Six-Gun Mine—was encircled by a growing number of people:

townsfolk hurrying up, miners' wives and children.

The Baders moved forward, too. All three men stopped, about fifty feet separating the brothers from McLeary.

"It is my understanding, Mister McLeary," one of the Stoughtons—McLeary guessed it was Tom—said, "that you have challenged these men. My employees. Is that true?"

"I told the bastards to haul ass or they'd wind up dead—just like the others."

Stoughton nodded his head. He was an elegant man in his late forties, impeccably dressed in black, with a snappy bowler hat. He held a silver-tipped cane, upon which he rested his folded hands. His driver, a nondescript black man, sat quietly next to him. "How unfortunate," Stoughton said.

"It don't have to be this way."

"Are you prepared to back down, Mister McLeary?" Stoughton asked in feigned surprise. "I was given to believe that you were not such a man."

"I ain't. But you can stop it. You hired these idiots. You can send 'em packin'. Their fight's over."

"I'm afraid I can't do that."

McLeary shrugged and nodded.

"Well," Stoughton sighed, "I see that this must play itself out. Will the miners back you?"

"How?"

"If you lose, they go back to work and quit all this nonsense of unionizing?"

"Yes!" McGregor roared, overriding any grumble of discontent that might erupt from the miners.

"No!" Pete Bowers snapped, shoving forward till he was next to McGregor. "No!"

McGregor turned to him. "Get back away from me, goddammit."

"I am one of the founders of this union, and I will not place my fate in the hands of that man." He pointed an accusing finger at McLeary, who had craned his head around to watch.

"No," McGregor said loudly, making sure everyone heard him, "you'd rather put your fate—and that of all the men—in the hands of the Stoughtons, wouldn't you, you traitorous son of a bitch."

There was a gasp from the crowd, and Bowers blanched. "Don't listen to him," Bowers squawked. "He don't know what he's talkin' about. He's—"

"It's true, goddammit," McGregor snapped. "In fact, he's the one responsible for little Martha's death. And old man Tyler's . . ."

He was drowned out by the roar of anger that steamed out of the angry miners. Bowers bolted, trying to get toward the Stoughtons, where he might find refuge. But half a dozen miners grabbed him and began pummelling him, till McGregor's repeated shouts finally overcame the noise, "Leave him be!"

The miners stood, holding Bowers in tight-fisted grips.

"We'll deal with him later," McGregor said with finality, not brooking any argument. He was in charge now, unafraid of leading. McGregor turned to face the Stoughtons. "I said we will back this man till the end, Mister Stoughton," he declared loudly. His tone let the miners know they must be behind him.

Tom Stoughton nodded. He tapped his driver on the arm and pointed to a spot nearby where they would be out of the line of fire. He stopped when McLeary shouted, "Wait!"

"Yes?" Stoughton asked, facing him. His face was passive.

"And when I prevail here? What happens then?"

"Then we negotiate with the miners, Mister McLeary," Stoughton said blandly.

"In good faith and honorably?"

"Yes."

McLeary believed him. He nodded, and Stoughton's driver pulled the carriage out of the way. It was followed by Alva's and George's carriages. McLeary's eyes stared balefully at the Baders. There was nothing to read on the Germans' faces. "Make your play when you're ready, boys," he said.

McLeary was calm, eerily calm. He usually was in situations like this. It was one of the reasons he was as good at what he did as he was. Afterwards he might find his mouth dry and palms sweaty. Or he might be forced to suppress a shudder.

But that was all afterward. Now he was calm.

The day was quiet, broken only by the steady hissing and regular thumping from the smelter off to his right, the snort or shuffle of a horse, or an occasional cough.

Arnie—on his brother's left—moved a few feet more in that direction, so there were maybe two yards between him and Alf. He spit tobacco, but McLeary never took his eyes from those of the brothers, flicking from one set of dull brown eyes to the other. He would not be distracted by anything.

Three hands went for three pistols at almost the same instant. The Smith and Wesson American seemed to leap into McLeary's hand of its own accord. He had thumbed back the hammer and was firing almost before he realized he had moved. His arm was a blur to those watching. Then McLeary felt the comforting bucking the the familiar pistol in his hand.

Several shots rang out. Arnie, the younger and faster of the two Baders, flew back as three .44-caliber bullets ravaged his stomach, a lung and the heart. He fell backward in an undignified sprawl, his body jerking in the throes of death.

McLeary, too, was spun around by the impact of a bullet. He gasped as the heat of it ripped his side. As he fell, he heard several screams, and he thought that Molly's voice was among them.

He rolled, not wanting to present a still target to the slower, but more deadly, Alf Bader. Two bullets kicked up dirt next to him as he struggled to rise. He finally lurched up onto one knee, swinging the Smith and Wesson around. He braced his gun hand with the left, and quickly squeezed off the final two shots in his revolver.

But Bader was running and was not an easy target at this distance with a pistol. McLeary saw the gunslinger flinch, as if hit.

McLeary leaped up and ran, spurs ringing, toward Bader.

Bader reached the crowd bunched up against the low rocky hills around the mine. He grabbed a woman—poorly enough dressed to look like a miner's wife, rather than a townswoman—and swung her around in front of him as a shield.

There were screams from the crowd, and from the woman.

He snapped off two more shots, and McLeary figured Bader was down to one cartridge in the Colt he carried. McLeary shoved the Smith and Wesson away, and from the back of his gunbelt, he pulled one of the Colt Peacemakers he had taken from an enemy. He believed it was from the man who had tried to kill him—was it only three weeks ago—in the meadow on the eastern slope of the Rockies. But it didn't matter.

The pistol felt unfamiliar in his hand, but still, it was comfortably balanced. And it was more powerful than the .38 Colt Lightning in the shoulder holster.

"Come no closer," Bader shouted in his thick German accent. He pressed the muzzle of his pistol against the woman's head. The woman was pale as fresh snow, but silent. She struggled some, until Bader mumbled something to her.

McLeary stopped. His side hurt, but he could not spare the time to look down and see how bad it was. He did not feel very weak, so he could not have lost much blood yet. And he was still calm, despite the flood of adrenaline rushing through his veins.

"It's all over, Alf," McLeary said harshly.

"Bullshit. *Nein.*"

"Yeah, it is, boy, and you goddamn well know it. You put that piece down and let the woman go, you might get off alive."

"So you are afraid to kill me, *nein?*"

"Let the woman go, Alf." McLeary raised the Colt and thumbed back the hammer. It was, he knew already, a well-cared-for weapon. The hammer came back easily, and the cylinder turned smoothly.

"Or vhat?"

"Or I'll blow your goddamn brains out here and now."

"Hah! You vill not endancher dis voman."

"I ain't the one endangerin' her, boy."

"Let the woman go, Mister Bader," Tom Stoughton commanded. "It is all over, as Mister McLeary said. There is no point in continuing with this."

"Go to hell," Bader replied.

Time seemed to freeze. It was mostly up to Alf now, and

there was nothing he could really do other than let the woman go. Or kill her, thus leaving himself in the open with an empty pistol.

"I vant my horse," Bader said. "So I might get avay from here."

"Someone bring up Mister Bader's horse," Stoughton ordered. He knew—had known since before arriving this morning—that the use of the regulators was all over. He had pinned his fleeting hopes on this one last play—the Baders against this deadly Charlie McLeary. Now even that hope was gone, and he could see no use in prolonging this, or in endangering an innocent woman's life. He had let himself be talked into this by his youngest brother, and now he regretted all the bloodshed that had flowed—especially the blood of the innocent.

McLeary waited, sweating in the heat of the day. The Colt was braced in both hands, and never wavered. Someone moved toward Bader with the gunfighter's horse.

Alf Bader's eyes flickered in that direction for less than a second, and in that instant, McLeary fired. The bullet shattered Bader's head, inches from the woman's, showering her with blood and brain matter. The impact also snapped the gunman back, jerking his arm away from the woman at the same time. The woman fell to the side as Bader's dead finger involuntarily flexed on the trigger. The weapon fired, the bullet digging harmlessly into the ground.

The woman screamed. With a grim smile of satisfaction, McLeary sank onto his knees in the dirt.

Chapter 31

Charlie McLeary and Molly Stoughton strolled along Silver Street arm in arm. It was hotter than blazes, with the sun shining bright and unsparing. But they did not mind. Nor did Bodie Wheeler and Alice Van Leuewen, who meandered the busy, noisy street with them.

And noisy it was. It had started before dawn that morning, when someone had fired off a small keg of gunpowder at the mines in Squaw Gulch, awakening the whole town so the revels in honor of the nation's one hundred and second birthday could begin.

When McLeary had gotten up and stretched, he felt a new man. His leg still hurt a little from the graze wound he had taken there three nights earlier, and his side, where he had been shot by Alf Bader two days ago was sore.

He had been fortunate that time. The bullet had plowed a shallow trench along his left side, glancing off one rib, which cracked. There had been a lot of blood, and a considerable amount of burning pain. But it was not a serious wound, and after he had gotten back to the house, the doctor had come to fix him up.

McLeary was fine now, though mildly uncomfortable with the bandage wrapped tightly around his midsection and the still stinging irritation of the wound itself.

Wheeler was fine, too, though his arm remained in a sling from the slug that had carved a chunk out of his right bicep.

Both men were dressed in new clothes: McLeary in dark-blue wool suit, a black derby perched jauntily on his head, a flowery velveteen vest, string tie, arm garters—a pair given him by Molly—new, black, pointed toe boots, and a string tie. Wheeler wore a checked wool suit, a brown derby covering his thatch of hair, a plain, brown vest, an ascot, and hand-tooled brown boots.

The women were more than the match of the men, though. Molly wore a low-necked, off-the-shoulder satin dress of silvery-gray trimmed with dark blue lace and pearl buttons. From under the lace-trimmed hem of the dress peeked high-heeled, black, button-side shoes.

Alice was dressed similarly, though her dress was a creamy tan satin, bordered with chocolate brown.

Molly's honey-blond hair and Alice's almost black tresses were curled in long ringlets. They made, the two men thought—and from the looks the other men cast at them, everyone thought—a spectacular pair, these two women. Molly, small, slim, fair of face, with her delicate features; Alice, taller, fuller of bust, darker of complexion. McLeary had never been so proud, and Wheeler looked happy enough to about burst.

Even if he had burst, it would have caused little consternation this day. There were people all over, and constant, raucous activity. Children shot off their firecrackers and various other minor explosives, like redheads and double-headed Dutchmen. There were foot races and horse races in the streets, each accompanied by much screaming, shouting and betting.

The Pick and Shovel had been rebuilt—hastily and with little regard to aesthetics. The temporary tent saloon had come down, and in the cleared lot, there were wrestling and boxing contests, and, on occasion, dog fights and crowing cock fights.

Earlier, the foursome had visited the mines themselves—shut down for the festive holiday—and watched for a while as the miners exhibited their skills at mule packing and rock drilling in hopes of winning one of the many prizes. Duncan McGregor and his partner had won the double-jacking contest. McGregor had started off holding the large iron drill, well-placed in the rock, while his partner slammed away with a heavy sledge hammer. After thirty seconds they switched, and McLeary was amazed that they never missed a beat; back and forth, until they were done, sweating and beaming.

All the people walking Silver Street were in a joyful mood,

and the recent unpleasantness between the miners and the mine owners seemed forgotten. And why not? There was a circus setting up in a pleasant glade at the south end of town, and this afternoon there was scheduled a baseball game between the men of the Squaw Gulch mines, and those of the mines up in Silverton. The field would be in a marshy glade on the east side of town, between the last of the buildings and the humped up peaks of the mountains.

The foursome strolled up and down the street, taking in the sights, McLeary and Wheeler wagering a bit here and there on a race or wrestling match. They spotted McGregor, who was full of both good cheer and bad whiskey.

"Congratulations on winnin' the double-jackin' contest before," McLeary said with a grin.

"Thanks." McGregor's eyes were bright, but he did not sound drunk at all.

"How are things goin' in your talks with the Stoughton brothers?"

"Done," McGregor said proudly, drawing himself up to his full five-feet-five.

McLeary was not surprised.

McGregor shrugged and said, "They knew they were beaten—all except that bastard . . . I'm sorry, ma'am, your husband."

"It's quite all right, Mister McGregor. He is my husband no longer, other than in name. As soon as I can manage it, I will be divorcing him."

"A sad state, ma'am. Anyway, Tom and Alva pretty well knew they were beat and—"

"You didn't rake 'em over the coals did you?" McLeary asked with a grin.

McGregor smiled. "Nah. It was good advice you gave us—to not kick 'em when they were down," he added seriously. "We got the four dollars a day we wanted, and we got them to agree to keep the Chinese out. They can keep the ones already workin' in the mines, but they agreed not to bring any more in. And we compromised on the hours. We had been talkin' all along of not workin' more than eight hours a day. That was what we wanted. We been workin' ten, and the Stoughtons wanted to keep that. We split it, and we'll be workin' nine."

"Sounds like you did all right, Duncan."

"Yeah." He chuckled, happy. "Hell, we even invited them Chinese boys to our celebrations here."

McLeary nodded, then asked, "By the way, whatever happened to Pete Bowers?"

McGregor got a funny kind of look in his eyes. "As you might well know, Mister McLeary," he said slowly, "there's an awful lot of things can happen to a man works the mines. Accidents, you know. Machinery mucks up, timbers fall, rockslides, cave-ins. Well, it was unfortunate, but I'm afraid Mister Pete Bowers had himself one of those 'unfortunate' accidents."

McLeary was not surprised. Wheeler only grinned. "His wife and young 'uns gonna be all right?" McLeary asked.

"Hell, yes." McGregor laughed. "Probably better. It might be a good thing Pete had an 'accident.' Emma heard about his treachery, and he would've had a devil of a time at home."

McLeary laughed, and the others joined in.

"Soon's his body was pulled out of the mine and laid to rest, Emma said her good-byes and took up with a widowed German with six of his own young ones. I expect they'll be married soon's they wait a decent interval—like a week."

McGregor wandered away, laughing, his bottle of whiskey clutched tightly in one small, powerful fist.

They had lunch at Lankshire's, dawdling over the fried chicken and seared steak, and coffee. Outside, after they had walked awhile taking in all the activities, Molly clutched McLeary's arm and tugged till he brought his ear down toward her. "I want to go home," she whispered.

He looked at her, alarm coursing through him—until he looked at her hazel eyes and saw the lust blazing deep inside them. He grinned, and they walked—hurriedly—back to the house, leaving Wheeler and Alice to stroll around.

They met Wheeler and Alice coming in as they were heading back toward the festivities. It was almost dusk when they all met up again and entered a bulging Lankshire's Restaurant for supper. When they walked outside, Molly said, "I forgot my little binoculars, Charlie. I'm gonna run back to the house and get them."

"I'll come with you."

"No, you can stay here. You wanted to see that boxing match over at the Silver Nugget."

"All right," he said doubtfully, dampening the little fear that flickered up inside him.

"I'll be all right."

He nodded. "Just be quick, though. The circus shows start pretty soon."

"I will." She hurried off, with Alice at her side.

McLeary and Wheeler pushed into the Silver Nugget. It was mobbed in the saloon, and they had to shove their way through in order to watch the boxing match in the makeshift ring set up in the center. It was over quickly, with the Consolidated Silver and Mining Company champion knocking out the Silverton Mining Company champion in only ten minutes.

As McLeary and Wheeler were leaving, a raggedly dressed boy of about eleven came up to them and asked, "Are you Mister McLeary?"

McLeary said, "I am, boy. What can I do for you?"

"Got a note for you." He handed it to McLeary, and then turned and ran away.

McLeary watched him for a moment, before Wheeler said, "Well, *open* it, dammit."

McLeary unfolded the paper. In the pale light coming through the window he saw a note written in a soft, exact hand.

"Well, for Christ's sake, Charlie, what does it say? Who's it from?" Wheeler demanded, exasperated.

McLeary grinned. "It's from Molly. Says she wants to meet me at somethin' called the Old Animas Building. You got any idea what that is?"

"Nope. Sounds like she's fixin' to ravish your tender person again, this time in some new place. Probably got somethin' special planned out for you." He grinned and winked.

"Reckon so. Guess I'll have to ask about to find this place. You gonna stick here?"

"Yep. It's where Alice will be expectin' me, unless," he added with another lecherous grin, "she's got some of the same ideas as Molly."

"Maybe, Bodie. I wouldn't put it past neither of them to pull somethin' like this. Now you be good, you hear." McLeary strolled off. He wandered a bit, not wanting to disturb anyone who looked to be busy, or having too good a time. But after five minutes or so of fruitless wandering, he stopped someone who looked like he wasn't too drunk and still had some sense left in him. He asked.

The man pointed a wavering finger south. "Go down to Third Street and then over to Animas, then south to First Street. It's the last buildin' there is."

"Thanks." He walked off hurrying a little, not wanting Molly to get bored waiting for him. Still, it was another ten minutes' walk. Though his rendezvous was on the fringes of the town, there were still plenty of people about, and the noise of the celebrating was loud. But from what he could see as he approached the Old Animas Building, it looked to be deserted. He grinned. Leave it to Molly to pick such a place—an island in the middle of all the activity.

Fortunately, he thought, as he reached the place, the moon was bright enough to let him see a little. There was a side door open, hanging crookedly. He grinned again and pushed his way in. "Molly," he called, eager now. "Molly?"

He heard a rustling farther back in the old wood building, and he smiled, heading for it. Then he saw a small flickering light way off in the back.

"Bodie, where's Charlie?" Molly asked, touching the big man on the arm.

He turned, startled. "What?" he mumbled. "What are you doing here? What do you mean, 'Where's Charlie?' " He was confused.

It was her turn to be surprised. "Where's Charlie?" she demanded. "Don't fool around, Bodie, please." There was fear in her voice, a deep-seated fear, as if the worst nightmare she had ever dreamed was unfolding into reality before her eyes.

"He went to meet Mol—you. What're you doin' here?"

"We were supposed to meet here, remember?" The iciness clutched at her heart.

"But the note."

"What note?"

"Charlie got a note from you sayin' to meet him at the Old Animas Building. We just assumed you were plannin' . . . you wanted . . . well, you know."

"I didn't send any note." The fear was a clutching, grabbing, choking thing now, shutting off her wind, making her dizzy.

"But . . ." Wheeler was still confused, but he was starting to catch on.

"Dammit, it's a trick. It's George. It must be," she cried.

"Reckon so. Where is this place?"

"No time to explain. Alice ran back for something just after I left. She ought to be here any second. She knows where it is. I've got to go. Got to run. Warn my—" She started crying.

"Stop it!" Wheeler snapped. "There ain't no time for such nonsense. You go on and find Charlie. I'll be along fast as I can run soon's Alice gets here."

Molly nodded. She turned and took two steps, but stopped when Wheeler called her. When she turned back, he was holding out a .38-caliber Pocket Colt. "Take this," he ordered. "Just in case."

She nodded again, too numb to think. She dropped the pistol in her purse. She turned again, gathered up her skirts in her hands, and then ran. She headed across Silver Street, then west on Fourth Street. It was only a little less crowded here. Frantic with worry, Molly grabbed the first docile-looking horse she found.

She ignored some shouts behind her as she hauled herself into the saddle, pulling her skirts up so that generous portions of black-stockinged legs showed. She kicked the horse as hard as she could.

The animal bolted down the street. Molly skidded around the corner onto Animas Street, the horse's hooves fighting for purchase on the dusty ground. As she raced along, she prayed she would be in time.

From a block away, she could just see McLeary entering the side door of the abandoned building, and she screamed his name several times; but he did not hear her as he disappeared into the building. Molly slapped the horse's neck with the reins.

She tore around the back of the building, where there was another fallen-in door. The horse was not even fully stopped when she slid off the animal, sprawling as inertia worked on her. She scrambled up, heart racing, her blood pounding in her ears.

Her hands shaking, she grabbed the small Colt revolver out of her purse and then dropped the satin drawstring bag that matched her dress. With ragged breath, she eased into the building. Hurrying, scared beyond belief, she heard a noise and saw a dim light. She moved as if in a trance, feeling that she was not really herself—that she was really floating up above, near the crumbling ceiling, watching as someone else moved quickly, determinedly, through this rotting building owned by her husband.

She heard McLeary calling her name, sounding a little annoyed, as if he was tired of playing a game. She opened her mouth to yell to him, when she saw a movement in the shadows to the left. Then there appeared the brief glinting of dim light on a gun barrel.

It became clear to her in an instant. She surprised herself with her lucidness. George Stoughton had set this trap, sending a forged note to McLeary, signing it Molly, telling McLeary to meet her here. He left the lantern on in one room to attract McLeary, who would move toward it. And Stoughton waited in another room, gun ready, to kill him.

Molly could see Charlie now, moving slowly, inexorably toward the lantern-lighted room. If she yelled, George would leap out from his hiding place and gun down McLeary where he was. No, she decided in that fractional instant of time, she must handle this one alone.

She took three quick steps, silent, until she had a clear view of George. Her husband, eyes glinting in the soft reflection of the lantern in the next room, was waiting, a shotgun at his shoulder, braced on a rotting timber from the building.

Whispering a quick prayer, she lifted the Colt in shaking hands. Her breathing came in erratic puffs, and she sucked in a good strong breath to try to steady herself.

"Charlie!" she screamed.

It had the desired effect of making George start in fright and surprise. In the next instant, three things happened: McLeary dived behind a pile of fallen lumber, George fired off one barrel of the shotgun, and Molly cocked and fired the Pocket Colt.

McLeary was safe behind the lumber, and the shotgun blast sprayed the wood instead of him. He popped up over the rubble quickly, Smith and Wesson in hand. He saw George falling, a section of his head gone, and Molly, apparently calm as ice, holding a small Colt in both hands.

Molly was numb inside, but at the same time she was calm and perfectly lucid. With one thumb atop the other, she cocked the Colt and fired again.

George had not yet hit the ground when the second bullet from Molly's Colt ripped through his carotid artery, sending up a roaring geyser of blood.

She was cocking the pistol for another shot at the lifeless, though twitching, body of her husband, when McLeary reached her. He grabbed the pistol out of her hand. He slid his own Smith and Wesson away. Then he uncocked the Colt and stuck it in the back of his belt, under his suit jacket.

He opened his arms, and Molly came into them willingly. "I . . . I . . ." she sobbed.

"You saved my life, Molly," McLeary said calmly.

"But I killed him," she wept.

He walked her outside. "And now we're free," he said firmly.

She looked up at him, tears glinting on her lashes. And she smiled.